WITHDRAWN

STONE
COLD
HEART

Center Point
Large Print

Also by Laura Griffin and available from
Center Point Large Print:

Far Gone
Desperate Girls

**This Large Print Book carries the
Seal of Approval of N.A.V.H.**

STONE COLD HEART

Laura Griffin

CENTER POINT LARGE PRINT
THORNDIKE, MAINE

This Center Point Large Print edition
is published in the year 2019 by arrangement with
Pocket Books, a division of Simon & Schuster, Inc.

Copyright © 2019 by Laura Griffin.

The text of this Large Print edition is unabridged.
In other aspects, this book may vary
from the original edition.
Printed in the United States of America
on permanent paper.
Set in 16-point Times New Roman type.

ISBN: 978-1-64358-181-1

Library of Congress Cataloging-in-Publication Data

Names: Griffin, Laura, 1973- author.
Title: Stone cold heart / Laura Griffin.
Description: Center Point Large Print edition. | Thorndike, Maine :
    Center Point Large Print, 2019.
Identifiers: LCCN 2019006523 | ISBN 9781643581811 (hardcover :
    alk. paper)
Subjects: LCSH: Large type books.
Classification: LCC PS3607.R54838 S86 2019 | DDC 813/.6—dc23
LC record available at https://lccn.loc.gov/2019006523

For Ann

STONE COLD HEART

CHAPTER 1

Grace hurried to keep up, stumbling in her borrowed sandals. At least she managed not to fall on her face. Half a block ahead, her cousin's veil fluttered behind her as she led the charge to the next bar.

Grace had liked the steampunk place, especially because they didn't have a bouncer. But Bella had gotten bored and wanted to go somewhere with a band. It was Sixth Street, after all—the nightlife capital of Austin, the live-music capital of the world, supposedly.

Grace's thighs chafed together as she race-walked to catch up with Bella's friends, all blond and all sorority sisters, including a Sienna, a Sierra, and two Rileys. Grace had sat beside Sierra at dinner and learned that she was an intern at a B-to-B marketing firm in Dallas—whatever that meant. Grace hadn't gotten much from the conversation. The woman had basically stopped talking once she figured out that Grace was not only underage but also a student at a podunk community college.

They reached the bar, a warehouse-style building

with a rooftop deck. A guitar chord ripped through the air above them as the band warmed up. Their entourage pressed close to Bella as she neared the door. She flirted with the bouncer, drawing his attention to the BRIDE sash draped over her breasts. He smiled and waved them in.

A man bumped into Grace, jostling her sideways.

"Hey, sorry," he slurred.

Grace stepped around him just as the Rileys disappeared through the door. Grace rushed to follow, but the bouncer grabbed her arm.

"ID?"

She unzipped her wristlet and took it out. The bouncer plucked it from her hand, and Grace held her breath as he studied it. It wasn't bad. Actually, it was good. It had a real Texas seal and a bar code on the back. The bouncer looked from the photo to Grace and shook his head.

"Sorry." He handed it back.

"What do you mean?"

"Can't let you in with that."

"But—"

"Step back." He reached over her for another girl's license. She looked sixteen, but she was thin and pretty. He barely glanced at her before waving her through.

Burning with humiliation, Grace stepped away from the door. She looked up at the rooftop deck and took out her phone.

Crap, what to write? She decided to go for lighthearted.

My ID didn't work! Followed by three crying-face emojis.

Grace tucked the ID away and stood in the sweltering heat, waiting for Bella's response. Would she come down and sweet-talk the bouncer? Round everyone up to go to another bar? Yeah, right. Grace wasn't betting on it.

A text bubble popped up as Bella started to respond. Then it disappeared.

Grace bit her lip. Sweat pooled in the cups of the tight strapless bra she'd worn with her off-the-shoulder blouse. She waited a minute. Two. Three. A bitter lump lodged in her throat. She should have known this would happen.

Grace took a deep breath and texted again: *no worries see you back at the hotel later!*

She waited another minute, but still no response. Clutching the strap of her wristlet, she set off down the street. She held her head high, as though there was nowhere she'd rather be right now than walking down Sixth Street all by herself. Grace blinked back tears. The hotel was eight blocks away, maybe nine, and the straps of her shoes cut into her skin.

She never should have come. She didn't know these people, and she couldn't afford it. She'd come for Bella, but her cousin had been too wrapped up in the wedding plans to even talk to

11

her. Now Grace had wasted not only a weekend she could have worked but thirty dollars' worth of gas, plus her share of the hotel room.

She stopped on the corner and looked around. Where the hell was the hotel? It had to be close. She took out her phone to check the map.

An SUV pulled over, its window rolling down.

"Hey, you call for a ride?" the driver asked. He wore a baseball cap and a blue button-down shirt that matched his eyes.

Grace noted the sticker on his windshield. "No, not me."

He smiled. "Would you like one?"

"I don't have the app, sorry."

He looked her over. "Tell you what, I'll make an exception. You can pay cash. Where you going?"

"The Marriott."

"Five bucks."

Grace hesitated. She should walk. It couldn't be more than a few blocks away. But thinking of her raw feet, she reached for the door.

The back seat was clean and spacious. It smelled like piña coladas and faintly of vomit. She noticed the pineapple-shaped air freshener dangling from the rearview mirror.

Grace checked her messages as he pulled away from the curb.

"You here for the festival?"

She glanced up. "What?"

12

"The music festival?"

"No. A bachelorette party."

"Where you from?"

"Houston," she lied.

A text came in from Bella. Two frowny emojis and then, *ok c u soon!!*

Of course, she'd waited until now to respond, when there was no chance of Grace ruining their plans.

Grace should have listened to her mom. She'd always said Bella was selfish. Well, she'd never said those exact words. But she knew what her mom thought of her own sister, and she'd said, *The apple doesn't fall far from the tree with that one.*

They turned into an alley, and Grace glanced around, startled. "Um, the hotel's on Brazos Street?"

"Shortcut."

His eyes met hers in the rearview mirror, and Grace's skin went cold.

She pulled out a twenty-dollar bill. "Actually, just drop me off here, thanks."

He turned into an even darker alley beside a parking garage. Grace's throat went dry as he rolled to a stop.

She lunged for the door, but it wouldn't open. Her heart hiccuped as he turned in his seat and reached back.

Pain blazed through her, and she reeled sideways. She couldn't move, couldn't breathe. She tried to lift her head.

Another jolt fired through her body, this one bigger and brighter, like grabbing a live wire. White-hot pain seared her. She couldn't move or hear, but she tasted blood and smelled her clothes burning.

And then there was nothing.

Nothing, nothing, nothing, only black.

CHAPTER 2

It was a beautiful wedding, as weddings went. Quaint country church. Polished wooden pews. Antique stained glass, with thick beams of light shining through. But the best thing about it was its brevity. Barely an hour after the first organ notes, Sara Lockhart was standing under an oak tree at the Magnolia Bistro ordering a glass of wine.

"Buy you a drink?"

Sara glanced up as her lab assistant stepped over.

"Thanks, but it's an open bar," she said.

"I'm kidding." Aaron turned to the bartender as Sara collected her wineglass. "Shiner Bock."

The bartender popped the top off an icy bottle, and Sara stuffed a tip into his jar. Careful not to snag a heel, she led Aaron across the cobblestone patio to a patch of shade under an awning.

"So, where's the happy couple?" Aaron swigged his beer.

"My guess? Still stuck at the church taking pictures."

Sara sipped her wine and looked Aaron over. At

six-two, he was a head taller than she was. His spiky hair had been tamed with gel today, and he wore a navy suit that hung loose on his lean frame.

Aaron was Sara's assistant at the Delphi Center Crime Lab, where they worked in the forensic anthropology department, fondly referred to as the Crypt. Aaron typically wore jeans and T-shirts or dusty coveralls if they were out in the field.

"What?" he asked.

"You clean up nicely."

"You're surprised?"

"Not at all. I'm just not used to you in a suit."

"You clean up pretty nice yourself," he said. "Don't think I've ever seen you in a dress before."

She looked down at her short black wrap dress. She'd heard it was bad luck to wear black to a wedding. But it had been this or the gray suit she wore to court, and she couldn't bring herself to show up to a party looking like an attorney.

She glanced up. Aaron was watching her steadily, and she reminded herself that they were coworkers. No flirting. Of course, that applied to every man she knew here, so she was in for a dull evening unless she wanted to mingle with the groom's friends. Which she should. Definitely. The whole point of coming was to meet people.

The conversation lagged, and Sara eyed the

door, wishing for the bride and groom to appear. The sooner they arrived, the sooner festivities could commence in earnest, and the sooner she could sneak out.

A buzz emanated from Aaron's pocket. He looked relieved for the interruption as he pulled out his phone.

"Sorry. Mind if I . . . ?"

"Go ahead."

He stepped away to take the call, and Sara turned her attention back to the courtyard filling up with guests. Even with the misters going, it was *hot*. Texas-in-July hot. Most of the men had already tossed their jackets over chairs and rolled up their sleeves.

From her meager slice of shade, Sara scanned the patio. Mason jars filled with red, white, and blue snapdragons dotted the tables. In a nod to the upcoming Fourth of July holiday, every center-piece included glittery red-and-blue sparklers. Sighing, Sara wished again that she could leave soon. It wasn't the heat or the standing-alone part that made her uncomfortable; it was the wedding. The nuptials. The promise of wedded bliss, for-ever and ever, amen. After running out on her own wedding and dealing with the aftermath, she felt cynical about the entire ritual. Usually, she kept her feelings buried, but today's festivities had brought everything bubbling to the surface. Subtly, she checked her watch. She wanted to chug her chardonnay and take off, but she forced herself to stay put and paste a smile on her face as she watched the crowd.

A man caught her eye from across the courtyard. Mark? Mitch? He worked in the DNA lab, but they'd never been introduced. And crap, he was coming over.

Her phone chimed, and she whipped it from her purse. "Hello?"

"Dr. Lockhart?"

"Speaking."

"I'm—" Noise drowned out the voice as the bride and groom made their big entrance. Brooke looked radiant in her fitted ivory gown, and cheers went up from the crowd as Sean pulled her in for a kiss.

"Sorry," Sara told the caller. "Just a sec."

She ducked around the side of the restaurant and found a narrow walkway near a back door. Through a window, she saw waiters and cooks rushing around the kitchen.

"I'm sorry, go ahead."

"I'm Detective Nolan Hess, Springville PD."

Sara's pulse quickened at the tone of his voice, and she dug through her purse for a pen.

"I'm at White Falls Park," he continued. "That's on the outskirts of—"

"I know where it is. What can I do for you, Detective?"

"A couple of hikers discovered some bones

this evening. The ME gave me your number. We could use your help out here."

"Which ME?"

"Doc Froehler over at the Travis County ME's Office. They handle our cases."

"Okay. Are you sure they're *human* bones? People often mistake—"

"There's no mistake. How soon can you be here?"

"You mean tomorrow?"

"Tonight."

She glanced at her watch again. "Well, we've only got a few hours of daylight left."

No response.

"I could make it if I left now." No pen in her purse. Only a lipstick, damn it.

"Sounds good. What's your vehicle?"

Sara gritted her teeth. She didn't mind leaving the wedding, but his pushiness was another story. Then again, she had yet to meet a detective who *wasn't* pushy when he wanted something. Which was pretty much always.

"I drive a black Explorer," she said. "Why?"

"I'll tell Tom, the park ranger. We shut the park down early. You know the way?"

"I can find it."

"Come to the west entrance, off Route Twelve."

"West entrance. Got it."

"Oh, and Doc? Bring sturdy shoes. You'll need them."

• • •

She took the interstate north from San Marcos, then cut west toward Springville, which had been a farming community before the fast-growing city of Austin began to encroach. Scattered farms gave way to trailer parks, then modest neighborhoods with names like Oak Grove and Shady Creek. Then the real money kicked in, and she passed a series of subdivisions with dramatic entrances. Saddle Ranch. Belmont Hills. Churchill Downs. There wasn't a horse in sight, or even a pasture, but luxury cars abounded. Sara navigated half a dozen congested traffic lights before the highway narrowed and she spied a sign assuring her that White Falls Park was only ten miles ahead.

She was losing daylight. She nudged up her speed and glanced at the quiet cell phone on the seat beside her. Nolan Hess had been determined that she come tonight. She could only guess why. Depending on the age of the hikers who discovered the bones, he might be worried about word leaking out on social media, which would cause headaches for his investigation.

Was that the only reason, though? She'd never worked with Hess before, but he'd been confident the bones were human. Sara was keeping an open mind. The Delphi Center forensic anthro unit got all sorts of bones. She'd known veteran law-enforcement officers who'd sent in remains they insisted were human, only to be told they belonged to a cow or a deer or even a raccoon.

A rural sheriff's deputy bringing bones to the lab was one thing, and it happened all the time. A police detective calling Sara on a Saturday and insisting that she drive a hundred miles to view bones in situ was another. Nolan Hess was adamant, and he was in a hurry.

Sara scanned the rolling hills. Away from sprinkler systems and lawn crews, the ground was brown and thirsty. Oaks and cedars dotted the landscape, along with the occasional herd of cattle. The cows took shelter wherever they could, under trees and near fence posts, waiting listlessly for the temperature to dip.

Sara turned onto Highway 12 and soon spotted a sign pointing to the west entrance of White Falls Park. She took the turn, trading smooth asphalt for a pitted road that was several decades past needing attention. After a few jaw-rattling potholes, she reached the west gate. A rusted swag of chain blocked the way.

No gatehouse. No attendant. Cursing, she shoved her Explorer into park and got out to look around. She walked over to the chain, examined it a moment, then unhooked it from the metal pole. After driving through, she got out and reattached the barrier, not that it provided much of a deterrent.

She proceeded through a parched valley flanked by steadily rising cliffs. The terrain here was rugged. Hard. She was glad she had her hiking boots with her. She still needed to change clothes, but she hadn't wanted to take the time to pull over.

Another sign appeared, offering a choice between WHITE FALLS LOOP or PARK HEAD-QUARTERS. Sara opted for headquarters, taking a road that made a gentle ascent to the top of a plateau. She came to another sign—yet another decision point, but this time she had help in the form of a red-and-blue flicker on some distant cliffs. Pointing her car toward the emergency lights, she followed the road through some scrub and brush and turned into a gravel lot where vehicles were parked haphazardly. A dusty white pickup, several old hatchbacks, a green Suburban with the logo for Allen County Parks District on the door. Sara pulled into a spot beside a police cruiser where a uniformed officer sat talking on his radio. He didn't spare her a glance as she got out.

Sara zeroed in on a woman with blond dread-locks seated on a railroad tie near the trailhead. The woman swiped tears from her cheeks as she talked to a shirtless man crouched beside her. He wore cargo shorts and climbing shoes and had a brown pouch attached to his belt.

"Park's closed, ma'am."

Sara turned to see a man in an olive-green park ranger uniform striding over.

"Hi," she said. "I got a call from Detective Hess with Springville PD."

He stopped and looked her over, frowning. "Who are you?"

"Dr. Sara Lockhart from the Delphi Center Crime Lab." She reached into the car and grabbed her wallet, flipping it open to show him her official ID, because her little black wrap dress wasn't helping her credibility. "Are you by chance Tom?"

"Tom left," he said, resting his hands on his hips.

"Okay. And where is Detective Hess?"

"At HQ." He looked her over again, glaring hard at her shoes. "Stay here."

With that, he trudged up the hill toward a small brown building.

Sara looked at the sky as the last flicker of sun disappeared behind the cliffs. The canyons around her shifted from warm yellows to cool grays. The cool was an illusion, though, and the day's heat radiated up through the thin soles of Sara's patent-leather heels.

She surveyed the scene, taking note of the emergency workers. A man dressed in hiking gear and a red T-shirt handed the dreadlocks woman a bottle of water. He eyed Sara across the parking lot, looking not exactly hostile but skeptical.

Sara walked to the trailhead, where a map behind plexiglass told her she was at the top of Rattlesnake Gorge. Beside the map was a litany of prohibitions: overnight camping, campfires, alcoholic beverages. The list went on.

A coil of blue climbing rope sat on the ground nearby, and she stepped over for a closer look. Heeding the numerous warning signs, she stayed a safe distance from the cliff's edge.

Boots crunched on gravel behind her—the man in the red shirt.

"Who set up this rappel?" she asked.

"I did." He offered her a handshake. "Bryce Gaines. I'm with ACSAR."

"ACSAR?"

"Allen County Search and Rescue. I heard you say you're from the Delphi Center. So you're here about the body, I'm guessing?"

Interesting word choice. Sara nodded at the couple across the parking lot.

"Are those the hikers who found it?"

"Climbers, actually. But yeah." He combed his shaggy brown hair from his eyes. "They were down there in Rattlesnake. Boyfriend was in the lead. He was halfway up the wall when she spotted the body. She tried to climb out, but then she got panicked and froze up on a ledge. Boyfriend called for help." Bryce nodded at the rappelling station. "We went down after her, got her in a harness, and hoisted her out of there."

"You and . . . ?"

"Guy from my team. By the time we got her up, the police were here, the rangers, everyone wanting a statement. Word travels fast." He shook his head. "We had a hiker go missing a while back. Guess they're thinking it might be her."

"And did you see the remains when you were down in the gorge?" She didn't want to use the word *body* at this point. It would only fuel rumors.

"I didn't stop to explore. Just got her tied in and out of there. I was worried she might have another panic attack, and that's a long drop."

Sara looked at the woman again. "Is she injured?"

"Nah, just freaked out. Evans—that ranger you met—he won't let them leave yet. Think he plans to slap them with a fine for illegal climbing."

Bryce's phone buzzed, and he pulled it from his pocket. "Sorry, I have to take this."

"Sure."

He stepped away, and Sara looked at the climbers. The man had a Mayan sun god tattooed on his arm. No longer looking so distraught, he and his girlfriend were busy with their cell phones. Posting about their adventures? Ordering a pizza? Who knew. She'd let Hess worry about that. Right now, she had work to do.

She retrieved the duffel she kept in the back of

her Explorer and ducked into the bathroom near the trailhead. After changing into her blue Delphi Center coveralls and hiking boots, she returned to her SUV and made some selections from her evidence kit: gloves, tweezers, several glass specimen jars. She didn't have a headlamp, so her mini-Maglite would have to suffice. She loaded everything into a black zipper pack and clipped it around her waist, then grabbed her digital camera and looped the strap around her neck.

Sara walked to the cliff's edge and crouched to examine the rappel setup, ignoring the drop-off just inches away. The anchor consisted of two bolts, which would distribute the load, both drilled directly into the rock face.

Bryce ended his phone call and walked over.

"These are expansion bolts?" she asked.

"That's right."

"Mind if I borrow your harness?"

"Depends," he said. "You know what you're doing?"

"Yes."

"You realize there's a trail that goes down there, right? Moderate grade."

"I saw the map. Two-point-six miles." She nodded at the rope. "This is faster."

He picked up the harness and handed it to her. "You want a helmet?"

"Any chance you have one with a headlamp?"

"Absolutely."

He trekked off to a green hatchback, and Sara shifted her attention to the hardware, checking for fissures in the metal.

"It's bombproof," Bryce said, returning with the helmet. "Nothing's going anywhere."

Sara stepped into the harness and buckled it around her waist. Bryce checked the fit and nodded.

"Hey!"

Ranger Evans was back now, his face reddening as he charged across the parking lot. "What do you think you're doing?"

"Going down there." She snugged the helmet on her head.

"That scene's off-limits. Authorized personnel only."

"I'm a board-certified crime-scene investigator." She tightened her chin strap. "Did you tell the detective I'm here?"

"Yeah, but—"

"If you've got a problem, take it up with him."

"But you're not authorized—"

"Springville PD summoned me to this location. It's their jurisdiction. I need to examine this scene before nightfall, and we're burning daylight." Sara stepped around Evans and clipped the belay device into her harness. She double-checked the system and made sure her carabiners were locked.

The ranger stalked away, and Bryce shook

his head. "Guy's a prick," he muttered. Then he looked Sara over. "Everything locked?"

"Yes."

"Okay, it's a hundred-forty-foot wall. Slight overhang at the top. Ledge about two-thirds down, case you need to stop."

"I'm good."

She approached the edge and turned her back to the abyss. Holding the brake strands in her right hand, she leaned back until the rope was taut, positioning her body as though sitting in an invisible chair. Her heart thudded as she adjusted her grip.

First a long, deep breath to help her focus. And then she took the most unnatural of steps—backward off the cliff.

CHAPTER 3

Sara used the rope like a brake as she walked down the wall and reached the overhang Bryce had mentioned, a distinct curve as the rock sloped inward. Her stomach clenched as she dipped her foot down and felt nothing but air. It was a leap—part faith, part science, but always nerve-racking—as her leg dangled and she leaned into the void. She fed more rope through the belay device until her toes touched stone. The wall curved again, and she was able to press the soles of her boots flush against the rock.

Sara looked straight ahead, studying the striations in the limestone as she walked down, nice and easy. Weeds and saplings clung stubbornly to the rock face. She didn't look down. Instead, she focused on the honeycomb texture and felt the residual heat coming off the rock. Sweat slid down her temples. She concentrated on her breathing and on keeping her fingers away from the sharp teeth of the belay device as the rope slid through. Sweat beaded at her temples, and not only from the heat.

Sara had been on a volunteer search-and-rescue team when she was in grad school. She hadn't rappelled in years, but she remembered the basics, and the details were coming back to her—such as that tight, sickly feeling in her stomach as she gripped the brake strands, slowly feeding the rope through. She was more than one hundred feet up, and as a forensic anthropologist, she knew what that sort of fall could do to the human body.

The gorge was narrow here—only sixty feet across, give or take, so more than twice as deep as it was wide. After several long minutes, she reached the ledge where Bryce had rescued the stranded climber. It was a small outcropping, barely a ledge at all, and she noticed the faint shoe prints in the dirt there. She didn't stop.

Down, down, down. Her pulse pounded. Her mouth felt dry and cottony. The space around her grew cooler and dimmer, and she peeked over her shoulder to survey the gorge's shadowy floor.

A great gust whipped up. Startled, she lost her grip on the brake strand and dropped abruptly, then jerked to a halt. A black cloud *whooshed* around her, swooping, flapping, squeaking, and she hunched forward and squeezed her eyes shut.

Bats. She clenched her teeth as thousands of little winged mammals swirled around her. Seconds ticked by. Minutes. When the air was still again, she opened her eyes and gazed up at the black cloud curling against the lavender sky.

Deep breath.

Peering over her shoulder, she searched the base of the wall and spotted the dark maw of a cave. Her heart did a flip-flop.

Not much scared her. She wasn't afraid of snakes or rats or creepy-crawly insects. She could handle musty bones and decomposing flesh. But tight spaces got to her. And she desperately hoped the remains she'd come for weren't tucked back in that hole.

She continued down the wall, alert now for more surprises, such as a loose rock tumbling down on her head. At last, the wall sloped toward her, and her feet touched ground. Relief flowed through her, and her stomach muscles relaxed. She unhooked herself from the rope and unfastened the harness.

"Off rappel!" she called toward the top.

Bryce hollered down and gave the rope a tug.

Sara stepped away from the wall and did a slow three-sixty, taking in the setting. She paused to listen. No flap of bat wings. No hiss of a rattler. The gorge was silent, and for a moment, she simply stood there, surrounded by the hot summer breeze and the pungent smell of guano.

Two hours ago, I was at a wedding, she thought. Some days, her job was surreal.

Sara pulled out her flashlight and beamed it in all directions, trying to get a sense of where the climber might have been standing when she spotted the bones or the body, whatever had sent her into a panic.

Dropping into a crouch, she aimed the flashlight across the ground at an oblique angle. White rocks of all shapes and sizes made up the floor of the gorge, but the terrain was too uneven to expect much in the way of footprints. Sweeping her beam over to the wall, she spotted some initials scratched into rock: *JM & CL.* She shone her light on the wall nearby. Metal glinted. Someone had hammered pitons into the stone—a definite taboo in a park where climbing was prohibited.

Sara stepped closer, scanning the rocks. Was this where they'd started their ascent? She looked around for more clues.

A flash of white caught her eye. She moved closer, switching on her headlamp. Fabric fluttered in the slight breeze. She made her way across the floor of the gorge, and with every step, her stomach tightened with dread.

A cranium protruded from the dirt.

As she reached the spot, Sara's mind kicked into gear with a long list of tasks. At the top of that list was documentation.

Shoot your way in, shoot your way out. The CSI mantra had been drilled into her. After removing the lens cap, Sara lifted her camera and took the first of what would be dozens, maybe hundreds, of pictures tonight.

Snap. Snap. She inched closer, studying the scrap of fabric and the partially buried bones. *Snap. Snap. Snap.*

She lowered her camera and knelt in the dirt, and a familiar mix of pity and outrage washed over her.

Nolan Hess had been right. The remains were human.

But this was no missing hiker.

"Is it her?"

Nolan trekked down the steep slope, surprised he was still getting reception. "Don't know," he told the police chief over the phone.

"Did the anthropologist ever show?"

"Yeah."

"Well, what'd he say?"

"*She* just got here. And I haven't talked to her yet. She's down in the gorge."

Hank Miller cursed. Nolan scanned the trail for loose rocks, but it was hard to see in the dimness.

"I need something, Nolan. Sam Baird's been ringing my phone off the hook since seven o'clock."

"Mine, too." Looking ahead, Nolan caught a flicker of light through the trees.

"And the mayor's calling me. I want an update tonight."

"You'll know something soon as I do," Nolan told him.

The flicker moved back and forth like a pen-dulum, and Nolan stopped to wait, turning on his flashlight so he wouldn't spook her.

"Call me later," Hank said. "I'll be up."

"Will do."

Nolan slid his phone into the pocket of his jeans as Sara Lockhart hiked up the path. According to Evans, she'd shown up dressed for a cocktail party. Now she looked like a miner coming in from a long day. She wore a helmet with a lamp attached—either she'd switched it off, or it had run out of juice—and the knees of her coveralls were brown with dirt. Even with her sleeves rolled up to the elbows, she had to be suffocating in this heat.

She stopped in front of him. "Detective Hess?"

"Call me Nolan." He offered his hand, and she gave it a firm shake.

"Sara Lockhart."

She pulled off the helmet, and honey-colored hair spilled around her shoulders. In the stark glare of the flashlight, her eyes were an impossi-ble shade of green. Nolan tried not to stare.

He cleared his throat. "Thanks for coming. So, what have we got down there?"

"Human remains." She wiped her brow with her forearm. "Advanced decomposition."

"A skeleton?"

"Not quite. There's still some desiccated soft tissue."

He waited for more, but she just looked at him. "Male? Female?"

"I don't know yet," she said. "But based on the personal effects I could see, it's probable we're dealing with a female."

Nolan sighed as he thought of Sam Baird and the raw pain he'd heard in the man's voice message.

"Again, that's *unconfirmed*," she added.

Lightning flashed, and they both looked up. Thunder rumbled in the distance.

"I didn't know it was supposed to rain tonight," Sara said.

"It's not, at least not according to the forecast." Nolan looked around at the arid landscape in the rapidly falling darkness. Ten more minutes, and it would be black as tar. He looked at Sara. "Flash floods can be deadly out here, though. I don't recommend we spend any more time in the gorge tonight."

"I wasn't planning on it."

She stepped around him and continued up the path. Surprised, he trailed behind her. She wasn't tall, but she had long strides, and her hiking boots had seen plenty of use.

"This is a delicate recovery." She looked over her shoulder at him. "I'll need people, equipment. I won't be able to get everything on-site until tomorrow."

He hoped to hell she meant morning, but who

knew how long it would take for her to get people and gear all the way from Delphi? Nolan had never visited the world-famous crime lab, but he knew it was in San Marcos, a good two hours away. The Delphi Center sat on several hundred acres of ranchland that had been converted into a forensic anthropology research center, also known as a body farm.

They reached the top of the trail, and she stopped to look around. "Did Bryce leave?"

"Who?" he asked.

"The search-and-rescue guy."

"Gaines. Yeah." They were on a first-name basis already. "ACSAR cleared out about half an hour ago. Weekends are busy for them."

Sara nodded and surveyed the parking lot. The hatchbacks were gone, leaving only Nolan's truck, the park district Suburban, and a black SUV. Sara pulled some keys from her pocket, along with a cell phone.

"Bars! Hallelujah." She smiled up at him. "I wasn't getting any reception down there."

"Yeah, it's like being in a cave."

Her smile faltered, and she looked down at her screen. "Let me just get a message to my assistant. I need to give him a heads-up about tomorrow."

Nolan watched her nimbly work her phone with one hand while with the other she popped the locks and opened the cargo space of her vehicle. A breeze swept over them, and he caught the scent of her perfume—something soft and feminine, totally at odds with her grimy coveralls and rugged old boots. Nolan watched her, impressed by her brisk confidence. She'd only just arrived, and already she'd taken charge of the scene. After finishing her message, she tucked the phone into her pocket and tossed her helmet into the back.

"So this recovery," he said. "How long will that take?"

"Depends. Could be as quick as a day. Maybe two."

Two days? Nolan bit back a curse. "Any idea how long she's been down there?"

"The sex is unconfirmed, Detective."

"That's Nolan. Any idea how long the *bones* have been down there?"

She unclipped the pack around her waist and added it to the growing pile of gear. "Again, I can't be sure yet, but I'd say six months, at least, possibly more."

Six months or more. So, the remains might belong to Kaylin Baird, and then again, they might not. Nolan raked a hand through his hair.

She grabbed a bottle of water and offered it to him.

"No, thanks."

"I won't be able to tell you anything for certain until I'm back to the lab." She twisted the top off the water and took a gulp, watching him. "These aren't the sort of remains you just pick up and zip into a pouch. They're partially buried. We're talking about an excavation."

"I get that."

She gazed up at him, unapologetic about the delay. He shouldn't have been surprised—she was a scientist.

"Look, Nolan, I understand you have a million questions. I work with investigators all the time, so I know how it goes. I'll get you answers as soon as I can."

He liked that she was using his first name. He *didn't* like that she was holding out on him. He was one-hundred-percent certain she knew more than she was saying.

She looked at her watch, a chunky, masculine thing much too big for her small wrist.

"And now I have a question for *you*."

"What's that?"

"Any chance this town has a motel?"

CHAPTER 4

"Did we cover everything?" Sara asked.

"I think so."

"Thanks again, Aaron." She pressed her phone against her shoulder as she rummaged through her duffel bag. "And sorry to drag you away from the wedding."

"I was leaving anyway. Brooke and Sean already took off."

"Okay, see you tomorrow, then. And text me if you have trouble finding it."

They hung up, and Sara tossed her phone onto the bed with a sigh. It sounded like Aaron was leaving the party alone, which was too bad. He was one of the few people at work who had even less of a social life than she did. Aaron avoided happy hours and always seemed perfectly content to eat lunch at his desk. Sara knew the feeling.

She went into the bathroom and unwrapped the tiny bar of soap beside the sink. Despite the worn carpet and faded bedspread, the Morningstar Motor Lodge was reasonably clean, which was all she ever hoped for in a cheap motel.

She scrubbed her face and arms, then eyed her reflection in the mirror as she dried off with a towel. Her hair—which she'd so carefully styled this afternoon—was messy and windblown, and she twisted it into a knot. Her growling stomach reminded her she hadn't eaten in hours, and she wistfully recalled the cocktail shrimp and wedding cake she'd planned to have for dinner tonight. She checked her watch: 11:45. If she hustled, she could probably still get a bite before everything closed for the night.

She grabbed her purse and her room key. Stepping into the oven-hot air, she counted only five other vehicles in the motel lot. The front office was dark, along with the diner next door. Sara glanced across the street and saw the grocery store was dark, too, and its parking lot completely deserted.

"Crap." She sighed and looked around.

A dusty white pickup turned left at the intersection. It swung into the motel lot, and Sara's nerves did a little dance.

Nolan Hess. The detective was tall and powerfully built. He had warm brown eyes and an easygoing smile, but underneath all that was an edge. The man had that hyperalert attitude that Sara always associated with cops.

He glided to a stop in front of her, and something about his arm resting on the door of his truck sent a warm flutter through her stomach.

"Settling in okay?" he asked.

"Yes. Actually, no. Is there a drive-through still open where I can get something to eat?"

"Not a one."

"Maybe a Walmart?"

"Nope."

She sighed. "What about a convenience store?"

"I know a gas station that's probably open. Hop in."

She stared at him. She'd grown up in the city, where you didn't accept rides from strange men, badge or no. It was an ironclad rule, drilled into her by her overprotective father, who was a commander in the Coast Guard.

Screw it, she was hungry. She walked around and climbed into the passenger seat.

"Thank you."

"No problem."

She fastened her seat belt, suddenly self-conscious about her filthy coveralls and dusty hair. Nolan pulled out of the lot quickly, and she looked at his hand on the steering wheel. No wedding ring, but she'd noticed that already.

He glanced at her.

"I talked to my assistant," she said. "We're all set for tomorrow."

He nodded. "What can we do?"

"Keep people out of the park, mainly. Bone recovery sites tend to attract onlookers. And sometimes treasure hunters."

"We're on it. Tom barricaded the gates, and we've got officers patrolling tonight to make sure things stay quiet."

"Good." She only hoped Tom's idea of a barricade was something more than a rusty chain.

"So, how's it look so far? I assume we're dealing with a homicide?"

"We shouldn't jump to that conclusion," she said.

"So . . . suicide? Accidental fall?" His voice was skeptical.

"Until we've done a full excavation, I won't have sufficient evidence to make that determination."

"But you're experienced," he said, clearly opting for flattery. "What's your gut so far, based on what you've seen?"

"I don't know yet," she insisted. "I won't have conclusive answers for you until I get the bones to the lab."

He fell silent, as though letting it go. For now, at least. But his impatience was palpable.

She stole another glance at him. He had prominent cheekbones and a square jaw—an undeniably attractive combination. Some women swooned over big muscles, but Sara was a sucker for good bone structure.

Not that he was lacking in the muscles department. He had wide shoulders, and she liked the way his big hand rested casually on the gearshift. Simply driving his truck, the man exuded confidence.

He pulled into a gas station, and Sara immediately spotted the CLOSED sign posted on the door.

"Damn it," she muttered. Was a day-old hot dog and a toothbrush too much to hope for?

Nolan parked and shoved open his door. "Come on."

Sara slid from the truck as he walked over and tapped his knuckles on the door. A fiftyish woman in reading glasses looked up from behind the cash register, and Nolan gave her a wave. She walked around the counter to unlock the door.

"Evenin', Mary Jo."

"Nolan." She smiled and held the door open. "Working late tonight?"

"Yes, ma'am." He stepped inside, and Sara followed him into the air-conditioning. "Any chance you got some of that coffee?"

"I was just about to pitch it. Want me to make a fresh pot?"

"I'll take whatever you got left. Mind if we have a look around?"

"Of course not." She looked at Sara over her reading glasses. "Help you find anything, hon?"

"I'm fine, thank you." Sara turned down an aisle, leaving Nolan to chat up the shopkeeper as she looked for a few necessities. She found a travel toothbrush kit, a box of granola bars, and a cellophane-wrapped turkey sandwich. She'd skip the beverages and make do with the water she had back in her room.

Glancing over the row of shelves, she saw the shopkeeper was now deep in conversation with Nolan. The woman turned to look at Sara, and her serious expression let Sara know they were talking about the bone discovery. Springville was a small community, and the news was probably all over town by now.

Sara made her way to the front and set her items beside the register.

"It's on the house," the woman said with a wave.

"Oh, I couldn't."

"I insist." She looked at Nolan. "Y'all take care now. Say hi to your folks."

"Thanks for the coffee." Nolan nodded and lifted his cup as he pushed open the door.

"She didn't have to do that," Sara said as they walked to the pickup. Nolan went around and opened the passenger door—a display of manners that left her speechless.

"She wanted to," he said. "She knows why you're here, and she wants to help."

"Still, I feel bad."

"Don't worry about it."

They drove back to the motel, which was on the far west side of town, and Sara took in the view. All the storefronts were dark, which seemed unusual for a Saturday night.

Sara wasn't used to small-town friendliness or gifts from strangers or men opening doors for her. But Nolan seemed at ease with all of it.

She looked at him. "Did you grow up here?"

He nodded. "Grew up, moved away, came back."

"It's a nice town. Quaint."

He made a noncommittal sound.

"You don't think so?"

"Looks can be deceiving." He glanced at her. "Crime is on the rise. Meth labs, human trafficking, sexual assault. We've got everything."

"Less than the city, at least."

He lifted an eyebrow but didn't comment, and a silence settled over them. Sara looked out the window again, tearing her gaze away from him. Everything about him was so masculine, and she kept catching herself staring at his mouth, his neck, his hands. She had to stop it. She was here to work, not to flirt.

"Thanks for doing this," he said. "I understand we pulled you away from a party?"

"A wedding."

He winced.

"It's okay."

"Family?" he asked.

"A colleague of mine. And it's not like we're best friends or anything. Really, it was a courtesy invitation. I moved here not long ago, so I'm the new girl at work."

"Moved here from . . . Maryland?"

She blinked at him. "Rockville. How'd you know that?"

"Your accent."

"Damn. I thought I got rid of that."

He shrugged. "My grandmother's from Bethesda."

He turned into the motel parking lot and pulled up to the sidewalk. "It's not exactly the Ritz, but the diner next door does a good breakfast."

"The manager told me." Sara gathered her items and looked at him across the dim truck cab. And for the first time, she noticed the creases around his eyes and the shadow along his jaw. He'd had a long day, as she had, but still he seemed energized. She wondered about the coffee he'd picked up and whether the officers patrolling the park tonight included him.

"We'll start early tomorrow," she said. "Before the heat sets in."

He nodded. "Up with the sun."

The expression caught her off guard. It was one of her dad's favorites, and Sara suddenly missed his voice. Maybe she should call him tomorrow. Catching up with her parents would take her mind off the lonely motel room. They'd be full of news about her brother and her nieces, which was sure to take her mind off tomorrow's grim task, too.

"What's wrong?" Nolan asked.

46

"Nothing. Thanks for the ride." She opened her door.

"Thank you for coming out tonight."

"No problem."

Another nod. "Good night, Sara."

She felt his gaze on her as she walked to her door and slid in the key card. He waited until she was safely inside before pulling away.

Nolan thought about her as he returned to the police station.

Sara Lockhart was smart. Headstrong. And those big green eyes were going to be a distraction from what he needed to be focused on right now—leading a murder investigation. Because no matter how cagey Sara acted, Nolan knew in his gut that they were dealing with a homicide, and this case had the potential to rock his community to its core. According to Mary Jo, news of the bone discovery in White Falls Park had already spread like brushfire.

Nolan's thoughts went to Sara again. She was beautiful, no getting around it. She was assertive, too, and she refused to be pressured, which was good and bad. Bad because he was impatient. Good because when he finally did get her conclusions, he felt confident they'd be the result of careful study. He had to respect her methods. Having seen more than one major case fall apart at trial due to sloppy lab work, he knew the importance of precision and accuracy.

Nolan spotted a familiar gray truck as he neared the police station.

"Shit," he muttered. Instead of parking in his usual space, he pulled up alongside the truck and gave the man behind the wheel a nod before getting out.

The driver's-side window was down, and Nolan walked over.

"Evening, Sam."

"Nolan."

The man's eyes were bloodshot. He'd been crying or drinking, maybe both.

Sam leveled a look at him. "I heard about the bones."

Nolan nodded. "Want to come in for some coffee and we can talk?"

"I don't need coffee. I need you to shoot straight with me."

"All right." Nolan stepped closer. "I'll tell you what I know. About five o'clock, two hikers discovered some remains in Rattlesnake Gorge."

Sam's gaze didn't waver.

"We got an expert out there, a forensic anthropologist, and she confirms the bones are human. They'll be excavated tomorrow, but so far, we don't know whether this is a male or a female, and there's nothing to indicate ID yet."

Sam looked ahead. The man was fifty-one, only fifteen years older than Nolan, but the past year had added a decade. Losing a child took a brutal toll. Nolan had been working for a year to find the family some answers, but so far, he'd failed, and that failure ate away at him every day. There was no getting away from it. In a town this size, the reminders were everywhere.

Sam reached to the seat beside him and picked up a manila envelope. "When Kaylin was nine, she got thrown from a horse. Broke her arm in two places. These are the X-rays."

Nolan took the envelope, feeling awkward as he looked down at it.

"Give that to your expert," Sam said. "See if it speeds things along."

"I'll do that."

Sam started up the truck. "Call when you know something, day or night. You've got all our numbers."

Nolan put his hand on the door. "You okay to drive?"

Sam gave him a hard look, then put the truck in gear and backed out of the space. Nolan's chest ached as he watched him drive away.

Pain surrounded her like water.

Grace was floating in it. Swimming in it. Drowning in it. Only she couldn't move.

She couldn't see. Couldn't hear. The pain was thick and heavy, pressing hard against her skin, flattening the air from her lungs.

Grace's head pounded. It was like a hangover but worse—like the morning after she and her friend Ava had raided the liquor cabinet, taking a shot from every bottle so her parents wouldn't notice anything was gone.

My parents. Oh, God.

Grace's eyes filled with tears, and she squeezed them shut.

Her eyes had been open. She realized that now. She could open and close her eyes, and everything remained pitch-black.

Where am I?

The question sent a zing of panic through her. She had to get out.

She tried to move her arms. Nothing. Her fingers. Nothing. Each of her limbs felt weighted down. She couldn't even move her toes, and just the effort made the pain intensify.

She tried moving her tongue. It felt thick and swollen, and she realized there was a gag inside her mouth. Moving her tongue around as much as she could, she tasted something sour, maybe vomit. And something else, too, something sweet. Grape but not like the fruit—more like the purple cold-medicine kind. Had she been drugged?

She tried to wet her lips, but her tongue was too dry. The corners of her mouth felt parched and stinging, same as her throat.

A sudden movement, and she jerked sideways.

I'm in a car.

The burst of clarity brought a wave of relief. But it turned to despair when the next thought came: *Where is he taking me?*

He.

Grace pictured the blue eyes, the blue shirt, the blue arm reaching back. Terror shot through her like an electric jolt. He'd used a stun gun on her.

Another bump, and the side of her foot scraped against something. She was barefoot. What about her clothes? Another zing of panic, because she couldn't *see* anything. But then she registered the sharp point near her armpit. Her strapless bra. The underwire protruding through the fabric. The familiar feel of it poking into her skin gave her a speck of comfort.

Another bump. And then another. Her knee knocked against something hard as the vehicle bounced and rattled. They weren't on a road, at least not a good one.

Where is he taking me?

The car slowed. Grace's heart skittered. Her breath came in shallow gasps. *Don't panic. Don't panic. Breathe, breathe, breathe.*

The car rolled to a stop.

CHAPTER 5

When Sara arrived at the park at 6:45, Nolan was already there, leaning casually against the back of his pickup with a coffee cup in hand. She pulled into the space beside him and got out, looking him over. If not for the gun and the badge clipped to his belt, he could have passed for a hiker in his all-terrain boots and khaki tactical pants. The layer of stubble on his jaw was even thicker now.

"Morning," he said.

"Good morning. How'd it go here last night?"

"Pretty quiet. We had some mountain bikers around sunup, but I turned them away."

Sara went around to the back of her SUV and opened the cargo door. "Did you sleep out here?"

"Biggs—he's one of our officers—he and I traded shifts. Mine started at four."

She grabbed the thermos she'd filled from the coffeepot in her motel room. "Can I top you off?"

"Definitely."

She unscrewed the cap, and he held out his mug.

"So what's the plan?" he asked as she poured.

He looked her over, brown eyes alert, and seemed eager to get started.

"My lab assistant, Aaron, is coming at seven with gear and grad students." She replaced the top and set down the thermos. "We'll haul everything down, set up a tent to protect from the elements, and begin our work."

"No rain in the forecast. Fact, you're probably aware we've hardly had three inches out here all summer."

"The tent is for the sun, mostly. I don't want my people getting heatstroke."

A low groan of an engine made Sara turn toward the road as a white van came into view. Aaron turned into the lot and pulled into a space beside Sara's Explorer.

"They're early, too," she said.

Aaron got out, eyeing Sara and Nolan. The van door slid open, and a pair of anthropology grad students piled out. Keith and Julia had been handpicked for this job. Both were known for their physical stamina and attention to detail.

Sara introduced everyone, and they started dragging big plastic tubs from the back of the van. Aaron slid poles through the handles, so they could share the weight as they made the long trek down to the excavation site. With Nolan's help, they got everything to the bottom of the gorge in one trip.

After dropping off the last tub, Nolan excused

himself to take care of something in town, promising to check back later. His departure came as a relief. Sara didn't mind getting a hand with the gear, but cops were impatient by nature and tended to get in the way.

Keith and Julia unloaded tools while Sara and Aaron went to work on the tent, assembling the frame with well-practiced movements.

"Helpful detective," Aaron observed.

Sara shot him a look.

"He going to be down here all day?"

"No idea," she said.

After the tent was up, Sara stepped over to examine the recovery site. Spiderwebs glistened with dew, and Sara swatted them away as she knelt for a closer look.

"This ground's hard," Aaron said. "It's going to be a bitch getting our stakes in. Could take all morning just to get the grid set up."

"I know." Sara looked up. "Hand me that mallet, would you?"

It didn't take all morning but half. After staking out the burial site, they used string to divide it into quadrants. By ten o'clock they were digging, and by noon they were fully immersed in the painstaking process of unearthing the half-buried bones and clothing.

The work was hot and tedious, and Sara lost herself in it. Some people listened to music or audiobooks, but Sara preferred a natural sound-track. She liked the quiet drone of the cicadas, the whisper of wind through the canyon, and the soft rasp of bristles as she dusted off bones with her boar's-hair brush.

The sun blazed down. The temperature climbed. Sara ignored the sting of sweat in her eyes as she carefully uncovered an ulna.

"Fractured," she murmured, more to herself than to anyone. With his earbuds in, Aaron was oblivious to her commentary.

Sara sat back and sighed heavily. Then she reached for the camera sitting under the cool shade of the little tent she'd erected for it. She snapped a few pictures of the bone, careful to document the jagged edge, before using a pair of bamboo tongs to lift the shard from the dirt. She never used metal tools directly on bone, wanting to avoid leaving marks that might later be mistaken for signs of violence.

She placed the bone in a cardboard box beside her.

"He's back."

She looked at Aaron. "What?"

He plucked out his earbuds. "And he brought company."

Sara turned around. Her heart skittered as she saw Nolan coming down the path carrying a six-pack of bottled water. A woman walked beside him—dark-haired, petite, dressed almost exactly like Nolan in a navy T-shirt and khaki tactical pants, with a badge and a gun on her hip. Her baseball cap said SPD across the front.

Nolan's gaze met Sara's as he deposited the water beside the tent. She stood and shook out her stiff legs, dusting her hands on her coveralls as Nolan and the woman approached.

"I'd like y'all to meet Natalia Vazquez," Nolan said.

"Call me Talia." She peeled off her sunglasses and nodded at Sara, then Aaron. She had brown-black eyes and a friendly smile.

"Talia's the other full-time detective in my department, and she'll be working this case with us."

Sara introduced her team, starting with Aaron, who was suddenly at her side, eagerly shaking hands with the pretty detective. From under the tent, the grad students looked up from their sifting screens and waved.

Nolan turned to Sara. "Talia wanted to walk the scene, get a look at your setup here."

"I'll show her," Aaron said.

"And I wanted to have a word." Nolan nodded away from the group, indicating he wanted a private conversation.

The sun was almost directly overhead, but Sara found a narrow strip of shade close to the wall. Her clothes were saturated, along with her baseball cap and even her ponytail. She pulled the hat off and wiped her brow with her forearm as she looked up at Nolan.

"Thanks for the water," she said.

"No problem. You're getting some sun."

"I just put block on." She glanced at Aaron beside the excavation pit, then back at Nolan. His hands rested on his hips, and his expression was serious. "What's up, Detective?"

He waited a beat before answering. "How's it coming?"

"Slow."

He nodded. "I heard what you said last night about needing confirmation. But I want to get a look at those personal items."

"Personal items?"

"Whatever you've got so far."

Sara stared up at him for a long moment, reading the determination in his eyes.

"You seem to think you might know who it is."

"A young hiker went missing last year," he said. "Kaylin Baird. There's a chance it's her."

"A chance?"

"Problem is, her backpack was found in another park about twenty miles east of here, so it doesn't quite add up. But still, there's a chance, and her family's hoping."

Hoping. The word put a pang in Sara's chest. She couldn't imagine the nightmare of having a child disappear and going without answers for so many months or years that the discovery of bones was a reason to *hope.*

"I can show you what we have," she said, "but you know personal items can't be used to establish ID."

"I realize that."

"For positive identification, I need fingerprints, DNA, or dental records, and in my line of work, I don't usually see fingerprints, unless I'm dealing with a water recovery." She paused. "Do you know if she's in the system?"

"Fingerprints? No. She was never arrested."

"Not that system. I mean the database. NamUs, the National Missing and Unidentified Persons System. Did the family submit a DNA sample?"

"I'm not sure. I know they were made aware of it back when Kaylin went missing, but I don't know if they ever followed up."

"Find out." Sara nodded at the tent. "In the meantime, if you want to take a look at what we've got so far . . ." She ushered him over to the folding table where recovered items had been sorted into cardboard trays. Four of the trays contained various bones and bone fragments. The last tray held remnants of gray fabric and a heeled sandal. The leather straps were discolored, but they'd once been white.

Nolan stepped up to the table, zeroing in on the sandal. Sara read the disappointment on his face.

"We haven't found the other one." Sara picked

up the ruler she'd used for scale when taking photographs. "The heel is six centimeters. It's hard to imagine someone hiking or even walking out here in shoes like that for any length of time."

He stared down at the items. "What about the fabric?" He looked up. "It's from her clothes?"

"Again, the sex is unconfirmed."

His eyebrows arched.

"I know it seems far-fetched, but I once worked a case where bones and women's clothing were found in a well, and police were about to arrest a nearby resident for killing his wife, who'd been missing. But the remains turned out to be a male prostitute—dressed as a female—who'd been kidnapped and murdered. I really can't tell you anything with certainty until we get all this back to the lab. At that point, I can get you the Big Four." Sara ticked them off on her fingers. "That's age, sex, race, and stature."

"Any chance you'll be back at the lab tomorrow?"

"I don't know. This is a time-consuming process, and there's no cutting corners." She nodded at Keith and Julia, doggedly sifting through every scoopful of dirt she and Aaron had removed from the grave. "Everything from the pit has to be sifted for clues—a wad of gum, a cigarette butt, a scrap of duct tape. The tiniest bit of evidence could be a critical lead. This work takes time."

Nolan studied the fabric, which had a sheen to

it. The cloth was rotted and discolored, likely the remnants of a dress or a long blouse based on the shape of the garment.

And again, not what you would expect a hiker to be wearing.

"Cause of death?" he asked.

"I don't know. Nothing obvious, though, such as a bullet through the skull. As for manner of death, again, it's unclear at this point. I haven't ruled out suicide or accidental death. Maybe this person was out here sightseeing and stepped off a cliff."

Nolan looked at her, his expression grim. He wanted answers. And she planned to give them to him, but she needed time to study the remains and confirm her initial findings.

"When did Kaylin go missing, exactly?" she asked.

"May sixth of last year. Fourteen months ago."

Yet another factor that didn't line up. Sara wasn't sure of the postmortem interval yet, but everything she'd seen so far pointed to a PMI of less than fourteen months.

Nolan combed his hand through his hair and stepped back.

"This family's desperate," he said, clearly frustrated. "You have no idea."

"I do." She held his gaze.

"This girl's parents are begging me for information, and I have to give them something, even if it's bad news. These people are in agony."

"I understand. That's one reason I do this work, Nolan. I know how excruciating it is for people, and I promise to get you some answers. We're working as fast as we can."

He looked at her for a long moment, and Sara knew he was desperate, too. And not just for answers about Kaylin. If these bones weren't hers, he was potentially looking at *two* victims in his jurisdiction.

Nolan was a leader. She'd sensed that about him from the moment they met. He held himself accountable for everything that happened in his jurisdiction.

He rubbed the back of his neck as he stared down at the lonely white sandal that had been ravaged by the elements.

"I left an envelope on the front seat of your car," he said. "It's X-rays from when Kaylin was a child. Her parents are hoping they might help with the ID."

"Thank you. I'll take a look."

Nolan's attention shifted to the burial pit, then back to Sara. "How can I help?"

"Well, the water's a big help."

"I'm serious. Give me a shovel, and let me pitch in with the real work."

Sara had expected the offer. "Are you trained in bone recovery?"

"No, but you can teach me."

"This isn't the place. Come visit us at the lab, and we can put you in a class with some grad students."

"There has to be something I can do for you."

Sara gazed up at him, once again seeing the determination in his eyes. "Well, there is something. I've been putting it off because I'm a bit squeamish."

"You? Squeamish?" He smiled. "You dig up corpses for a living."

"Yes, well, I'm claustrophobic. Do you have any problem with tight spaces?"

"No. Show me what you need."

Ignoring the curious looks from Keith and Julia, Sara retrieved a pair of flashlights from the equipment bin and handed one to Nolan. She grabbed her camera from beside the burial pit and looped it around her neck.

"This way."

She led him under the shadow of an overhang and tromped along the floor of the gorge, acutely aware of his large male presence beside her. Given his size, he was probably going to regret volunteering for this. Sara spied the carved initials on the rock face and pointed to the yawning black opening about five feet above the ground.

"You want me to check out that cave?" he asked.

"Considering its proximity, we should definitely look to see if there's any physical evidence associated with our crime scene."

He was already climbing over the large rocks leading up to the mouth. He crouched down and ducked his head.

"Entrance is pretty low."

She joined him on the rocks. "Think we can squeeze through?"

"Sure."

He beamed the flashlight into the opening. "Gets bigger inside. Here, point your light for me, would you?"

Sara switched on her flashlight and aimed it into the blackness. Nolan tucked his light into the back of his pants. He then duck-walked inside, somehow managing not to fall on his butt, as she certainly would have.

"I can stand up in here," he said.

Sara switched off her flashlight and tucked it into her bra. She took a deep breath and followed Nolan's lead—although she opted to go on her hands and knees. When she made it inside the cave, Nolan offered her a hand and helped her to her feet.

The air was cool and smelled of sulfur. A shiver ran through her. Nolan had room to stand, but still the space seemed impossibly small. Sara's stomach clenched as she thought of the immense weight of rock above their heads.

Nolan was watching her. "You okay?"

"Fine."

He pointed his light at the icicle-shaped rock formations dripping from the ceiling. "Look at that."

"Stalactites." Sara swept her flashlight beam over the floor. "And stalagmites, too."

"I can never remember the difference."

"Just remember *C* for ceiling, *G* for ground." Sara ventured a few steps deeper into the cavern, noting the milky puddles on the floor made from water and mineral deposits.

Nolan walked away, and Sara instinctively followed him, still freaked out to be in here. His presence helped calm her nerves, even though he took up a lot of the limited space.

"Look." He pointed his light at the remnants of a small fire. Nearby, a burned-down pillar candle sat in a pool of dried wax.

"Looks like this is a hangout." Sara set down her flashlight and lifted her camera to snap a photo of the candle.

Nolan stepped away to examine some graffiti on the wall. Sara walked up behind him and dusted a spider off his shoulder.

"What? Shit!" Nolan lurched away.

"Just a spider."

"I freaking hate those things."

"Arachnophobia."

He glared at her, and she smiled.

"Don't be embarrassed—it's the most common phobia."

She knelt to take a photo of the graffiti. The crude pentagram had been carved into the limestone by something sharp, a knife or maybe a car key.

Stepping away again, Nolan inspected the remaining corners of the cave. "That's about it. No bones. No tunnels leading anywhere." He shone his light at the ceiling, illuminating a terrifyingly large swath of black. "Just some bats."

Sara shuddered.

Nolan aimed his light at her. "You seen enough?"

"Yes. Let's go."

"You lead."

Sara duck-walked through the opening, somehow managing not to fall on her butt. Standing up, she blinked at the sun and felt ridiculously grateful to be back in the sweltering heat.

Nolan emerged from the cave and flowed to his feet with the sort of natural athleticism Sara had envied her whole life. She would bet he'd played sports in high school, maybe even college, and probably had a gaggle of girls lusting after him. In high school, Sara had been a science geek and a late bloomer—completely invisible to guys like Nolan.

He dusted his hands on his pants, then glanced over. "What?"

"Nothing."

"So what do you think?" he asked. "Worth the effort?"

"Definitely. I can check the cave off my list. I like to be thorough."

He stepped closer, smiling, and rested his hands on his hips. "How come I knew that about you?" His voice was deep and low, and she couldn't look away from his warm brown eyes.

She cleared her throat. "Thanks for helping."

"Anytime."

The silence stretched out. They stood in the sun, staring at each other, and the only sound was the low drone of locusts.

"Sara."

She whipped her head around. Aaron crouched beside the pit with Talia. He looked from Sara to Nolan, then waved them over.

"You need to see this."

CHAPTER 6

The Delphi Center parking lot was surprisingly crowded, considering it was the day before the Fourth of July. Sara would have thought most people would be taking a long weekend, but apparently not.

She swiped her way into the building and waved at the security guard as she crossed the lobby. With its soaring Doric columns and shiny marble floors, the Delphi Center reminded Sara of the university where she'd once worked. The difference here was the people. They had a certain energy that had been lacking in academia. People weren't only acquiring knowledge but were doing something with it, applying tidy scientific theories to the utter mess of modern life. It's what got Sara up in the morning, and she didn't miss her university job one bit, because she believed in the mission here.

The murmur of jazz music greeted her as she neared the anthro lab. She stepped into her office and tried to find a spot for her tall iced latte on her cluttered desk. Not seeing an inch of free real estate, she set the cup on Kelsey Quinn's desk, which had been uncharacteristically clean for the past two weeks.

"Hey, you're here," Aaron said from the doorway. He wore a white lab coat over jeans and a T-shirt.

"Sorry I'm late. Had to stop for caffeine." Sara grabbed her lab coat off the hook behind the door. "You ray her yet?"

The remains had been a *her* since the pelvis was unearthed yesterday afternoon. Because of the flared iliac blades and wide subpubic angle to accommodate childbirth, Sara had quickly determined the remains were female.

"All finished," Aaron said. "X-rays are up on my laptop."

"Great. Any messages?"

"No."

"I'm expecting a phone call from Dr. Underwood sometime today."

His eyes widened. "*Clifton* Underwood?"

"Yeah."

"Well, I haven't heard anything, and definitely nothing from him. The phone's been silent."

After a gulp of coffee, Sara followed him into the lab and stopped short when she saw the bones spread out on a table. "You cleaned them already?"

He shrugged sheepishly. "I've been here since this morning."

"You didn't have to do all that."

"I know."

"Thanks. Wow."

Cleaning bits of flesh from a skeleton was a messy, stinky process that involved boiling batches of bones in a giant kettle. It wasn't the worst part of the job, but it certainly wasn't her favorite.

She followed Aaron to his notebook computer, which was open on the black slate counter. He tapped the mouse to bring the screen to life. Half a dozen X-rays appeared, two rows of three.

"Not a lot to see, unfortunately."

Sara frowned at the images, hoping to spot anything to contradict his assessment. But as she'd observed down in the gorge, the skeleton displayed no obvious cause of death, such as a bullet hole or a compression fracture to the skull. She tapped the skull image to enlarge it but didn't see any traces of metal left by a projectile.

"No bullet wipe," she said.

"None anywhere."

"And we never recovered the hyoid."

"Nope."

She glanced across the room at the table. "Let's have a look at the hands."

Sara surveyed the skeleton—what they'd recovered of it, anyway. They'd collected a grand total of 152 bones, which wasn't bad, given how long the remains had been exposed to the elements.

Sara stood for a long moment, studying everything. Aaron had done a nearly perfect job arranging the bones. She moved a metacarpal from the right hand to the left and then rotated a tarsal bone in the foot.

Of the 206 bones in the human body, fifty-four were in the hands, and they often told a story. Pulling a magnifying glass from her pocket, Sara leaned over the right hand and studied the phalanges.

"No parry wounds that would indicate she fought off a knife attack." She walked around the table and examined the left hand. "I wish we had that hyoid."

Not all strangulation cases resulted in a broken hyoid, but some did, and it could be a useful indicator for cause of death.

No such luck in this case.

"I couldn't come up with anything," Aaron said.

"I'll keep looking." She glanced up as he checked a text on his phone.

"So, listen—"

"Feel free to take off," she said.

"Are you sure?"

"Absolutely. You worked the weekend."

"I don't mind or anything, but I've got an Ultimate game later, so—"

"Go. And thanks for everything. You went above and beyond."

"Okay, well, I sent you the films, so check your email." He shut down his computer and took off his lab coat as Sara returned her attention to the hands.

"You can come, you know."

She looked up, and Aaron was watching her from the doorway.

"What's that?" she asked.

"The game. It's a bunch of us from Delphi—me, Ben, Roland, Laney. We play every second Monday at five."

"Laney plays Ultimate Frisbee?" Sara tried to picture the pale-skinned cyber sleuth running around a field in the ninety-degree heat.

"Sometimes, yeah." He shrugged. "Or she watches from the sidelines with friends. It's a pretty good time, if you want to join us."

"Thanks, but I've got to give a lecture tonight." One she'd forgotten about until she woke up this morning and realized she hadn't pulled her slides together. She'd been distracted with her trip to Springville. "Maybe next time."

"Sure." But he lifted an eyebrow skeptically as he left the room.

Sara refused to feel guilty for turning him down. It was nothing personal. She really did have a presentation to prep for. But she'd turned down quite a few invitations lately. At some point, her coworkers would simply stop asking, and she'd miss her window of opportunity to make friends. Not that she absolutely *needed* a lot of friends at her workplace, but she spent most of her time here, so it seemed like the logical place to start.

The problem was that most of the people she'd met at work were already part of a couple. Kelsey, Mia, Laney. Brooke had been one of the few holdouts when Sara first moved here, but as of Saturday, she was married, too. And married people tended to try to nudge their friends into relationships. Sara wasn't interested. She was happily single.

Okay, maybe not *happily,* but at least *contentedly.* The last relationship she'd been in had turned her life inside out, and she didn't want another for the foreseeable future.

Sara bent over the bones again and examined the surfaces for any signs of trauma. There were plenty of fractures, but they were consistent with what she'd expect if an inert body was dropped from an elevation. She paid specific attention to the neck bones. A slight nick on the C4 vertebra piqued her interest.

Sara lifted the bone for closer examination. Then she took out a slide and secured the bone with a dab of putty. Turning on her microscope, she placed the slide on the stage and peered through the viewfinder.

A small mark was visible on the anterior surface of C4. But was it a postmortem artifact created by a scavenger? Or was it man-made? The lab's tool-marks examiner could probably tell her. But he wasn't here today, so she'd have to wait.

Sara switched off the microscope and returned to the table with her clipboard. She studied the pelvis, the joints, and the teeth, scribbling notes as she went. She'd promised Nolan an update on the Big Four, and she had a feeling he'd hold her to that.

Nolan Hess.

Detective Hess.

Like so many other cops she'd worked with, he had a strong, confident way about him that bordered on arrogance. Sara didn't mind, really. She liked assertive people, male or female. But along with his confidence, Nolan had something else she'd noticed.

Empathy.

She'd seen it in his eyes when he talked about Kaylin's family. She'd heard it in his voice when he pressured her to speed up her work so he could get them some answers. In Sara's dealings with cops, empathy was much rarer than confidence. It couldn't be learned. It came from the heart. Sara suspected it was one of the many things that made Nolan good at his job.

After making notes about age, sex, race, and stature, Sara got to a trickier question, post-mortem interval. She could ballpark it based on the bones, but to get Nolan something specific—

she hoped—she needed to consult some weather charts.

Sara turned to the table containing the assorted items that had been recovered with the bones. Everything had been sorted into flat cardboard trays, and Sara studied the contents: fabric remnants, three plastic buttons, the white sandal whose mate hadn't been found. Perhaps the most important item was a silver loop earring. Sara had swabbed it for DNA before placing it in a little plastic bag. The earring was small—less than two centimeters—but might be a big lead for investigators in terms of getting an ID. A photo of the earring would be uploaded to NamUs, along with everything else, in hopes of connecting the remains to an unsolved case.

When Sara was all out of distractions, she turned her attention to the last cardboard tray. It contained a tangle of purple twine that had been found near the wrist bones.

Sara stared down at the twine. Thinking about it had kept her up half the night, tossing and turning. Now, using a pair of bamboo tongs, she picked up the tangle, which was knotted in the shape of a figure eight. The twine was caked with dirt, and the ends were frayed. After carefully unearthing it at the gravesite, Sara had studied it, photographed it from every angle, and swabbed it for DNA. The twine might be key to the entire case.

Or it might not. Maybe she was doing what she'd warned Nolan about, which was jumping to conclusions with insufficient evidence.

The phone rang, jolting Sara from her thoughts. She abandoned the trays and rushed to the lab line.

"Osteology."

"Sara."

The familiar voice filled her with relief. But her relief quickly turned to apprehension.

"Cliff, hi. Thank you *so* much for getting back to me." She paused. "Did you have a chance to look at the photos?"

"Yes."

That one word put a knot in her stomach. Clifton Underwood was her mentor, and she knew him well. He was about to confirm her worst fears.

"I examined your photographs, all eight of them."

"And?" She held her breath.

"As you can imagine, I found them rather alarming."

Talia caught sight of Nolan the second he stepped into the bull pen. He looked to be in a hurry, and she got up from her desk and walked over. He stood beside his chair, combing through a stack of reports.

"Can't talk right now," he said, not looking up. "I'm on my way out."

"Kathy Baird is here asking for you."

"Shit." He looked over her shoulder at the waiting room. He'd come in the back entrance, probably to avoid getting sidetracked talking to anyone.

"Joanne put her in Interview Two."

Nolan raked a hand through his hair, then checked his watch.

"Want me to send her away?" she asked.

He glanced at the interview room. "No. I'll talk to her."

Talia watched him, impressed that he didn't try to duck the meeting. That wasn't Nolan's way. He confronted things head-on, which was one reason she was glad he'd been her training officer ever since she earned her detective's shield and was promoted to the Crimes Against Persons Squad.

"Mind if I sit in?" she asked. Talking to families who had lost a loved one was one of the hardest parts of the job. "I want to see how you handle it."

"Suit yourself." He checked his watch one more time and then finger-combed his hair as he strode across the bull pen to the interview room, where the door stood ajar.

Kathy Baird was seated at a table with her purse at her feet and her hands in her lap. Not long ago, the woman had been a whirlwind of energy, organizing Springville's annual Bikes for Kids fund-raiser every Christmas. But Kaylin had gone missing last summer, and everything had changed. At first, she'd poured all her energy into the search, mobilizing hundreds of people to comb the park and pass out flyers. But as the months dragged by, all that energy had drained away, and now she looked haggard. She'd once been one of those athletic-looking women with a tennis tan and perfectly highlighted blond hair. Now her cheeks were gaunt. She'd let her hair go to its natural brown and had a thick streak of gray on the right side.

"Mrs. Baird." Nolan shook her hand as she stood up.

"Good to see you, Nolan." She smiled, but it didn't reach her eyes. "How are your folks?"

"Fine. Thanks. You know Detective Vazquez?"

"Of course."

Talia nodded and smiled as the woman sank back into her chair. Instead of the designer work-out gear she used to wear, she now wore a faded T-shirt and jeans. Talia took the seat across from her, but she wasn't paying attention to Talia. She was focused on Nolan, searching his face for any hint that there might be news.

"I'm here about the discovery in the park," she said.

Nolan took a chair and angled it so that he was facing her without the table between them. He looked Kaylin's mother directly in the eye.

"We recovered some bones in White Falls

Park," he said. "They were in Rattlesnake Gorge, on the far west side."

"Sam told me. Kaylin liked to hike there. She went there all the time."

"Yes, ma'am. I know."

"He said he gave you her X-rays. Can you tell whether it's—"

"We don't know anything conclusive yet. The remains were transported to the Delphi Center forensic lab. I'm on my way to talk to one of the specialists now."

Hope flared in her eyes, and she leaned forward. "Will you call me after? As soon as you know anything?"

"Yes, I will."

"And you gave them the X-rays?"

"I did."

She leaned back in her chair, and her shoulders sagged. Her attention shifted to Talia, and Talia was struck by the deep sadness in her eyes.

"You know, I dream about her all the time. Almost every night." She smiled slightly. "It's something I look forward to."

Talia didn't know what to say. The comment seemed directed at her, and she darted a look at Nolan for help. He simply watched the woman patiently, as if he had all the time in the world.

"Well." She blew out a sigh and picked up her purse. "I won't keep you." She stood up. "You can call us anytime."

"I have all your numbers."

"I'll see myself out."

Talia watched her cross the bull pen and wondered if she noticed how everyone glanced away, avoiding eye contact. She was probably used to that by now.

She looked at Nolan. "She looks old enough to be Kaylin's grandmother."

"Stress'll do that to you."

"So, you're off to San Marcos?"

"Yep."

Talia watched his reaction. Was this a business trip only, or was there some other reason he was going, such as a certain forensic anthropologist?

She followed him back to his desk, unable to resist ribbing him. "Wouldn't it be easier to pick up the phone?"

"Easier but less effective. People can ignore a phone call." Nolan grabbed a stack of reports from his in-box and thumbed through. He met her gaze. "If you really want answers, you need to show up and talk to people face-to-face."

He was using his training-officer voice. She didn't mind, really. Nolan was a good mentor, and she was lucky to have him. Still, she had to give him crap when he got bossy.

"Thank you, Obi-wan," she said.

"Anytime." He smiled and grabbed his car keys, clearly eager to get on the road, which answered her question.

"Let me know how it goes," she said. "And say hi to Sara for me."

Nolan stood by the fountain, watching the quadrangle as the sky darkened and the fireflies came out. The university was quiet tonight, with only a trickle of students moving in and out of the library. He tried to remember the last time he'd been on a college campus. Probably during his patrol days in Austin when he'd been responding to some complaint at UT.

The door to the auditorium opened, and people filed out—mostly middle-aged and mostly without cell phones glued to their hands. The continuing-education crowd, and it really *was* a crowd. Dr. Sara Lockhart was a popular attraction.

She stepped outside, and Nolan knew the instant she spotted him. Her expression went from surprised to happy to wary, all in a few fleeting moments. Nolan focused on the second reaction as she approached him. She wore black jeans with a lightweight blazer, and her computer bag was slung over her shoulder. This was her college-professor look.

"What are you doing here?" she asked.

"Sitting in on your lecture."

"How did you find me?"

He smiled. "I'm a detective."

Her eyebrows arched.

"The event was posted on the university website." He nodded toward the building. "I saw it when I googled your name."

She smirked. "You were vetting my credentials."

"I was."

"Well, what'd you think?" She started walking, and he fell into step beside her.

"PhD in anthropology," he recited. "Associate professor at American University, followed by a stint with the International Forensic Anthropology Foundation. Very impressive."

"No, I meant the lecture. It's part of our summer series. Dr. Filburn asked me to do it and left the topic up to me. I worried it was a little much." She looked at him, and he was struck again by how green her eyes were. "What was your take?"

"Honestly?"

"Yes, of course."

"I was pretty blown away." And that was an understatement. He'd watched from the back of the room for forty minutes as she'd presented slides showing the mass graves she'd excavated down in Guatemala. Many of the victims were boys or young men who'd been caught up in gang violence. Some victims were killed simply because they were in the wrong place at the wrong time and had witnessed the carnage. When Sara got to the picture of a toddler-size skeleton, her impassioned words had moved people to tears. Even Nolan had gotten a lump in his throat.

"I'd never heard about it," he said. "And I keep up with stuff like that."

"Stuff like . . . ?"

"Murder. Violence. The twisted shit people do to each other."

They passed the admissions office and continued toward the parking lot.

"I'm not surprised you didn't see it in the news," she said. "Everything's infotainment now. This happened in a foreign country, and there's no celebrity connection." She glanced up at him. "Not to get on a soapbox, but it's something that bothers me."

They reached the street, and he stopped walking. "I got your voice mail," he said.

"I take it that's why you came?"

"I figure I'm not going to like what you have to tell me. If it was easy, you would have said it over the phone."

She sighed and looked out over the parking lot. Her honey-colored hair was smooth and shiny tonight, and she'd left it down. Last time he'd seen her, she'd been wearing a baseball cap and coveralls, and her nose was pink from the sun.

"There's a lot we need to go over," she said now. "We should sit down. How about somewhere close? Maybe Schmitt's Beer Garden?"

"You bet."

"I'll meet you over there."

• • •

Nolan insisted on paying for their beers, and they found an empty table outside under a giant oak. Strands of white lights wrapped the tree, casting a glow over the entire patio. With the misters going, it was almost pleasant outside.

Sara took a seat at the picnic table and shed her linen blazer. She wore a silk tank underneath, and the breeze felt good on her bare arms. She smoothed her hair self-consciously. She hadn't planned on a date. She'd skipped makeup and only added a spritz of Chanel before leaving home tonight. She didn't care for expensive clothes or makeup, but she spent a lot of time around bad smells, and French perfume was her one indulgence.

Nolan sat across from her. "You come here often?"

She smiled, and he shook his head.

"Sorry. That sounded like a line. I'm asking because the only time I've been here, I was with Alex and Nathan."

"Alex from our cybercrimes unit?"

"Yeah. I worked with her husband up in Austin way back when."

Alex's husband was a detective with Austin PD, and he had a ton of connections in cop circles.

"So, you started your career with APD?" Sara asked.

"Yep."

She squeezed a lemon wedge and dropped it into her glass. At Nolan's suggestion, she was trying a wheat beer from a local brewery. "How come you left?" she asked.

"Thought I might like the job better in a smaller city. You know, make more of an impact."

She sipped her beer, wondering whether that was the full story or if there was more to it. Some people joined a small department to rise through the ranks faster.

"And do you? Like it better?" she asked.

"Sometimes yes, sometimes no."

She looked at his fingers around the beer glass. He had capable-looking hands and a tan that suggested he spent a lot of time outside.

Sara's nerves fluttered. This wasn't a date. Not even close. But something about the way he watched her made her imagination take off. There was an undercurrent of attraction between them. Or maybe it was just her.

Her gaze met his, and he lifted an eyebrow. Okay, it wasn't just her. He was definitely giving her a *look*.

"You didn't answer my question," he said, deflecting the conversation away from himself.

"No, I don't come here much. Honestly, I don't go out a lot. At least, not to bars."

She'd just made herself sound like a nerd, but it was true.

"So what do you like to do for fun, Dr.

Lockhart?" He smiled slyly and sipped his beer.

"When I get time—which isn't often—I like outdoor activities," she said. "Hiking, rappelling."

"I figured that. Where'd you learn to rappel?"

"College. It's my favorite hobby. And in grad school, I joined a volunteer S-and-R team." She sighed. "What else? Oh, salsa dancing."

He arched his brows.

"You don't like salsa?" she asked.

"Dancing's not my thing. I'm more into sports."

She tried to guess which one. Football, maybe? He had the tall, trim build of a receiver. Or maybe he'd been a runner. He certainly had the long legs for it.

And now she was thinking about his body again. She sipped her drink to distract herself. This *wasn't* a date. It was a business meeting. He was here for her expertise.

"How is it?" he asked.

"The beer? It's good." She cleared her throat. "So, Nolan, I'm preparing my report, and I've got most of the basics covered at this point. But there are a few things I wanted to talk through."

He nodded.

"First of all, it isn't Kaylin Baird."

Disappointment flickered in his eyes, and she realized the Bairds weren't the only ones who had been holding out hope that the bones belonged to Kaylin. Nolan had to know that the chances of finding Kaylin alive after fourteen months were slim, so his most realistic hope was to get her family some closure and move forward with the investigation.

"The remains are female, likely Caucasian—"

"Likely?"

"Ancestry is based on data collected over many decades. But more and more, we're living in a melting pot, so the lines are blurred."

"Okay."

"As for age, looking at cranial sutures and tooth development, I'd say very early twenties. Possibly even as young as nineteen. And stature—she was somewhat shorter than average, about sixty-two inches. We recovered some soft tissue, as I mentioned, but it's desiccated and discolored, so not necessarily reliable in determining race. However, from the bits of hair we have, we know she was a brunette."

Sara watched him, waiting for him to absorb all this. She had done some googling of her own and knew from several news stories that Kaylin Baird was a five-foot-four blonde.

"Another important factor is PMI," she said.

"Postmortem interval."

"That's right. The condition of the remains reveals a lot. I can tell you she most likely died between six and ten months ago. But I'd like to provide you with something more specific than that, and I keep coming back to her location."

"In Rattlesnake, you mean."

"Yes, down in the gorge. In that particular location, buried the way she was under sand and debris."

He tilted his head to the side. "I've been thinking about that, too. It didn't look like a man-made grave."

"Exactly. And the site is remote. Not near a highway. I can't see anyone hauling a body down there, on a two-point-six-mile trail, so it seems more likely she was dumped off a cliff and her body ended up there as a result of natural forces."

"In other words, you think she was dumped upstream and then washed down in a flood?"

Sara nodded. "It's a possibility, yes."

"October ninth of last year. That's the last flash flood."

CHAPTER 7

"You looked it up already," Sara said, surprised.

He nodded. "We got six inches of rain in four hours."

They really had been thinking along the same lines, and Sara felt relieved. So often she had to spend time and energy bringing detectives around to her conclusions, but Nolan was already there.

"It's a theory, and I can't be certain," she added. "But what really supports this idea is the bones themselves."

His brow furrowed. "How do you mean?"

"They show trauma—fractures consistent with an inert body being dropped from an elevation. So the body could have been dumped off a cliff upstream. But when it was subsequently buried in sand and debris, the skeleton was *intact*. That's the key. If decomposition had been advanced at the time of the flood, the connective tissue would have been mostly gone when the floodwaters hit, and we would have found the bones scattered. Or maybe never found them at all."

"That narrows our time frame," he said.

"Exactly. Now we're talking about a PMI of

nine to ten months. In other words, her body was dumped shortly before the last flood on October ninth."

"A four-week window for the murder. That helps me a lot."

She felt a wave of satisfaction. One of her core objectives was to help investigators as much as she could. She liked the spark in Nolan's eyes, as though he couldn't wait to run with this lead.

"This is great. Thank you."

"Glad to help." She sipped her beer again, watching him.

"So what's your next step?" he asked.

"As of this moment, she's a Jane Doe. But I have DNA, which I'll submit to the missing-persons database, see if we can get a hit. I'll also submit her dental X-rays."

"I'll be in touch with law-enforcement agencies, starting local and then moving farther out." He paused. "I assume you're treating this as a homicide?"

"That's right."

"Okay, what else?" he asked.

"What else what?"

"The purple string at the gravesite." He watched her closely. "That's important. I could tell by your reaction when Aaron found it and called us over."

He was right, the twine *was* important, but she wasn't ready to talk about it yet. If she voiced her suspicions, she might throw his investigation into a tailspin, and for what? She could be wrong. She was still waiting on feedback from Cliff Underwood, as well as the cordage expert at the Delphi Center.

"I'll get back to you on the twine."

"That's it?" His voice had an edge.

"I'm still checking into a few things. I'll update you as soon as I can."

He just looked at her.

"I've barely had this case two days, Nolan. You need to give me some time here. We have to be meticulous. We can't be pressured into providing incomplete—or, worse, inaccurate— information."

He gave a slight nod. "Fair enough."

She could tell he was skeptical. And impatient. But he had more than enough information now to move forward, and the answers she needed would be coming soon.

She hoped.

"I'll get you more info as soon as I can," she said. "Probably by tomorrow."

"I'll hold you to that."

He looked at her for a long moment, then slid his glass away. "I had better get back. I need to go by the Bairds' tonight."

She ignored the tug of disappointment as he stood up. Of course, he had to get back now. He had work still to do and a two-hour drive ahead of him. Silently, they walked to the parking lot together. His dusty white pickup was right beside her black Explorer.

She popped her locks and lingered near the bumper. Despite their friction over the case, she'd enjoyed hanging out with him, and she didn't want it to end. Which was ridiculous. She had work left to do tonight, too.

He eased closer, and her pulse picked up. "Thank you for giving up your weekend," he said.

"It's no problem. Thank you for the beer."

He held out his hand. She shook it and felt a warm rush as his fingers closed around hers. Their gazes held, and she had the odd sensation of being pulled into him, even though they didn't move.

He stepped back. "Keep me posted, Sara."

"I will."

Sara lived in a vintage building that had been a paper factory before it was converted to loft apartments. The place had a lot going for it— charming brickwork, a prime location, affordable rent. What it didn't have was parking, and Sara leased a space in the lot behind the bakery next door.

She grabbed her computer bag and locked her car, eyeing the dark corners of the parking lot for anything suspicious. In many ways, San Marcos was an idyllic college town, but as Nolan had pointed out, looks could be deceiving.

She walked past the bakery and was surprised to see a white SUV roll to a stop at a meter across the street. Kelsey Quinn slid out and gave her a wave. Sara waved back as her coworker waited for a break in traffic and hurried across the street.

"Didn't know you were back," Sara said.

"Just got in."

Kelsey was tall and slender. She wore jeans and a sleeveless white shirt that showed off her new tan. Her auburn hair was pulled up in a ponytail.

"How was Belize?" Sara asked.

"Restful. How's everything here?"

"Fine. Not exactly restful, but we've managed to juggle it." Sara paused, searching Kelsey's face for clues. She wasn't in the habit of stopping by, so something had to be up.

"Sorry to just drop in," Kelsey said.

"Not at all. Want to come up?"

"For a minute, yeah. I won't keep you."

Sara tapped her entry code, ushered Kelsey into the tiled lobby, and led her to the stairwell.

"Elevator not working?" Kelsey asked, glancing at the antique cage with an ornate door.

"It's temperamental."

Sara's second-floor unit was the first door on the left. She unlocked it and let Kelsey inside.

"Hey, you changed it," Kelsey said, looking around.

"Finally got around to unpacking." Sara dropped her computer bag on the armchair and went into the kitchen. Her place was all one room, with a long granite bar dividing the kitchen from the living area. Her bed—currently unmade—was pushed against the exposed brick wall to maximize living space.

"It's a mess, I know."

"You should see my place." Kelsey set her purse on the counter and glanced around.

"I'm out of wine, but I've got juice, tea. Think there's a Corona in here somewhere," Sara said.

"I'll have tea, if it's handy."

"Hot okay?"

"Sure."

Sara took out a kettle and filled it with water as Kelsey stepped over to a shelf filled with anthropology books. She seemed intrigued by the titles. Kelsey had been over once before to pick up a report, but everything had been in boxes.

Kelsey looked at a small wooden statue of a rice god, guardian of the harvest, which had been given to Sara on a visit to the Philippine rice terraces. Sara displayed it on her top shelf beside a Virgin Mary triptych—which would have made her devout grandmother frown with disapproval. Sara was too much of a scientist to believe in superstitions, but for some reason, she liked having guardians from two totally different cultures keeping watch over her home. She found them comforting, and they reminded her of special people in her life.

"Are these Salvadoran?" Kelsey asked, studying a row of painted figurines.

"Guatemalan."

"That's right. You spent a summer down there, didn't you?"

"A year."

Kelsey wandered over to the kitchen and leaned on the bar. "How was that?"

Sara took her time answering. "Heartbreaking."

Kelsey nodded knowingly. She had spent a summer in northern Iraq and had seen her share of atrocities as well.

"But educational, too. And I met some amazing people."

"I bet."

Sara waited for the water to boil and for Kelsey to get to whatever was on her mind.

"I'm sorry for leaving you guys in a lurch," Kelsey said. "Two weeks is a long time, I know. I've never taken a vacation that long."

"It flew by."

"For me, too." Kelsey smiled, but her eyes looked worried. "I really needed the break." She paused. "You know, I probably should have told you this, but several months ago, I had a miscarriage."

Sara stepped closer. "I'm so sorry. I had no idea."

"No one did." She shook her head. "It's fine now. Well, not *fine,* obviously, but better. We're going to try again soon."

Sara didn't say anything. She didn't know what the correct response was. Through some light-hearted teasing at work, she'd picked up on the fact that Kelsey and her husband were trying to have a baby. She hadn't realized they'd lost one.

"How is Gage doing?" Sara asked.

Kelsey tipped her head to the side. "You know, most people don't ask about him." She paused. "Gage is . . . okay. It's been hard for him. Not only losing the baby but seeing me hurting." She looked at Sara. "You've never been married before, right?"

"I was engaged once, but it didn't work out."

Kelsey waited, and Sara felt oddly compelled to explain, which she didn't usually do. "We'd been engaged almost a year, and then a few months before the wedding, I started to panic. I had all these doubts about, you know, spending my whole *life* with someone. I kept thinking, 'What if I change? What if he does? What if this isn't a good fit?'" She stopped talking, surprised she was sharing all this. Maybe she was doing it because Kelsey had let her in on something painful. "I couldn't shake the doubts I was having, so finally I told Patrick what was on my mind. Maybe things would have worked out between us if he'd reacted differently."

"How did he react?"

"He was angry. And when I suggested we postpone the wedding, he freaked out. Told me I couldn't do that to him or our families. And him telling me I *couldn't* just reinforced my doubts about our relationship. I felt trapped. So I broke up with him, quit my job, and moved to Guatemala."

"Just like that?"

"Just like that." Sara sighed. "Which was very hurtful to a lot of people. In retrospect, I should have handled it better."

She remembered her mom's reaction. *What on earth is wrong with you? You have something good, and you throw it away with both hands.* Sara's mom hadn't understood her reasoning any more than Patrick had, and Sara had stopped trying to explain.

"What's that look?" Sara asked.

Kelsey smiled. "I never would have pegged you for a runaway bride. You always seem so level-headed."

"Well, it was impulsive, you're right." Her decision hadn't been logical. For the first time in her life, she'd completely ignored logic and followed her gut. She was still following it, which was why she'd taken the Delphi Center job in Texas, where she knew exactly no one and her family was fifteen hundred miles away.

The kettle whistled, and she moved it to a

back burner. She took down two cups from the cabinet and dropped a tea bag into each of them.

"Wow, how'd we get on this topic, anyway?" She looked at Kelsey. "You didn't come here to talk about my dysfunctional love life."

Kelsey took a seat at one of the bar stools. "I heard about White Falls Park. Sounds like you guys had a tough day out there."

"We did."

"Good recovery, though?"

"One hundred fifty-two bones, along with some personal effects." She slid Kelsey's tea in front of her. "Chamomile. No caffeine."

"Thanks."

"We're analyzing the twine now."

"I heard." Kelsey's brow furrowed. "Bindings?"

"Looks like it."

"Aaron told me it's a homicide."

"Yes."

"And Nolan Hess is the lead?"

Sara was surprised. "You know him?"

"Just by reputation." The corner of Kelsey's mouth ticked up. "Alex's husband is friends with him. I hear he's hot."

Sara pictured Nolan's strong fingers wrapped around his beer earlier. And the way he'd gazed down at her when he said good night.

"I *also* hear he's a bit of a hard-ass, so I'm sure he won't be happy to see this." Kelsey took her phone from her purse, tapped in a code, and slid it across the counter.

Sara stared down at the screen, not sure what she was looking at. It was a video showing a bird's-eye view of something. A rocky canyon? A creek bed?

"What—" The question vanished when she saw the blue tent. "Is this our *dig site?*"

Kelsey nodded.

Sara's stomach filled with dread as what could only be a drone camera flew closer to the pit. Aaron was hunched over the northwest quadrant with his boar's-hair brush. He leaned back and wiped the sweat from his brow.

The camera zoomed in on a cranium.

"What the hell?" Sara looked at Kelsey. "Who took this?"

"Some kids, I'm guessing. A student in my Anthro 101 class sent it to me."

Sara stared down at the image, which would likely end up on TV. Meaning that Jane Doe's family, whoever they were, would someday get a look at their daughter's skull being pulled from the dirt. A hot lump of anger lodged in Sara's throat.

"Where was this posted?" Sara asked.

"My student saw it on Twitter, but it's probably made the rounds by now. I wouldn't be surprised if it turned up on the news tomorrow."

"Unbelievable. This poor family."

"I called our cybercrimes lab and asked Alex about getting it taken down, but I'm not sure what good that will do since it's already gone viral. When you talk to Hess, you might want to let him know whatever security he had at that crime scene was compromised."

"Damn right I'll let him know."

CHAPTER 8

Nolan bypassed his desk and went straight to the break room, where he filled a mug with coffee before heading into the meeting. Hank and Talia were already seated at the conference table.

"You two keep your radios on today," the chief instructed as Nolan grabbed a chair. "We're liable to be busy."

Triple-digit heat combined with alcohol meant a spike in tempers and assaults. Plus, they were anticipating the usual holiday-related uptick in motor-vehicle accidents.

"The sheriff's office already has one fatality," Hank said.

"Jeez, it's only ten," Talia said. "DUI?"

"Plain stupidity. Some guy was cliff jumping over at Dove Lake. Guess no one told him about the drought." Hank turned to Nolan. "All right, catch me up. What do we know from the bone doc?"

"The victim is a female, probably early twenties, most likely Caucasian," Nolan said. "Height approximately five-two, and she's a brunette."

Talia sighed. "Not Kaylin Baird."

"No." Nolan looked at Hank. He'd already called the chief last night with the news after visiting the Baird family.

"And it's definitely a homicide?" Talia asked.

"That's right. She's still working on cause of death. Hopes to have that soon."

"How soon?" Hank asked.

"I'll get an update later today." If Sara didn't call him, Nolan planned to track her down. "A DNA sample's been submitted, so we'll see if we get any hits in the database."

"That's *if* she's been reported missing," Hank said, homing in on a scenario that had been eating away at Nolan. They got a lot of migrant workers in the area, and many of them avoided police. "There might not be a report on her, much less a DNA sample," the chief said. "What'd she say about time of death?"

"Nine to ten months ago," Nolan told him.

"So, between September and October of last year." Hank shook his head. "Case is ice-cold. And we've had no MPs in that time frame."

"I'll put out some feelers in the community," Talia said. "I can talk to Father Uribe."

"Good idea." Nolan opened the file folder in front of him. "Meantime, I'm going to check in with some of the park regulars. The climbers, the mountain bikers."

"Don't they have a climbing ban?" Talia asked.

"Yeah, but people do it anyway," Nolan said. "I'll ask around, see if I can find anyone who remembers anything unusual from last fall."

"Ha. You'll be lucky if they remember last week," Talia said. "Those kids are baked half the time."

"What about the video?" Hank asked.

"Video?" Talia looked at him.

"Some kid posted a video of the remains being dug up," Nolan told her.

"Where the hell'd they get that?"

"Sent a drone over the gorge. I haven't seen it, but I hear there's a close-up of the skull."

"I saw it," Hank said. "Damn thing was on the news this morning. The bones were blurred out, but still. It'll come back to bite us if we ever get an arrest in this case."

"Bite us how?" Talia asked.

"A defense attorney will say our crime scene was penetrated," Hank told her. "Contamination of evidence, whatever they can think up."

"That's crazy. How are we supposed to keep out a drone?"

"I've seen crazier." Hank folded his arms over his chest. "Anyway, this video's all over everywhere."

"Are you worried?" Talia looked at Nolan.

"About some video? No. What I'm worried about right now is getting an ID on this victim."

Brad Crowley poked his head into the conference room and looked at Nolan. Crowley was a rookie, but so far he showed potential.

"You have a call," he told Nolan.

"Who?"

"A ranger out at White Falls Park. He's going apeshit." Crowley glanced at the chief. "Sorry. He's, um, really worked up about some lady who just showed up there. A Dr. Lawler, and he says she's unauthorized?"

"Dr. Lockhart," Nolan said. "What's she doing there?"

"I don't know, but she brought a cadaver dog."

Sara eyed the hikers and picnickers as she unloaded gear from her SUV, but no one seemed to notice her. She grabbed her backpack and slung it over her shoulder. She'd opted for yoga pants and a pink tank top today, wanting to keep a low profile.

Sara scanned the woods past the sign at the trailhead. Peaches and her handler had gone ahead, the German shepherd bounding down the path, eager to explore this new part of the park.

A green Suburban pulled into the lot, and Sara bit back a curse as Ranger Evans got out. He walked over and glowered down at her.

"I called the police chief."

"Thank you. That saves me the trouble." She smiled up at him, shielding her eyes from the sun.

"Where's your dog?"

"In the woods."

"Unleashed dogs are prohibited in the park, and that's a minimum fine of two hundred dollars."

"Except for service dogs."

"What's that?"

"Service dogs. Check the sign at the trailhead if you don't believe me. And working police dogs are permitted to be off leash in the presence of their handlers."

The ranger's face reddened, and Sara wondered about his blood pressure.

"Tom told me that dog of yours dug up a bone," he said.

Sara stepped back and nodded at the cardboard tray containing a small gray metacarpal. "See for yourself."

Evans peered down at it. "Probably just an animal."

"That's right. And a human is an animal."

"But—"

"My team and I plan to be here all day, Mr. Evans. Possibly longer, if you continue to impede our work."

"We'll see about that. I could have you arrested for trespassing within the hour."

"You're welcome to try."

He strode back to his vehicle, and Sara stared after him as he peeled out of the lot with a spray of gravel.

Sara took out her metal detector and propped it on her shoulder. Then she locked her doors and started down the trail. The grade quickly became steep, but the path was shaded by oaks and cedars. Mockingbirds chirped overhead as she made her way down. The trail had a lot of switchbacks, and she set an easy pace to avoid twisting an ankle on loose rocks.

"Sara."

She turned around, and her heart skittered at the sight of Nolan approaching. She was happy to see him, but she managed not to grin like an idiot. He was dressed casually in jeans and a golf shirt, but there was nothing casual about his expression as he stopped and gazed down at her, hands on hips.

"Heard you were back in town," he said.

"Let me guess. Evans?"

Nolan lifted an eyebrow. "You do something to piss him off?"

"My mere existence pisses him off. I'm a woman intruding in his little fiefdom."

Nolan studied her face, and his whiskey-brown eyes looked serious. "You should have called me."

"I was going to."

"What's with the canine unit?" He nodded at the metal detector. "And what's that for?"

"I'll explain if you've got a minute."

"Wouldn't be here if I didn't."

She started down the path again, and he walked beside her.

"As I mentioned yesterday, we were missing some bones at the recovery site. Some metacarpals, a tibia, several vertebrae. The dogs are better at this than we are."

"And did you find anything?"

"Only a finger bone. It was down in the gorge, about twenty yards from the recovery site. We did a thorough canvass."

"And now you're up here. Why?"

The trail ended at a clearing, and Sara looked around but saw no sign of Peaches or her handler.

"Seems logical." She took her phone from her pocket and pulled up the topographical map she'd been using. "We talked about the body originating upstream." She pointed to a place on the map near the entrance to the park where a small picnic area was situated beside a scenic overlook. "See this picnic spot on the map here?" She turned to her right and pointed to a nearby wall of limestone. "At the top of that cliff there? That looks to me like the optimal location. It's close to the access road, allowing for a quick getaway. Appears to be the perfect place to dump a body into this ravine."

"But you said she was intact." Nolan folded his arms over his chest. "What am I missing?"

Sara didn't say anything.

"You think there are *more* victims?"

"I think it's unusual." She tucked the phone into her pocket. "You've got a missing woman last seen in this park. You've got an unidentified woman's remains found here. Might not be a coincidence."

"You make it sound like we've got a serial killer on the loose."

She just looked at him.

His eyebrows shot up. "Is *that* what you think we're dealing with here?"

"I don't know yet."

His eyes sparked. "I need a better answer than that, Sara."

A low yelp had her turning around. Peaches bounded up the path, followed by Raul, her handler. The dog stopped at Sara's feet and gazed up at her expectantly.

"Good girl! Look at you!" Sara crouched down and rubbed her ears. She glanced at Raul, and her heart sank. "What is it?"

"We got a hit."

Sara, Raul, and Peaches spent the entire afternoon searching, only stopping twice for breaks. The tree-lined ravine was shaded, which mitigated the heat factor, but dense vines and thorny undergrowth covered the steeply sloping walls. Sara swatted at the leaves as she moved through the thicket where Peaches had discovered a cranium. She scoured the ground but found nothing new, and she'd been over this section three times now.

"Sara?" Raul called from the top of the ridge.

"Coming!"

Sara looked around and sighed. It was a steep hike out. She could follow the creek bed until it intersected the hiking trail, but that would take three times as long. Grabbing a sapling, she hauled herself up, trying to avoid razor-sharp thistles. Not that it mattered at this point. Her arms were covered in scratches from tromping through the brush all day.

After ten minutes of climbing and pulling, she reached the top, where Peaches waited with her tongue hanging out. Her tail thumped as Sara approached.

"She looks tired," Sara said.

Raul nodded. "She's beat. I need to get her home and hydrated."

"It's almost five. I can't believe she lasted so long."

"She's a worker."

They trekked back to the base of operations they'd established near the picnic area. A uniformed officer—Crowley was his name—stood guard beside a Springville PD pickup truck. The tailgate was down, and a flat cardboard box in the truck bed held an array of bones. Sara surveyed the assortment.

"You found another femur?" She looked at Raul.

"It was south of that big boulder. Don't worry, I photographed it from every angle."

"Good." Sara grabbed a clipboard and added the femur to the inventory.

"Detective Hess just called, ma'am."

Sara looked at Crowley as she peeled off her latex gloves. The officer's blue uniform was soaked with sweat, but he hadn't complained about being stationed in the scorching heat all afternoon.

"What'd he say?" Sara asked.

"He's wrapping up some business at the firehouse. Said for you to meet him back at the station."

Sara didn't comment. She'd planned to stop by there anyway, but she preferred to be asked, not ordered. Nolan had been brisk with her since Peaches first started alerting on bones all over the ravine. After the fourth hit—a mandible that was clearly human based on the fillings—Nolan made the call to shut down the entire park and then summoned several uniforms to the scene to help cordon off the area. Around noon, Talia arrived, and Nolan left to handle something in town. From what Sara gathered, the police chief had called a meeting with people from the park district and the sheriff's office to talk about the latest bone discovery.

Sara retrieved some water from her SUV and walked over to the pickup. She offered Crowley a bottle and gave two to Raul, who crouched beside Peaches and helped her drink straight from the container. When she finished, he opened the second bottle for himself.

"You two should head out," she told Raul. "I'll get the equipment loaded for transport back to the lab."

"You need help with anything?"

"No, I got it."

Raul gave her the Delphi Center camera he'd been using and then tossed his gloves into a nearby trash bin. He opened the door to his gray pickup, and Peaches jumped in the front, clearly eager to go.

With Crowley's help, Sara got everything packed into the back of her Explorer. The officer looked faintly sick as Sara wrapped the cranium in gauze and loaded it into a separate cooler for transport. The cranium was a gold mine, evidence-wise, and she didn't want to risk it getting knocked around.

Sara hitched herself up behind the wheel and plugged her dead phone into the charger. She was tired and sweaty, and her lips tasted like dirt. She wasn't looking forward to this meeting with Nolan.

Buzzing the windows down, she let the wind whip around her as she wended her way through the park. Her AC was on the fritz again, and she really needed to get her car into the shop, but she never had the time. Her black '98 Explorer was on its last leg, but she couldn't bear to give it up. She used it so much for hauling remains to the lab that people called it her hearse.

Sara pulled up to the main exit. A ranger—not Evans, thankfully—was stationed there and opened the gate as she approached.

"You're closed down for the day?" she asked.

"Yes, ma'am. We'll be closed tomorrow, too. Chief's orders."

"I might be back then," she told him. "If so, I'll call ahead."

"Yes, ma'am."

Sara's phone chimed as she reached the highway. Aaron.

"Hey," she said.

"I've been trying to reach you."

"My battery's been dead."

"Okay, well, check your email. That report is in from the tool-marks examiner. I forwarded it to you."

"I thought you were off today?"

"I am, but I checked my email from home. And heads-up, word is that APD pulled a floater from Lake Austin."

"Damn. Really?"

"Cops are saying suicide. Guy jumped off a bridge, and they say he left a note. But you know how that goes. It's a homicide until it isn't."

"I'm back in Springville," Sara said. "And I'll probably be here tomorrow, too."

"You found something? Why didn't you call me?"

"You're off today, and anyway, Raul and Peaches were here to help."

"Well, you could have called me." Aaron paused, and Sara could tell he felt slighted. "Anyway, don't worry about the floater. TCMEO's got it."

The Travis County Medical Examiner's Office sometimes requested help with bodies recovered from the water, particularly those where identification was difficult.

"You sure?" Sara asked.

"That's what I heard. I guess he wasn't in long. If you want—"

Aaron's voice cut off. Sara looked at her phone and cursed. She'd call him back when she had more battery.

Pulling into town, she passed the Morningstar Motor Lodge with its flickering VACANCY sign. She fought the urge to pull in and get a room. She could have used a long, hot shower. Not to mention a nap. But she was nowhere near finished for the day.

"And miles to go before I sleep," she muttered.

She reached the Springville police station, a

surprisingly new building with a glass atrium and a limestone facade. She'd expected something small and humble, but maybe the building reflected the city's expanding tax base. The landscaped parking lot was divided into two sections—a gated area for police vehicles and an open section for visitors. Sara pulled into a space near the flagpole and looked around.

Not too busy, considering it was a holiday. She'd expected the place to be crowded with drunks and scofflaws. Maybe Nolan's day had improved since she'd last seen him. Maybe his mood had improved, too. Their last conversation had been tense, and he'd seemed to think she was blowing him off. She wasn't. She just needed to be sure of some things. Detectives never understood that. They were impatient by nature, and certainty took time.

Sara reached for her duffel bag in the back seat. She used a wet wipe to freshen up and threw a clean T-shirt on over her tank top. Not great, but nothing short of a full scrub-down was going to make her presentable at this point. She grabbed the backpack she was using as a purse today, tossed her cell phone inside, and headed for the door.

The waiting area and the squad room were separated by a tall glass wall, and Sara immediately spotted Nolan standing at a desk and talking on his phone. As if sensing her arrival, he turned around and looked directly at her. He motioned for her to come on back.

Sara stepped up to the receptionist. The woman's headset suggested she might be a dispatcher as well. She wore a white T-shirt with a sequined American flag across the front, along with American flag earrings.

"Excuse me. I'm—"

"Dr. Lockhart." She smiled. "They're expecting you. Go right on in." She reached under her desk, and a buzzer sounded as the door unlocked.

Sara entered the bull pen and walked to Nolan's desk. He was talking to an older man now. White hair, sun-browned skin, paunch hanging over his belt buckle. In jeans and cowboy boots, he looked like a rancher, but his badge and sidearm said otherwise.

"Sara Lockhart, this is Hank Miller, chief of police," Nolan said.

Sara nodded. "Nice to meet you, Chief."

"Likewise. I hear you been busy at Little Rat."

"Little Rat?" She looked at Nolan.

"Little Rattler Gorge. The ravine where you were today. It leads into the big one."

"Yes. I didn't know it was called that." She looked at the chief. "Is there a place we can talk?"

The chief led the way past a glass conference room and ushered her into a room without windows. She appreciated the privacy, and her heart leaped for joy when she saw the coffeepot in the corner.

"Mind if I . . . ?" Without waiting for an answer, Sara grabbed a paper cup and poured.

"That's been there since this morning," the chief warned.

"I don't mind." Sara dumped in several sugar packets and took a seat at the table opposite Nolan and Hank. They watched her warily as she took a sip.

"We've got a microwave in the break room," Nolan said.

"It's fine."

Really, it was cold sludge, but she was too tired to care. She hadn't realized how light-headed she'd been until just that moment.

"So." Sara slid the cup away and looked at the chief. "I spent most of the day in White Falls Park working with a canine unit."

"The cadaver dog," Hank said.

"That's correct. Peaches—the German shepherd—she's the best in the business. I've seen her alert on a body twenty feet underwater. She first alerted on a metacarpal. That's a hand bone, about the length of a matchstick in this case."

"This is a different victim than you dug up Sunday?" the chief asked.

"That's correct." She glanced at Nolan, who was watching her with an unreadable look on his face. "We recovered forty-three bones today.

The remains include a skull, a pelvis, and two femurs, which is good news from an investigative standpoint."

Nolan lifted an eyebrow.

"The teeth are important for identification," she explained. "The shape of the pelvis indicates a female decedent. And the long bones help us determine stature and age."

Hank stared at her for a long moment. So did Nolan. Neither said anything, so she continued.

"Regarding the bones, no duplicates. In other words, I have no reason to believe we're dealing with more than one skeleton in that particular area. From what I've seen so far, I believe these are the scattered remains of one individual."

The chief looked at Nolan.

"Also, I don't believe that individual is Kaylin Baird."

Hank's brow furrowed. "You can tell already?"

"I'll confirm back at the lab. But I've seen Kaylin's dental records, and they don't match up with what we recovered today."

Nolan leaned forward on his elbows. "You're telling us we've got *two* separate bodies in White Falls Park, and neither one of them is Kaylin?"

"That's right."

"What about clothes or jewelry? Anything like that?" Hank asked.

"We zeroed in on a few objects using the metal

detector—stray coins, bottle caps—but I doubt they're associated with these remains."

The chief heaved a sigh. "These bones, how were they scattered, exactly?"

"It can happen any number of ways when a body is left in the open or buried in a shallow grave," she said. "Coyotes, feral hogs, carrion birds. I'll have a better idea when I get back to the lab and check for postmortem artifacts—scratches, teeth marks, that sort of thing."

The door opened, and the patriotic receptionist leaned her head in. "Sorry to interrupt. The sheriff is on line one, Chief."

Hank stood up and nodded at Sara, then walked out without a word.

The door whisked shut, and silence settled over the room. Nolan gazed at her, long and hard, and she got the feeling he could read her mind.

"You're holding back. What else do you need to tell me?"

Sara took a deep breath. "This situation is . . . disturbing."

"Damn right it's disturbing. We're talking about potentially three victims."

"There's something else."

His expression darkened as Sara unzipped her backpack and took out an iPad.

"I keep coming back to the twine we recovered Sunday," she said as she powered up the tablet.

"Did you find any today?"

"No, not today." She tapped the screen a few times, opening a photo of the twine from Rattlesnake Gorge.

"I've seen a lot of bindings over the years, and these are unusual." She slid the tablet in front of Nolan. "That isn't some haphazard knot; it's very intricate."

Nolan's brow furrowed as he stared down at the picture. "This is from the gravesite Sunday."

"Correct." She looked at him. "After analyzing the evidence, I believe this victim was kidnapped by her killer. I believe he bound her hands with twine so he could control her throughout the attack, which could have lasted hours or days. I believe he killed her—"

"How?" Nolan's gaze was sharp.

"I don't know yet." She paused. "I believe he killed her and then dumped her into that ravine where we were today, and her body moved downstream during a flood. After dumping the body, the killer could have been back on the highway in less than two minutes. And yes, I also believe he could have done it not just once but multiple times. Everything I've seen makes me think he's experienced and deliberate."

Nolan rubbed his jaw as he stared down at the photo.

"Let me show you something else." She tapped the tablet and opened another file, this one containing photos Clifton Underwood had sent in response to her email. She slid the tablet back to Nolan.

His face became a stony mask as he gazed down at the picture. It was a close-up of a woman's wrists. Her hands were bloated and discolored, her fingernails greenish-black. Her wrists were bound together with purple twine.

"This is the last time I saw similar bindings. I was a graduate student in Knoxville, working under one of the nation's top forensic anthropologists at the anthropological research center known as the Body Farm."

Nolan's gaze locked with hers, and the question burned in his eyes.

"It's an open case," she said.

He didn't react. He didn't so much as blink. He just looked at her.

Sara pulled the iPad back and opened another photo: yet another tangle of purple twine, this one on a stainless steel table in an autopsy suite.

"Five years ago, two bodies were pulled from a lake in western Tennessee. Rocky Shoals Park. The finds occurred eight months apart."

"Both victims were female?"

"That's right. One was identified as a nineteen-year-old runaway, Lena Langley. The second woman is still unidentified."

"Still?"

"Her DNA is in the database, but we've never

had a hit. I just checked for any updates. Neither woman's case was ever solved."

"You're saying—"

"I'm not saying anything definitive," Sara said. "Not yet. The twine we recovered Sunday is still being analyzed. And it's not that uncommon. Could be the similarities in the cases are purely coincidental."

Nolan looked at the photo again. "This theory—were you ever going to tell me?"

"I'm telling you now."

"You knew it this morning. Hell, you knew it on Sunday."

"I didn't want to alarm you if we didn't find more remains."

Anger flared in his eyes. "This is my jurisdiction, Sara. It's my *job* to be alarmed. Don't protect me from information, ever."

She drew back, surprised by his vehemence. But she shouldn't have been.

"You're right. I'm sorry." She watched him, noting his tense shoulders, the firm set of his jaw. "If there is a connection, we'll know soon enough. My contact in Knoxville is sending a sample of the twine for comparison. Our cordage expert at Delphi will analyze it and let you know."

"Same cause of death in both of these cold cases?"

"That's right. The killer used a garrote."

"A *garrote?* Jesus."

"The wounds show both women were approached from behind, and he wrapped some sort of wire around their necks. No gunshots. No blunt-force trauma. Just a wire."

Nolan shook his head. He looked at the photo again. "I want the case files. Both of them."

"I'll put you in touch with the lead detective." She watched him, wishing she didn't have to add to everything he was already dealing with.

"You believe these other cases are connected to Kaylin's," he stated.

"I don't know. But I'd be surprised if they're not."

Nolan leaned back in his chair and waited.

"According to news articles," Sara continued, "Kaylin was last seen by her friends in White Falls Park. So it's possible she saw something."

"You mean like a body being dumped?"

She nodded. "Or a suspicious vehicle in the park. Or maybe she personally knew the perpetrator, and she stumbled across something he didn't want her to see. Kaylin could be the key to everything."

Nolan raked his hand through his hair. He looked every bit as drained as she was, and he hadn't spent the day tromping around a ravine.

"One other thing," she said. "I'd like to see the other park where Kaylin's backpack was found."

He frowned. "Why?"

"It's a crime scene. I've been to quite a few over the years. Maybe something will stand out about it." She waited a beat. "It might help you to get a fresh perspective."

He watched her, clearly debating whether to accept her offer. Then he glanced at his watch. "It's almost six."

Sara shrugged. She wasn't planning to leave town anytime soon, but she didn't tell him that.

"Fair warning, I'm on call tonight," he told her.

"So am I. Let's go."

CHAPTER 9

They took Nolan's pickup, and Sara felt an odd familiarity riding in it for the second time. She tipped her head back against the seat and let her shoulders relax as he expertly navigated downtown traffic.

"Lot of calls today?" she asked.

"Not too bad." He glanced at her. "Yet."

"Things will probably get going soon."

The town whisked by, a blur of old-fashioned storefronts, many with red-white-and-blue bunting hanging in the windows. Most of the shops were closed, but people clustered on the sidewalks, and Sara noted a long line at the ice cream parlor on the corner. They passed a town square, where more red-white-and-blue decorated a gazebo. A band was setting up, and several food trucks were parked along the sidewalk. A crowd of people waited outside a silver Airstream with JETHRO'S BBQ painted on the side, and another food truck advertised corn dogs and deep-fried Oreos.

At a glance, it was a charming scene, a charming *town,* with so many residents out enjoying the holiday, oblivious to anything sinister happening close by.

"You want to hear more about the Kaylin Baird case?" Nolan gave her a sidelong look.

"I do."

"I take it you already read the basics online."

"I read what was in the paper."

"The *Gazette* or the *Austin-American Statesman*?"

"Both."

"Okay, so you know she disappeared fourteen months ago. It was a Saturday. She'd gone with a group of friends to White Falls Park, and they split up around eight A.M."

"Sounds early. What time did they get there?"

"Seven. It was five kids piled into a little white Kia. We confirmed that with the ranger who took their money and gave them a day pass. He remembers seeing Kaylin in the front passenger seat."

"Who was driving?"

"Luke Kopcek, her boyfriend."

Sara looked at him.

"Yes, we checked him out. No dice." Nolan turned left onto a highway heading southbound out of town. The neighborhoods gave way to sporadic houses and then undeveloped land. They crossed a bridge, and Sara spotted a sign for Lakeview Park.

"How far is this park from White Falls?" she asked.

"Twenty miles exactly."

He pulled into the turn lane and waited patiently as several carloads of people paid admission.

Nolan pulled up to the window. "Hey, Randy. How's it going tonight?"

"It's going." The ranger dipped his head down to peer inside at Sara. He wore the same green uniform as the White Falls rangers.

"Any citations?" Nolan asked.

"Two so far. Coupla kids shooting off bottle rockets near the soccer fields. Maureen took care of them."

"Good for her."

"Hey, I heard about White Falls. Is it true they're shut down tomorrow?"

"Rest of the week, looks like."

Randy shook his head. "Hell of a thing."

"Well, I'll let you get back to it," Nolan said, dodging more questions.

They proceeded down a two-lane road lined with oak trees. The topography was dramatically different from the park where Sara had spent her day.

"Is it all this flat?" she asked.

"Pretty much."

"How many acres?"

"One-fifty."

They reached a large clearing. Athletic fields

stretched in every direction. She scanned the landscape, counting five soccer fields, all occupied. Several baseball diamonds were busy, too, and the parking lots adjacent to them were crowded with cars.

Nolan took a right onto a narrow drive and curved around to a field where a baseball game was wrapping up. Players filed through the chain-link fence, guzzling water and sports drinks as a fresh team took the field.

Nolan pulled into an empty space beside a snow-cone truck. Sara climbed out and immediately smelled hot dogs grilling. Her stomach growled, but she ignored it as she surveyed the area.

People milled around a grassy clearing between the parking lot and the baseball fields. Beyond the fields was a green-and-yellow playscape and a covered picnic area, both bustling with people. Sara followed a curl of smoke and spotted the source of the hot-dog smell, and her stomach grumbled again.

"Over here." Nolan jerked his head toward a line of trees. A wooden sign marked a trailhead. Nearby was a trash can and a plastic-bag dispenser, along with a sign telling people to clean up after their dogs.

"A parent noticed the backpack here by the trailhead and turned it in to lost and found," Nolan said. "It sat in the office for a day, until someone went through it and found Kaylin's wallet inside."

"The backpack was here?"

He nodded. "Right under the map, according to the mom who turned it in."

"And how'd they track the mom down if she left it with lost and found?"

"She came to us when she heard the missing woman's backpack had turned up at the park. We interviewed her. Got all the details she could remember."

Sara studied the map behind protective plastic. It showed a 1.5-mile loop through the woods, ending back at the parking lot. Sara glanced around. "Busy place."

"That's right."

"He wanted it spotted quickly."

Nolan looked at her. "You're thinking it's a decoy meant to lead us to a different park?"

"Maybe. I assume this one was canvassed thoroughly?"

"Both parks were. But we spent extra time here dragging the lake."

"Lake?"

He nodded in the direction of the soccer fields. "Just south of the athletic fields is a man-made lake. It's a pond, really, but the park's named after it. We dragged every inch of it the week Kaylin went missing, then again two months later. Nothing."

Sara gazed out at the park where so many kids were playing, and she imagined how painful it must be for Kaylin's parents to come here.

"My dad was in the Coast Guard," Sara said.

Nolan looked at her. "Oh yeah?"

"Twenty-six years. He retired a while back." She glanced at him, not sure why she'd decided to tell him something personal. "He did a lot of search-and-rescue missions, which sometimes turned into search-and-recovery. And sometimes they never recovered anything, not even a boat. It was agonizing for the loved ones. All that waiting and wondering. And when you can't bring someone back home to their family . . ." She shook her head, remembering the defeated look on her dad's face when he would come home from one of those missions. "I think not knowing is the hardest."

Nolan didn't say anything, but she sensed he understood. She also knew he felt personally responsible for getting answers, because she felt that, too. So had her father.

Sara did a slow three-sixty, trying to commit the setting to memory. She took in the sights, the smells, the sounds, even noting the direction of the shadows falling across the parking lot. She took out her cell phone and snapped a few pictures of the area.

"This mom who found the backpack, did she remember what time it was?" Sara asked.

"Four in the afternoon. She'd just finished coaching her daughter's T-ball game."

"So she's a regular here?"

"That's right."

Sara took close-up shots of the sign and the trash can. She looked around again.

"Seen enough?" Nolan asked.

"Yes."

They returned to the pickup, and Nolan opened the door for her, catching a waft of her sweet scent as she slid into his truck. He liked showing her around, even if he didn't like the reason she was here. He was interested in her take on his case and her take on his hometown, too.

Sara quietly looked out the window as he made a slow loop through the park, passing the pond-size lake that had been dragged for Kaylin's body.

"Kaylin's parents were here during the search?"

He glanced at her. "Her dad was. Couldn't keep him away, even though we blocked off everything and started our work at the crack of dawn to avoid spectators."

"Desperate fathers have a way of showing up."

Nolan tapped his horn at Randy on the way out, and Sara heaved a sigh when they were back on the highway.

"What are you thinking?" Nolan asked.

"I don't know yet."

He tamped down his impatience. He wanted Sara's perspective, both because she was smart and because she had fresh eyes. She was well educated, too—much more so than the cops and CSIs he had access to in Allen County. Not that she was a snob about it, but she'd seen a lot in her travels and her humanitarian work, not to mention her time at the Delphi Center. She'd logged a lot of hours in the field, and Nolan respected her for that. It had to be soul-crushing work, and it required careful precision. Her pace drove him crazy, but he'd already decided her expertise was worth waiting for.

He glanced at her beside him, watching the scrub-covered landscape whisk by with a pensive look on her face. Her cheeks were pink from the sun. She had tiny scratches on her arms and a smudge of dirt on her face from tromping around the creek bed, and he couldn't remember the last time he'd felt so attracted to a woman. Every damn thing about her turned him on.

She looked at him. "What?"

"Nothing."

They drove in silence for a while, with traffic backing up as they neared Springville's first stoplight. Nolan swung into the Dairy Queen parking lot.

"What are we doing?"

"Getting dinner." He pulled into a space. "I'm guessing you missed lunch?"

"I had a granola bar."

He shook his head. "Sorry."

"Why on earth are you sorry?"

"I should have sent someone out there with sandwiches for you guys."

Sara slid from the truck and crossed the lot with him. "Yeah, right. I'm sure your officers have nothing better to do on a national holiday than cart food around."

"We take care of our emergency workers."

Nolan opened the door for a group of tween girls holding chocolate-dipped ice cream cones. The restaurant smelled like french fries, and his mouth started to water the moment he stepped inside. Sara ordered a ridiculous amount of food—which she insisted on paying for—and they found an empty picnic table on the patio.

Nolan unwrapped his double cheeseburger as Sara dug into her chicken tenders.

"Did you know White Falls Park is listed as one of the top mountain-biking destinations in the state?" she asked.

"Whose list?"

"A sportswriter out of Colorado, Will Merritt. He has a popular blog called *High Life*, and he recently did a piece about mountain biking gaining popularity in Texas."

"We get plenty of them through here."

Sara slurped her Coke. The food seemed to perk her up, and he was glad she was talking again.

"You're wondering if Kaylin was in with them?" He chomped into his burger.

"Or maybe her boyfriend?"

"From what I know, they were more into hiking and climbing," he said.

"Climbing's banned in the park."

"Doesn't keep people from doing it."

"Why bother with the ban?"

He popped a fry into his mouth. "County officials put it in place a couple of years ago after a sixteen-year-old fell to his death while free soloing. That's climbing without a rope. After the accident, his parents sued the county."

"Did they win?"

"No. But the lawsuit scared everyone pretty good, and the elected officials decided to try and head off anything like it in the future."

"So having a ban in place absolves them of liability, even if people ignore it."

"Something like that."

Sara looked out at the traffic on Main Street as she nibbled a french fry. Pickups rolled by and Jeeps and convertibles. People were out in full force, despite the lingering heat.

"What's on your mind, Sara?"

She watched him intently with those vivid green eyes, and he wished he could read her thoughts.

"I'm stuck on the locations and the timing," she said. "I keep thinking Kaylin's disappearance is directly connected to these other deaths. Otherwise, it's too much of a coincidence."

He didn't comment. The prospect that they were dealing with a serial killer weighed heavily on him.

"Also, I keep thinking about the park," she added. "Lakeview."

"What about it?"

"It's basically the opposite of White Falls. No cliffs. No plateaus. No hills. White Falls is rugged and remote, full of hidden canyons and hollows. Lakeview is flat as a pancake. It's all soccer fields and families."

"Today is a lot more crowded than usual, but you're right. It's generally dog walkers and sports teams."

"Did Kaylin have a dog?" she asked.

"No. Why?"

"I'm looking for a reason she might have been a regular at that park. If her friends were into climbing and hiking, White Falls would have been their place, and I definitely can't think of why she'd split off from the group and catch a ride over to Lakeview. My opinion? That backpack was planted there as a distraction."

Nolan didn't respond, just looked at her. He agreed with her assessment. But investigators had pursued the lead anyway, even giving it enough credibility to drag the lake twice looking for Kaylin's body. With so little in the way of leads and Kaylin's family frantic for answers, they hadn't had much of a choice.

"We're on the same page," he said.

She nodded. "What did her friends say about why she decided to split from the group that day?"

"She wanted to go off on her own. She did it a lot, according to them. Luke told her to call him when she was ready to meet up and head out, but she never called."

"I assume you checked the phone records?"

"The phone was in her backpack. No calls or texts from her to anyone that morning. Her friends said they figured maybe she bumped into some people she knew and caught a ride home or hitchhiked. She did that sometimes."

"Jesus." Sara closed her eyes.

"I know."

"Even so, I can't see Lakeview Park as her destination. Home, maybe. But not that park." She dipped a fry in ketchup. "That backpack is almost certainly a plant."

Nolan looked away. "In the last fourteen months, I've been through her case file over and over. Every interview. Every report. I keep trying to find a contradictory statement or a blip in someone's timeline or, I don't know, some detail that feels off. Sometimes it's the smallest thing that breaks a case open. But I keep combing through, and I keep coming up with nothing."

Sara watched him, and he wondered if he sounded bitter. He wasn't. But he was frustrated. He'd been trained by Austin PD to be thorough, methodical, and patient in his work, but patience had never been his strong suit.

Nolan watched her as she finished off her fries. "What?" she asked.

"I keep wondering why you're here."

She smiled. "You wanted a burger."

"That's not what I meant."

Her smile faded, and she looked away. "You know, when I was a kid, I wanted to be in the Coast Guard, like my dad."

He lifted an eyebrow. "What happened?"

"Turns out I get seasick. And then I took my first anthropology class and found my calling. It's different from what my dad does, but it's similar, too. The crazy hours. The stress. The grieving families." Her eyes turned somber as she looked down at her food. "You know, it's ironic. I work with the dead. That's my job. But I do it for the living." She shook her head. "It's torture for those families left behind when someone goes missing. All those unanswered questions. I'm one of the few people who can help, so I feel this bond with them. An obligation. And I can never seem to shake it. Those cold cases never go away, you know? They're always lurking in my mind, even when I'm working on something else."

Nolan stared at her, caught off guard by her

words. He knew exactly what she meant. It was as if she was in his head, reciting his thoughts.

She slid her basket away. "So, this cold case you're working on—I could help, if you like. I know you're short-staffed."

"First binder alone would take you all night."

"Not paperwork. People. We could make the rounds again. Reinterview the friends who were with Kaylin that day."

He leveled a look at her. "Don't offer unless you're serious. I'm liable to take you up on it."

"I'm always serious. In light of everything new with the bone discoveries, it makes sense to talk to them again. You have any idea where they'd be tonight?"

"What, you want to go now?"

She nodded. "No time like the present."

According to Nolan, the Swinging R Ranch had once been a thriving cattle operation before the heirs sold off the livestock and turned it into a private campground, complete with bathrooms, rec facilities, and RV hookups. The property was situated beside a high limestone bluff along a scenic stretch of Mesquite Creek.

It was nearly seven when they arrived at the gatehouse. The attendant had a dark braid down her back and a quick smile for Nolan.

"How's it going, Tammy?"

"Hanging in." The woman peered through the window at Sara. "Y'all looking for someone tonight?"

"Just passing through," Nolan said. "We won't be long."

"Sure thing, Ace."

He waved and rolled through the gate, and Sara looked at him.

"Did she just call you Ace?"

"It's an old nickname." He glanced at her. "I played baseball in high school."

"Were you any good?"

He shrugged. "Went to UT on a pitching scholarship."

"Hmm. Interesting."

"Why?"

"You're left-handed."

He lifted an eyebrow. "So?"

"My dad loves baseball—Orioles fan—and he always said never trust a left-handed pitcher. They're unpredictable."

He smiled. "Your dad's smart."

She looked out the window, trying not to picture him on a pitcher's mound, staring down a batter with his super-intense gaze. She didn't need any more sexy visuals in her head.

"They're packed tonight," she said.

"Yep."

Everywhere she looked were RVs and camper vans. They wended their way down a bumpy gravel road, and Sara surveyed the cars and tents divided by clusters of camp chairs.

"Is it my imagination, or is the neighborhood getting sketchier as we go?" she asked.

"The upper loop has electricity and water hookups. The lower loop doesn't, so it's cheaper, kind of a grunge crowd."

"Great. I'll fit right in."

The lower-loop campers were teens and twenty-somethings. They were dressed in shorts and swimsuits and congregated around fire pits with no fires in them.

"Burn ban?" Sara asked.

"It's county-wide. Been in effect since June."

The lack of campfires didn't seem to be diminishing anyone's fun. People were drinking, eating, and listening to competing stereos. They lounged on chairs and on car hoods—basically any surface available.

"There have to be a hundred cars here," Sara said. "They must make a fortune."

"Capacity's eighty, and yeah, they do. This is their peak weekend."

"And these friends of Kaylin's—do they live here?"

"Pretty much. They come and go, kind of on a rotating basis. It's sort of like a commune. At the time of her disappearance, Kaylin was living with her parents, but she spent a lot of time with her friends out here."

"And who are they?"

"Luke Kopcek, twenty-two. Tristan Sharp. He's twenty-four. And Kaylin's two closest girlfriends, Jill Ortega and Maisy Raines, both nineteen."

"And what do they do?"

"Whatever they can. Jill works at a coffee shop. Maisy, nothing in particular. Luke's a lifeguard, and Tristan works part-time at a boat-repair shop in town that's run by his dad."

"Anyone have a rap sheet?"

"No."

The road dipped lower, and they entered a tunnel of trees. On the other side was a line of ramshackle vehicles—an ancient pickup, a hatchback, a two-toned Oldsmobile with a Sierra Club bumper sticker. This campsite had no fire pit, and the activity seemed to center around a yellow VW van that was older than Sara.

People were lounging and milling about, and everyone turned to watch as Nolan rolled past their setup and pulled off the road.

"Do they know you?" Sara asked.

"I've been around."

She slid from Nolan's truck and scanned the scene. Music drifted over, along with marijuana smoke. Voices quieted as they approached.

Nolan stopped beside a shirtless man sitting in a low-slung chair. He had a cigarette in his hand and a tallboy at his feet.

"Luke," Nolan said with a nod.

"Detective." He squinted up at Nolan. "You here to arrest me?" He held up his cigarette. "It's tobacco, by the way."

"I don't care what you're drinking or smoking. I'm here with some questions."

From the corner of her eye, Sara saw several young men get up and duck into tents. Not feeling talkative tonight, apparently.

Luke—presumably the boyfriend who had driven Kaylin to White Falls Park the day she disappeared—got up from his chair. He was a head shorter than Nolan, but he had a defiant look in his blue eyes.

"I gave a two-hour interview Sunday. I got nothing more to say."

"This isn't about Sunday. It's about last May. The day Kaylin disappeared."

His attention turned to Sara, then shifted back to Nolan.

"I've got nothing more to say about that, either." He walked away, leaving Nolan and Sara staring after him.

Undeterred, Nolan turned to a man sitting in a hammock dangling from a nearby tree.

"Chris." Nolan nodded. "How's it going?"

"Fine."

"You seen Maisy around?"

"Last I heard, she was over at Mustang Wall."

"Where's that?"

"Other side of the creek."

"What about Jill?"

"Think she's in the van on her iPad." The kid nodded toward the yellow van. The doors were open, and a tarp had been erected to create a shaded porch. A sticker on the van's bumper said GOD BLESS JOHNNY CASH.

Nolan looked at Sara. "I'll talk to Jill first."

"I'll look for Maisy."

"There's a bridge down the road," he said. "Want me to show you?"

Sara shook her head. "I'm good."

"I can show you."

She turned to see a young man standing beside the pickup. He wore shorts and climbing shoes and had a coil of blue rope slung over his shoulder. Sara recognized the Mayan sun god tattoo on his arm.

"I'm Tristan." He stepped forward.

"Sara Lockhart."

"The bone lady. I know who you are."

CHAPTER 10

Sara glanced at Nolan, and he gave a slight nod. Yes, this was the same Tristan he'd mentioned earlier.

"I'll meet you at the wall when you finish here," Sara told Nolan.

She and Tristan started trekking down the road. He was short but muscular, carrying a bulky coil of rope as though it weighed nothing.

"So, what's Luke's problem?" she asked. "He seems to have a chip on his shoulder."

"He doesn't like cops."

"Why not?"

He gave her an amused look, then shook his head. "I don't know. Maybe you should ask him."

Sara looked around. The road had narrowed, and they seemed to have come to the end of the encampments. She heard gurgling water to her right, but scrub trees blocked the view of the creek. A massive wall of limestone rose up beside her, its top gold in the evening sun.

"Isn't it late to start up there?" she asked Tristan.

He shrugged. "It's a three-pitch climb. More of a sprint, really."

They neared some tall cypress trees, and Sara spotted the bridge Nolan had mentioned. It wasn't much, but neither was the creek beneath it due to the drought.

"Tristan, I understand you were with Kaylin on the morning she disappeared."

"Yeah?"

Unlike Luke, he sounded low-key instead of hostile.

"I'm wondering if you remember anything unusual about Kaylin that day?"

"How do you mean?"

Tristan motioned for Sara to go ahead of him over the narrow bridge.

"Did she seem upset about anything?" Sara glanced over her shoulder. "Distracted, maybe?"

"No."

They reached a dirt path through the trees, and Sara glanced up at the lacy canopy of cypress leaves.

"Watch your step," Tristan said as she picked her way over some exposed tree roots.

"Do you have any idea why she decided to hike on her own that morning?"

"You mean climb? That's what we were doing there, you know. Not hiking. We started at Rattlesnake Gorge, and then Kaylin went off exploring."

"She went by herself?"

"Yeah."

"Any idea why?"

"No, but I mean, that's Kaylin for you. She was always off bouldering or checking out some wall she wanted to try. She went off on her own a lot."

The sound of voices told Sara they were nearing their destination. The wall of rock to her right swept up sharply, and she paused to study it. It had to be three hundred feet at least. She spied a yellow rope dangling from the top, where it looked like someone had set up an anchor.

"This way." Tristan ducked under some low-hanging limbs, and Sara followed.

A trio of people gathered at the base of Mustang Wall. Two women in climbing helmets stood off to the side swigging from water bottles. A man at the base held the yellow rope in his hand and tipped his head back.

Sara looked up at the wall to see the climber. She was petite and built like a gymnast, and she wore a white helmet along with snug black yoga pants and a purple sports bra. Long dark hair streamed down her back.

"That's Maisy."

Sara glanced at Tristan beside her, noting the admiration in his voice. Sara tilted her head back to watch as Maisy floated up a rock face. Her movements were fluid, effortless, and she seemed to defy gravity as she used invisible holds to pull herself up.

And she wasn't attached to a rope. Besides the helmet, her only equipment was a pouch of chalk clipped at her waist. Sara looked at Tristan.

"She's free soloing?"

"Yep."

"No rope at all?"

"None."

Sara's stomach tensed. She watched as Maisy reached a leg up, securing her foot to a mere bump in the stone, and then moved her entire body up the wall. She was probably a hundred feet up with another two hundred to go.

"She's tiny," Sara said.

"Yeah." Tristan folded his arms over his chest. "It's not about big muscles, though. It's about flexibility. Core strength. Keeping calm under pressure."

And calm she was. Maisy reached behind her back and dipped her hand into the pouch of chalk. Then she reached up and wedged her fingers into a vertical crack in the stone. In one smooth motion, she hoisted her entire body up another expanse of rock. She made smooth, steady progress as her audience watched silently from below.

Sara stared at the overhang near the top, unable to imagine how anyone could get over it. They'd have to be Spider-Man.

"That Maisy?"

She turned around to see Nolan walking over.

"It is," she told him. Sara tried to read his expression to see if his interview with Jill had yielded anything, but his face gave nothing away.

Nolan looked at Tristan. "Will she hike down the back or rappel?"

"Rappel."

Sara looked up again, and her pulse started to race. Just the thought of what a drop like that could do filled her with dread.

Maisy moved swiftly over the rock, as though she belonged there. She extended her leg again, and Sara watched, stunned, as she sank into a full split, her tiny feet pressed against bumps in the stone. Sara's breath caught. Beside her, Tristan muttered a curse. She glanced over to see Nolan staring up, his face frozen.

Maisy reached back and chalked her hands one at a time. Then she stretched her arm up and found a hold. Her body flowed upward, moving gracefully over the stone until she reached the overhang.

Sara's stomach clenched as she tried to imagine the route. She had to go around. There was no other way.

"What the . . ." Nolan's words faded as Maisy reached an arm up, swung sideways, and then used the momentum to throw her leg over the outcropping of rock. The next instant, her entire body disappeared over the ledge.

No one moved or spoke. The air was thick with tension. And then a high-pitched whistle echoed down.

"She did it." Tristan grinned.

The man watching from the bottom let out a howl, and the women beside him clapped. Sara found herself clapping, too, even though her hands felt numb and her heart was still pounding just from watching the show.

Sara looked at Nolan. His jaw was clenched tight, indicating he'd been just as worried as she had.

"I'll check you guys later." Tristan smiled and walked off, clearly eager for his turn on the wall.

Sara glanced at Nolan. "You all right?"

"No." He shook his head, looking up. "If I had a kid who did that, I'd ground her for life."

She smiled.

"Anything from Tristan?" He turned to face her.

"Not much," she said.

"What's your read on him?"

"He seems genuine. I don't get the impression he's hiding anything."

"In other words, if he knew something, he'd tell us?"

"That was my take, yes."

"Mine, too," Nolan said. "I've talked to him several times now."

"You mentioned Luke has a solid alibi. What is it, exactly?"

"Witnesses saw him in the park all morning. Then he showed up on time for his ten-to-six shift as a lifeguard at a local pool. His story holds, and he even volunteered for a polygraph, which he passed with flying colors."

Sara held Nolan's gaze. Polygraphs weren't foolproof.

"I know what you're getting at," he said. "Always look at the boyfriend. But in this case?" He shook his head. "I'm not feeling it."

Pop! Pop! Pop!

Sara whirled toward the noise. It sounded like gunshots, but it had to be firecrackers.

Pop! Pop!

"Are those—"

"I have to go deal with that," Nolan said. "Last thing we need tonight is a brush fire. Meet you at the truck?"

"Sure."

"See if you can talk to Maisy."

He headed off, and Sara glanced back at the wall in time to see Maisy unhooking herself from the rappel. Tristan handed her a bottle of water, and she gave him a fist bump. Sara watched them talk for a few minutes, and then Maisy broke away from the group to walk over to a pile of gear. She pulled her helmet off and shook out her hair as Sara stepped over.

"Maisy?"

She looked up, instantly wary.

"I'm Sara Lockhart. Detective Hess and I stopped by to see if we could ask you a few questions."

Maisy glanced around, probably looking for Nolan.

"He went to check on some fireworks," Sara said. "You mind talking a minute?"

She shrugged. "I'm headed back to camp."

Maisy dropped her helmet on the pile of gear and dusted her hands, leaving streaks of white on her black pants. "You're the one who found the bones in Rattlesnake."

"I helped recover them."

"I'm friends with Liz. The one who spotted them down there?"

Liz had to be the woman with the dreadlocks.

"Think I saw her at the scene," Sara said. "How's she doing?"

"Pretty freaked-out."

They ducked into the shade of the cypress trees.

"Someone posted a video of it," Maisy said. "I didn't see it, but I heard it was pretty bad. It wasn't Kaylin, though, right?"

"The victim is unidentified. But it isn't Kaylin, no."

Maisy stopped and gazed up at her. She was

barely five feet tall, but the look in her eyes was fierce.

"The guy who did it, they think he might have killed Kaylin, too, don't they?"

"You think it's a guy?"

"Isn't it always?"

Sara didn't answer. She wanted to see if Maisy had something specific to say or if she was generalizing.

"That's what they're thinking, right? Hess? The cops?"

"We're investigating a possible link between the cases."

They started walking again, headed toward the distant sound of music coming from the campground.

"I understand you were with Kaylin the morning she disappeared," Sara said. "Did anything seem unusual to you?"

"No."

"Did she seem upset about anything? Any recent problems?"

Maisy sighed. "They asked me all this back when it happened. *No*. Kaylin was fine. Normal. She hadn't had a blow-up with her parents or anything. I mean, they disapproved of her, but that was nothing new."

"What did they disapprove of?"

Maisy snorted. "Everything. Her friends, her boyfriend. All the nights she spent camped out here. They wouldn't let her move out, but she may as well have. She spent all her time here anyway."

"What about Luke? Do you know why they didn't like him?"

Maisy didn't answer for a moment, and Sara wondered if she was protecting him.

"He got her into climbing, for one thing. And they didn't like that at all. They wanted her to go to college, but then she got into all this and decided she wasn't interested."

"On the day of her disappearance, I understand Kaylin went off on her own. You have any idea why?"

"I don't know. I've answered this question a hundred times. She just wanted to be by herself, you know, explore."

"Had she been in a fight with Luke?"

Maisy bit her lip, and Sara's pulse picked up.

"Not a fight." She stopped and looked at Sara. "I told Hess, they weren't fighting or anything. Not openly."

"But . . . ?"

"But there was friction." She shrugged. "There always was with those two."

"What was the friction about?"

She sighed. "Kaylin was independent. And she was better than him."

"At climbing."

"Yeah, she was the better athlete. I mean, yes, he taught her to climb, but she surpassed him.

She'd entered a few competitions, won a few awards. She'd started making plans. She was headed to El Cap."

"El Cap?"

"El Capitan in Yosemite. She wanted to free-climb the Zodiac. That's the southeast side."

"Kaylin told you this?"

"It's all she talked about. She was planning to spend the summer training, maybe hit some of the walls in West Texas, and then take a trip up to Yosemite in the fall."

"What did Luke think of this?"

"I don't know. He was probably jealous. He's good and all, but he's not up to something like that. And anyway, I doubt he could scrape together enough bank to make the trip. He spent all his money on pot. Kaylin wasn't like that. She'd been saving up tip money for months and months. She really wanted to do it."

They neared the campsite, and Sara stopped, not wanting the conversation to end yet.

"What was Kaylin's favorite place to climb in White Falls Park?"

Maisy thought for a moment. "Sangria. That's a wall on the east side of the park, the only thirteen in the area."

"What's a thirteen?"

"A five-thirteen. It's a difficulty rating. But they searched Sangria last year. They searched every inch of that park." Maisy looked away.

Sara waited, sensing she had more to say.

"I dream about her all the time."

Sara didn't respond. A breeze wafted through the trees, making the dappled shadows shift on the dirt path.

Maisy turned to Sara. "You think she's dead, don't you?"

"I don't know."

Maisy shook her head. "There were rumors she ran away. Or she got kidnapped and forced into sex slavery. I even heard someone say she was doing porn. It's all bogus, though." A tear trickled down Maisy's cheek, and she brushed it away. "I think someone killed her."

Sara's heart squeezed. She wanted to hug the girl, but she sensed she might clam up.

"You mentioned the problems with her parents," Sara said. "Do you think there's any chance she ran away?"

Maisy shook her head. Another tear slid down. "Kaylin didn't run away from anything. No way. It wasn't her style."

It was almost sunset as they left the camp, and Sara relayed her conversation with Maisy.

"Anything new?" she asked hopefully.

"The rivalry," Nolan said. "I hadn't heard about that before. But Luke's alibi is airtight, so I'm not sure it helps us."

She thought of what Maisy had said about

the friction between Kaylin and her boyfriend. Sara could relate. Sara's job had been a battleground between her and Patrick. He routinely canceled plans when he got "tied up at work" or had a "very important meeting," but if Sara's work ever infringed on their personal time, he would get pissy and lay guilt trips. It was not only exhausting to deal with but worrisome, too, in terms of their pattern together. Why was his career more important than hers? And why did he always expect her to cater to him and never the other way around? Their relationship had a major disequilibrium that Sara hadn't fully recognized until she was free of it.

Nolan dug his phone out of his pocket as they pulled onto the highway.

"Hey, it's me," he said as he put the phone on speaker and dropped it into the cupholder. "What's happening there?"

"Not much." The voice sounded like Talia's. "A couple public intox arrests down at the river-front."

"Anything else?"

"Not yet. I'm headed to the bluffs to see if they need a hand at the fireworks launch."

"All right. Do me a favor. Swing by the middle school on your way there and check the athletic field. Crowley busted some kids there earlier shooting off Roman candles, and we need to make sure they're not back."

"Anything else?"

"That's it."

"Okay, later."

Nolan hung up.

"All hands on deck tonight, huh?"

"That's what happens in a small department." He looked at her. "What's that smile?"

"You're good at giving orders. You auditioning for the chief's job?"

"No."

The firm response surprised her.

"Talia's a junior detective," he said. "She's my trainee."

"I see." Still, Nolan seemed to take the lead on a lot of things. "Hank is pretty hands-off. Or is that just my imagination?"

"He didn't used to be, but he's getting up there in years. And he's had some health issues lately."

"Why doesn't he retire?"

"Kaylin Baird is his grandniece."

"Oh."

"He intends to solve her case or drop dead trying." Nolan glanced at her. "His words, not mine."

Sara felt a pang of sympathy. She imagined how awful it would be to investigate a family member's case. The stress had to be intense, and Hank's age already put him at risk for heart problems.

She suspected Nolan was well aware of these

issues, as well as the vacuum that would surely be created when Hank eventually did leave, for whatever reason.

"Do you like working in the place where you grew up?" she asked.

"That was always the plan."

"What was?"

"Go through the academy. Get experience in a big department. Make detective. Then come back here and build something."

"Build what?" she asked, intrigued.

"A career, a life."

"And you started this plan when you were, what? Twenty-three?"

He looked at her. "Twenty-two. Why?"

"You set your goals young."

"So?"

"So, that's good." She shook her head. "My career path's been a lot more zigzag, I guess you'd say. I trained in forensics. Then I took a teaching job. Then I did humanitarian work, and now I'm working with law enforcement again. I'm kind of all over the map."

"Nothing wrong with exploring," he said. "There's a saying, 'Not all those who wander are lost.'"

She smiled.

"What?"

"That's Tolkien," she said. "I wouldn't have guessed you for a fan."

"Some cops *can* read, you know."

"If you say so."

He shot her a glare, and she realized she liked teasing him.

They neared the Morningstar Motor Lodge. The VACANCY sign still flickered, even though the parking lot looked crowded. Nolan drove through downtown and turned into the police station, which was busier than when they'd left. He slid into a space beside Sara's Explorer.

"I'm going to check out that wall tomorrow," she told him. "Sangria."

He turned to face her. The air between them felt charged suddenly. "You're staying overnight?"

"No reason to leave and come back." Plus, she had some things left to do tonight. But she kept that to herself.

"Are you going alone?" he asked.

"Sure. Why not?"

Nolan gave her a long look. "Let me know your plan."

Sara stared into his deep brown eyes, overcome with an odd sensation of being pulled into him again. The silence stretched out, and her pulse started to thrum. She couldn't be around him and *not* get distracted. His deep voice. His hands. His eyes when he looked at her intently, as he was doing now.

The phone buzzed from the cupholder. He checked the screen.

"It's Crowley. Sorry, I need to—"

"Take it." She pushed open the door and hopped out. "I'll be in touch."

Talia got a call as she neared the police station and was surprised to see the department phone number on the caller ID.

"Vazquez," she said.

"Hey, it's Joanne. You've got a visitor."

"Who?" Talia swung into the staff parking lot and found an empty space.

"You know that detective who called yesterday?"

Talia stared through the windshield, completely at a loss.

"The one from Austin?" Joanne prompted. "Detective Harper?"

"Crap, *Harper.* I meant to call him back. Are you saying he's *here?*"

"Standing right across the lobby." Joanne's voice lowered. "I tried to get him to wait in the break room, but he wouldn't budge."

Talia checked her watch. "Well, what does he want? It's a holiday, for crying out loud."

"He said he needs to talk to you or Detective Hess, and it's important."

Talia scanned the parking lot but didn't see any APD police units, marked or unmarked. Was he here on his personal time? She remembered what Nolan had told her about people ignoring phone calls and showing up in person when they wanted something. Talia hadn't ignored this detective—she'd fully intended to call him back—but she'd bumped it to the bottom of her list because she had so many other things demanding her attention.

"Thanks for the heads-up," she told Joanne. "I'm on my way in."

She scooped up her radio and the laptop she'd been using to file reports from the road. Approaching the entrance, she saw through the glass that the lobby was full—mostly mothers and girlfriends waiting to bail someone out, from the looks of it. She spotted the Austin detective immediately, and not just because he towered over everyone in the room. He had a sharp gaze, and it was fixed on her as she walked through the door. She didn't pretend not to know who he was.

"Detective Harper?"

"That's me."

She stuck out her hand, and he gave it a shake, swallowing her fingers in his big grip. He wore jeans and a golf shirt, but the badge and the gun on his hip told her he was on duty.

"I'm Natalia Vazquez, CAP Squad." She didn't mention that she'd been promoted to Crimes Against Persons only a few months ago. "Come this way."

Joanne buzzed the door open, and Talia led the detective through the bull pen, ignoring the curious glances from several uniforms. She started to take him to the break room, then changed her mind and veered toward the conference room, where they'd have fewer interruptions.

"Have a seat," she said.

Harper kept his gaze on her as he pulled out a chair. He wasn't just big but huge. Six-four, two-twenty at least, all muscle. His short-cropped dark hair made her think he had a military background.

Talia took the chair at the head of the table, trying to level the playing field a bit.

"What can I do for you, Mr. Harper?"

"It's Dax."

"Okay, call me Talia."

"I'm here about a case."

"Your message said something about a missing person? I meant to call you, but we've had our hands full around here."

He nodded. "I heard about the bodies."

"Bodies?"

"Another one today, right?"

She leaned back in her chair, watching him. They'd gone to great lengths to keep the latest recovery quiet for as long as possible. Maybe he had an in with the sheriff's office.

"Tell me about your MP," Talia said. "It's recent, isn't it?"

"Friday night," he told her. "Or early Saturday

morning. We haven't pinned it down exactly. This girl was last seen at Blue Brew. That's a bar on Sixth Street."

"Girl?" she asked, because men tended to use the term loosely.

"Grace Murray, nineteen," he said. "She was at her cousin's bachelorette party when she disappeared."

"So, barhopping, it sounds like. She have a fake ID?"

"They started the night at a Mexican restaurant, then went from there. The party split into two groups around eleven. From what I hear, Grace got carded outside Blue Brew, and that's when she was separated from the pack."

"Okay. And what does this have to do with us? You realize the recoveries we're dealing with are bones, right? They've been there a while."

"Alicia Merino."

Talia tipped her head to the side. "Who's that?"

"The body from Sunday. She's been identified as Alicia Merino, twenty years old, went missing from a bar in San Antonio last October second."

Talia bit back a curse. "Where did you get that?" And why didn't she have it?

"San Antonio PD," he said. "We've been swapping info on our missing-persons cases. The identification just came in, and they gave me a call."

Talia resisted the urge to check her phone. With the bones recovered here, Springville PD should

161

have been contacted first. Maybe they had, and Nolan hadn't told her.

"So . . . you're thinking what?" she asked. "Same MO? Same perp?"

"Could be."

"Don't you think it's a little early for that? I mean, just because both of them went missing from bars doesn't mean the crimes are connected."

He leaned forward on his elbows. "Here's what I think, Talia. I've got a missing teenager. And frantic parents. I've got no witnesses and no good leads whatsoever. I'm thinking if there's even the slightest chance these cases are connected, I need to pursue it, because there's a chance *my* missing person is still alive. That's what I'm thinking."

Talia watched him, struck by the fire in his eyes. He wasn't just checking a box here.

"All right, I hear you," she said. "How can we help?"

The hot water felt good on Sara's tired muscles. But the shower quickly turned lukewarm, and she jumped out after only a few minutes. She crossed her tiny motel room and let her towel drop as she rummaged through her duffel bag. After moisturizing her skin, she dressed in dark clothing—a black tank top and jeans—and pulled on her dusty hiking boots. The boots were chunky but well broken in, and the blisters they'd given her when she first wore them in Guatemala were a distant memory. Now they fit her like a comfy pair of socks.

Sara surveyed the evidence boxes on the dresser. She had doubted anyone would have the audacity to break into her SUV while it was parked at the police station, but the motel was another story, so she'd hauled everything inside for safekeeping. She grabbed her camera and checked the memory card. Then she zipped some equipment into her backpack, tucked her room key into her pocket, and headed out.

It was almost dusk, which meant police and firefighters would be preoccupied with fireworks displays across the county. Sara drove with the windows down, eyeing the horizon. So far, the night sky was empty.

She turned onto the familiar road. Reaching the west gate of White Falls Park, she saw no sign of a patrol officer. She'd planned to sweet-talk her way in if necessary, but instead, she simply got out and unhooked the rusted chain.

Once inside the park, she followed a back route to the picnic spot where she'd parked her Explorer for most of the day. The lot was empty now, and she pulled into the shadows under an oak tree. No reason to attract attention. She got out, gathered her equipment, and started down the trail, using only a small penlight to illuminate her path.

The air smelled of dust and juniper. She took a deep breath, expanding her lungs, which seemed to be stubbornly holding on to the day's tension. Murder cases got to her. Always. The effect was amplified this time by her emotional connection to the missing young woman, who—as Maisy had wisely noted—was most likely dead.

Sara wasn't a pessimist, but she knew the odds.

And then there was Nolan. Sara felt an emotional connection to him, too, and she didn't fully understand it. Two years ago, she'd broken her engagement and moved halfway around the world, shocking both herself and her family. Since then, she hadn't looked back, at least not with regret. She also hadn't given serious thought to dating again—hadn't even been tempted—until she met Nolan.

Not that she wanted to *date* Nolan. She didn't want to date anyone. But she was drawn to him. Unable to resist the magnetic pull she felt whenever she was alone with him.

Did he feel it, too? She was so out of practice she couldn't tell. Sometimes it seemed like he did. Other times his interest seemed like an illusion, the result of her overtaxed brain and her vivid imagination conspiring to make her life complicated. She had a new job, a new home, a new *life,* and the very last thing she needed was to be distracted by a small-town cop who lived two hours away from her.

But what if they had a fling? Nothing serious—just a night or two together. The mere thought of it put a flutter in her stomach, which told her it was a bad idea. Unprofessional. How could she focus on doing her best work if she was distracted by sex with the lead investigator? It could get complicated, fast. She definitely shouldn't go there. She was supposed to be working with him, not lusting after him, and it didn't matter how well he filled out a pair of Levi's.

Focus, Sara told herself as she reached the end of the trail. She dug through her backpack and traded her penlight for a larger flashlight. The creek bed stretched out before her, a weirdly lunar landscape under her bright beam. Once she felt oriented, she trekked across the rocks to the area where many of today's bones had been discovered—the pelvis, the femur, the ulna. Sara pulled on some orange-tinted glasses and switched the flashlight to ultraviolet. Slowly, carefully, she scanned the creek bed, tracing her beam over the rocks. Something caught her eye near a mesquite tree. Sara walked to it and knelt down for a closer look.

"Find anything?"

She jumped and turned around.

CHAPTER 11

"God, don't *do* that." She stood up as Nolan walked over. "You scared the hell out of me. What are you doing here?"

He stopped and gazed down at her, hands on hips. Even in the dimness, she could see he wasn't happy. "Thought I'd ask you the same thing."

"Searching for evidence."

"In the dark?"

"Some things fluoresce under alternative light sources—clothing dyes, footwear, sometimes even human teeth. You'd be surprised what you can find at night."

Nolan stared down at her, and she tried to regain her composure. She didn't like feeling rattled.

"What?" She turned and swept her flashlight beam around.

"It ever occur to you to avoid skulking around alone at night in a place where someone's been dumping bodies?"

She stopped and looked at him. "You want to help, or did you come down here to impede my investigation?"

"*Our* investigation. Give me a job."

She combed through her backpack and found another pair of tinted glasses. "Put these on. I don't have another UV light, but you can follow my lead."

"Yes, ma'am."

His fingers brushed hers as he took the glasses, and she felt a warm tingle. Ignoring it, she turned and swept her flashlight over some large rocks at the side of the creek bed. Returning to what had caught her eye, she realized it was only a candy wrapper.

"How'd you know I was out here?" she asked.

"I was making a loop through the park and saw your car."

"You guys patrol the park?"

"Lately we do."

"Good."

Sara took slow, careful steps along the side of the creek bed. Peaches had alerted on several bones right in this spot, so she was hopeful.

Nolan's boots crunched on the rocks beside her. She caught a faint trace of his scent—male sweat with a hint of shaving cream or maybe cologne. She wanted to ease closer, but she resisted the urge.

"Look," Nolan said.

She turned around. His gaze was trained on a distant cliff. Above it, Sara caught the glow of fireworks.

"Where is that?" she asked.

"Belmont Hills Golf Club. You drove by it on your way into town."

They watched a series of red, blue, and green starbursts. After a few minutes, Sara resumed her flashlight sweeps.

"So," she said, searching for small talk. "What's your family doing on this nice Fourth of July evening?"

He smiled, seeming amused by the question. "Well, let's see. My sister and her kids are camping on Padre Island. My brother is hosting his annual chili cook-off, which I'm not invited to."

"What, you don't cook?"

"No, I win every year. So this year, he suggested I take a shift."

"Your brother *un*invited you to his annual party?"

"He was kidding. Sort of. But then all this came up, and I ended up having to work anyway." Nolan steadied her arm as she stepped over a deep rut. "Let's see . . . and then there's my parents. They're at a picnic with some friends."

Picnics and chili cook-offs. It sounded like the sort of settled suburban lifestyle that might have been hers if she'd gone through with her wedding, and she felt a strange combination of wistfulness and relief.

"Sara?"

Damn, he'd asked a question.

"Sorry. What?"

"I said what about your family? Are they in Maryland?"

"Yeah. My parents and my brother's family. He's got twin girls, Ellie and Erin."

"You see them much?"

"No."

It had been since Christmas. She'd intended to fly up for a weekend, but she'd been busy with work, and all she'd managed to do was send birthday presents for the girls.

"I keep inviting them to visit, but I doubt they will," she said. "My parents are hoping this is temporary."

"What is?"

"My living here. This job with Delphi. They're hoping it's a phase, like when I moved to Guatemala."

"Is it?"

"No."

The word jumped out before she could think. But it was true. This *wasn't* a phase. She loved her job at Delphi and fully intended to stay.

"Anyway, I'll probably go visit them for Thanksgiving. My mom's already hounding me."

Nolan drew closer, keeping step with her. "Tell me about Guatemala," he said.

"What about it?"

"What was it like there?"

It was the second time she'd been asked that in less than a week. She swept the flashlight over the ground.

"It was hard," she said. "Stressful. There were so many lives lost, or else broken beyond fixing. I learned a lot from it."

"Like what?"

"Like . . . what my limits are. And that I could never go back to my cozy job at the university, where the most dire question was whether or not I'd make tenure. I realized I wanted to make more of an impact. Anyone can teach human osteology to undergrads."

"Not anyone."

"Well. Many people can. Not everyone's good at the forensic side of things. It's dirty. Smelly. The cases can be depressing. And there're the midnight callouts, the long hours, the distraught families." She looked at him. "*You* know."

"Yeah, I do."

"But I'm okay with all that. I guess that's why I feel obligated."

He stopped. She stopped, too, and looked up at him, studying the contours of his face in the dimness. Her pulse started to pound as he gazed down at her.

"What?" she asked.

He reached down and brushed a lock of hair from her eyes, and her heart flip-flopped. He turned away, and they resumed the search.

What had just happened? She shouldn't have gotten personal. But he sounded genuinely interested, and she didn't know why that surprised her.

"We have something in common," he said, and his low voice seemed to wrap around her in the dark. "We're both trying to prove ourselves."

"You?" She scoffed. "The hometown hero? Everyone loves you."

"Not everyone." He paused, and she waited for him to explain. "I left Austin PD under a cloud of suspicion. There were some allegations being investigated by Internal Affairs."

She stopped and looked up at him, surprised. "Were they legit?"

"No. IA cleared me."

"Good."

He looked away, and it seemed like there was more he wanted to say on the topic, but she didn't want to pry. Still, she was curious. What sort of "suspicion"? She wanted him to open up to her. But intimacy was a two-way street, and if he opened his life to her, he'd expect her to do the same.

Nolan shook his head. "This case has been hard on everyone. I intend to solve it. People need answers—although I don't think they're going to like what I find."

Sara eased closer. "How do you mean?"

"Well, you've probably heard the rumors. A

lot of people think Kaylin was kidnapped by a transient. A tourist. Some evil stranger passing through. But I believe he's local."

"Why?"

"I've got a gut feeling about it."

Sara watched him in the darkness. "People never want to believe there is evil and cruelty in their midst. They never want to think people they see day to day, people they trust, are capable of inflicting pain and suffering."

He nodded. "The folks around here are proud of this town. It's friendly and scenic. People look out for each other."

"Except when they don't."

"That's right."

He stared down at her for a long moment. Then he started walking again, sweeping the flashlight over the rocky ground, and Sara fell in alongside him.

Nolan halted. "Hey, look." He took a few paces and crouched down. "Shine that light this way."

She aimed the UV light at something beside the rock, a scrap of white fabric. Excitement flitted through her as she stepped over.

"Looks like a T-shirt," he said.

"Don't touch it."

Nolan shot her a look. "Wasn't planning to."

Sara unzipped her pack and took out a pair of latex gloves. She passed one to him and pulled on the other.

"It's stuck under the rock, looks like," Nolan said.

Sara took out her camera and a ruler for scale. After snapping a few photos, she moved the rock aside and picked up the garment. As suspected, it was a T-shirt. It had been white originally, but now the fabric was dirty and stiff, too crunched up to read the lettering on the front.

"I've got an evidence envelope in my truck," Nolan said.

"I've got one here." Sara pulled a folded envelope from her bag, and Nolan opened it so she could drop the shirt inside.

"It might not be hers," she said.

"True." Nolan stood up. "Then again, it might."

Sara stood up and looked around. Then they combed the ground for another half hour but saw no more evidence. After scouring the entire creek bed, they headed back to the parking lot. They didn't talk, just made their way silently up the steep path. By the time they reached the top, Sara was breathing hard and in need of another shower. Nolan wasn't even winded. She still didn't know what he did for exercise, but he was in excellent shape.

"I've got some water," he said when they reached the lot.

Sara followed him to his pickup. He popped his locks and reached across the front seat for a bottle of water. She set down her backpack and the evidence envelope so she could unscrew the lid and take a gulp.

"Any chance you can run the shirt back at your lab?" he asked.

"Sure." She watched his eyes. "You don't want to run it through the state crime lab?"

"I'd just as soon get the results back this century."

Sara took another swig and passed him the bottle. He set it on the hood.

"We'll run it for DNA, blood, anything we can find, but it might not belong to the victim."

"Then again, it might," he repeated.

She liked his optimism. The determination in his voice made her feel better about a case that was growing bleaker by the day.

He stepped closer, peering down at her in the darkness. He slid his hand around her waist, and her heart started to sprint.

"Nolan—"

He kissed her. No hesitation. He just leaned down and settled his mouth over hers, silencing whatever she'd been about to say.

She responded without thinking, and the instant she tasted him, she wanted more. He tasted sharp and masculine, a flavor she liked. Her hands slid up around his neck, and he made a low groan and pulled her closer. His fingers curved around her hips as she went up on tiptoes, pressing her breasts against his solid chest, and she realized they fit together perfectly, despite the height difference.

His mouth was hot. Hungry. He dug a hand through her hair and tipped her head to get a better angle. He kissed her deeper, but still she couldn't get enough of his taste and his scent and the hard feel of his body. Something inside her just reacted, like she'd been craving him without even knowing it.

He eased back, blinking down at her, and she saw the surprise on his face. He started to say something, but she cut him off with another kiss. He felt so good. He pulled her against him and slid his hand over her breast, and she felt the delicious heat of it through her clothes.

How how *how* had she gone so long without this?

He jerked back suddenly.

"Shit."

"What?" she asked, disoriented.

"Sorry." He eased her away from him, and she heard the faint squawk of a radio in his truck. He pulled the door open and grabbed the receiver. "Hess."

Sara turned away, not listening to the garbled response. She tugged down her tank top, which had ridden up, and brushed her hair from her eyes.

She was at a crime scene. She was here to collect evidence, and instead she was kissing the lead detective on the case. What the hell was she doing?

"Sorry." He slammed the door and stepped over. "I have to go in."

"Of course. I'll just . . ." Flustered, she bent down for her backpack and the evidence envelope. He bent to help her, and she bumped her head against his chin on the way up. "Ouch."

He held her arm to steady her and gazed down. "You all right?"

"Yes, fine." No, she wasn't.

"I'll call you when I finish tonight."

"Don't."

His eyebrows tipped up.

"I'll be asleep." She stepped away, holding the backpack in front of her. "Early start tomorrow, seven A.M."

The radio in his truck started squawking again, and he turned and scowled at it.

"I'll talk to you tomorrow."

"Sara—"

"Good night."

CHAPTER 12

Nolan was up with the sun. He downed some strong coffee and checked his phone to make sure he hadn't missed anything overnight. Then he threw on his running clothes and stepped outside.

His six-year-old neighbor sat on the steps of the porch next door. Emmett had his dog beside him and his feet propped on his skateboard. At the sound of Nolan's screen door, the dog perked up and trotted over.

Nolan waved at Emmett. The kid waved back.

"Is your mom up?" Nolan asked, making sure to face him. Emmett was deaf, but he could sign and read lips. The boy pointed at the house, where his mother was probably making breakfast or getting ready for work.

Lori Davies was a single mom. Like Nolan, she had inherited her house from a grandparent. Unlike Nolan, she still owed money on it, and she worked two jobs to keep up with the payments. She probably could have found something cheaper at one of the new apartment complexes, but that would mean giving up her yard and her rabbit hutch, and Emmett loved animals.

Thor was sniffing around Nolan's feet now, wagging his tail, as he sensed a run in his future.

"Mind if I take Thor?"

Emmett shook his head, and Nolan ducked back inside to grab the leash off the table by the door, where he also kept a pile of plastic bags for the two or three times a week he took the dog jogging.

"Thirty minutes," Nolan said, and Emmett waved.

They set off at a brisk pace, with Thor close to Nolan's side. Part greyhound, part mutt, the dog was lean and wiry. He had a lot of energy, and Lori was always glad for him to get some extra exercise.

Nolan spent the first mile getting the kinks out. He hadn't run all week, and his body felt it. He passed a park with a playscape and a basketball hoop. No suspicious people or vehicles. The place was deserted except for a lone guy using the chin-up bar.

Nolan hung a left onto a winding road that hugged a creek. Giant cottonwoods offered shade, and the ground was covered in kudzu. Thor liked it down here, but Nolan had to keep the leash short so he wouldn't dart into the brush.

Nolan picked up the pace. His breathing settled into a rhythm, and he thought of Sara.

He'd caught her off guard when he kissed her. It wasn't something he really thought through—he just did it because she was gazing up at him, and it felt right. After a few seconds, she'd relaxed, and that was when things heated up. She'd responded with her whole body—her mouth, her arms, her hips—and he'd been so consumed he'd lost track of where he was. He'd lost track of everything but how much he wanted her.

Nolan couldn't remember the last time he'd been so turned on, and it was a problem. Sara was far away, and not just in terms of geography. She had walls up. He'd sensed it from the beginning, although he didn't know why. Getting her to open up wasn't going to be easy.

Not that he minded. Nolan liked a challenge. But this one came at a tough time. He wished he'd met Sara eighteen months ago, when the biggest thing on his plate had been a serial flasher going around town. Or even last fall, when he'd been working with a DEA task force closing in on a meth ring.

What he had now was bigger. And personal, because of the Baird family. Even beyond that, it was personal because it threatened the very heart of his hometown. Nolan had made it his goal to help hold back the tide of drugs and violence and callousness plaguing the cities around him. For the first time since he'd moved back, Nolan saw the true scope of what he'd set out to do.

The problem was he liked Sara. A lot. He liked

the way she tasted. The way she felt. He liked the way his truck smelled like her after she'd ridden in it. And the attraction wasn't just physical. He admired what she did, too, and how she did it. He'd come to understand that her careful, meticulous process wasn't something meant to drive him crazy, even though it did. It was who she was. She was thorough and methodical and dedicated to her work. Last night was a case in point. She would leave no stone unturned—literally—in her search for answers. Sure, Nolan was dedicated to his work, too, but that was different. He knew these people. This was his home. Sara worked nights and weekends in the blazing sun, and she did it for perfect strangers because it was the right thing to do.

Thor pulled at the leash, and Nolan reined him in. As his shoes pounded the asphalt, he thought of his last serious girlfriend. He and Michelle had gone from being partners at work to off-duty friends to having an intense sexual relationship that nearly ended Nolan's career when she was brought up on corruption charges. Nolan thought of how naive he'd been then and how much he'd taken for granted. Growing up surrounded by people with integrity, he didn't see when someone close to him didn't have any. The whole thing had blindsided him. Michelle wasn't who he'd thought she was, and her betrayal still felt like a gut punch.

Never again. Next time he got involved, he was going in with eyes wide open.

Nolan hung another left, taking a street that would loop back past the park. He sped up his pace, letting his thoughts wander, and, of course, they went to Sara. He thought about her mouth and her body and her fingers combing through his hair. The last mile was a blur, and then he was back at his house, sweaty and winded and greedy for the day. He took Thor inside, where he unhooked the leash and went to the kitchen to fill a bowl with water. The dog lapped it up as Nolan filled a glass for himself.

His phone buzzed, and he recognized Sara's number.

"Hess."

"It's me. Are you up?"

Just the sound of her voice made his heart thud, and he knew he was in trouble.

"I've been up," he told her. "You said seven, remember?"

"Well, I couldn't sleep, so I got here at six."

"Where are you?"

"The Sangria rock wall."

He put his glass down. "What's wrong, Sara?"

"You need to get out here."

Sara heard him before she saw him. The low rumble of his truck moved past her, and he pulled onto the shoulder. Sara kept her gaze on the digital display, wishing the numbers would tell a different story.

The truck door slammed. She turned around and saw he hadn't wasted time shaving after she called.

"What happened?" he asked gruffly.

"I started at the wall. Sangria." She nodded at the rock face that gleamed rosy-pink in the morning sun. "Maisy said that's where Kaylin liked to climb."

Nolan didn't even look. He was frowning down at the device in her hands.

"When I was there, I noticed this bike trail I didn't know was here. It's not on the map."

Nolan looked over her shoulder now at the landscape behind her. Dirt had been shaped into steep mounds and ramps—an obstacle course for BMX bikes.

"It's soil, Nolan." She stepped closer. "Not hard like the rest of the park. Everything else I've seen here is rock, but then there are these few acres of dirt. Do you get what I'm saying?"

"What is that?" He nodded at the device in her hands.

"Ground-penetrating radar. It picks up anomalies."

"Anomalies?"

"Soil disturbances. Pockets of air, loose dirt." She paused. "When a body decomposes, the tissue breaks down, creating a space underground."

He stared down at her, not even blinking.

"You're sure?" he asked.

"Not yet. But the reading I'm getting is pretty indicative."

"You're telling me you think there's a body buried here?"

"At least one, maybe more."

Talia squeezed her unmarked sedan between two patrol cars. Nolan's truck was across the street just beyond a black RV with the Delphi Center logo on the side.

She got out and looked around, unnerved by the crop of blue tents that had sprouted overnight.

"Talia."

She turned to see Nolan striding over. He had a phone pressed to his ear and latex gloves covering his hands.

"Yeah, I know. She's here now." He ended his call and shoved the phone into his pocket.

"What's with all the tarps?" she asked.

"Sara's idea. She doesn't want any more drone footage leaking out."

Talia glanced at the anthropologist, who was on her knees beside a pit, collecting something with a small tool. More people in blue coveralls worked a pit just a few feet away.

Dread tightened Talia's stomach as she looked at Nolan. "How many graves are we talking about?"

183

"Two so far," he said. "Did you get what we needed in San Antonio?"

She held up a thumb drive. "You have a computer here?"

"This way."

Nolan peeled off his gloves as he walked past her. He tromped up the stairs to the RV. Talia followed him inside and was smacked by a wall of cold air. The place was frigid. Aaron stood at a counter, tapping away on a laptop computer.

"Nice digs," she said.

Aaron glanced up. "Welcome to our mobile laboratory, otherwise known as the Ice Hut."

"This computer free?" Nolan asked. Without waiting for an answer, he sat down at a workstation tucked between a cabinet and a mini-fridge.

"Help yourself."

Talia handed Nolan the thumb drive, then grabbed a rolling desk chair and pulled up beside him.

"I got copies of all the reports, the interview transcripts, everything," she said. "But the main thing you need to see is the video. Here, let me navigate." She reached around him for the mouse and clicked open the only video file on the thumb drive.

Grainy surveillance footage showed a bar parking lot. A neon sign within the frame said RICO'S.

"This bar is on the north side of town, several blocks off I-35."

"Twenty-three fifty-two," Nolan said, reading the time stamp at the bottom of the screen.

"Watch," Talia said.

On the video, a line of people filed out of the bar, several not too steady on their feet. All were men. But then a woman stepped out.

Nolan leaned closer.

"That's not her. Just wait." Talia glanced up as Aaron left the RV. Quiet settled over the room. Nolan stared at the screen, and the only sound was the low hum of the refrigerator beside them. Talia had a sudden craving for something cold to drink.

"Think they'd mind if I grab something?" She reached for the door.

"They keep evidence in there."

"Ew. Never mind."

Nolan tapped the screen. "That's her—the girl who just exited. Alicia Merino."

Talia leaned closer. "You're good. I hardly recognized her. She doesn't look like her driver's license photo."

The woman had straight dark hair that trailed all the way down her back. She wore a sleeveless white shirt and a short black skirt that made her legs look long, even though the police report put her at five-two. Alicia had a phone in her hand, and she was texting away, not paying attention to

185

her surroundings as people streamed in and out of the bar.

"Watch what happens," Talia said, though she didn't have to. Nolan's eyes were glued to the screen.

Alicia glanced up from her phone. She said something to someone off camera, then shook her head. She looked down, then back up again. For a moment, she didn't move or talk. And then she stepped forward, moving out of camera view.

Nolan muttered a curse.

Rico's parking lot was still, no traffic going in or out. The door to the bar opened again, and a couple stepped outside.

"There." Talia hit pause as a white SUV pulled out of the parking lot. "That's them."

Nolan leaned forward. "You sure?"

"No, but SAPD is. They zoomed in on the image, and they believe it's Alicia in the passenger seat."

"Go back."

Talia moved the footage backward, then hit play again.

"Can we enhance it?"

"This is already enhanced. But they've examined it repeatedly, and they say it's her."

Nolan leaned back, folding his arms over his chest as he watched the frozen image. A muscle in his jaw tightened.

"They're right, Nolan. It's Alicia. Look at that

hair. And the white shirt, no sleeves? It's her in that vehicle. She caught a ride, and it's the last time anyone saw her alive."

"Besides her killer."

"Right."

The door to the RV opened, and Sara stepped inside. She was on the phone and hardly glanced in their direction as she took over the laptop Aaron had left open on the counter.

"I've got it right here," Sara was saying. The knees of her coveralls were dirty, and her boots were coated with dust. She stripped off a pair of gloves and gave the keyboard a few taps. "Okay, ready?" She rattled off a series of numbers.

Talia shot Nolan a puzzled look.

"GPS coordinates," he said.

"I realize that, but it's worth a try." Sara glanced at Nolan, and something in her eyes softened. Then she turned away and propped her phone on her shoulder, freeing her hands to type.

"They give you any crap down there?"

Talia looked at Nolan, startled by his question. He meant the San Antonio detectives assigned to Alicia's case.

"They were territorial," she said. "Didn't stonewall me, though. Mainly, I think they want a look at what we have on our end. I told them about the missing person in Austin, and they already knew."

Sara walked out, and Nolan's gaze followed her. Talia studied his expression.

"You look pissed off, Nolan. What's wrong?"

"You mean besides the fact that we've got some sick dirtbag using our town as his personal dumping ground?"

"Yeah."

Nolan shook his head. "Nothing."

"Bull." She watched him, determined not to talk until he shared what was on his mind.

"Okay, I'm frustrated. This thing keeps snowballing on us." He combed his hand through his hair. "But I'm glad SAPD gave this up. It's the best lead we have so far, hands down."

"This?" Talia frowned at the monitor. "But we can't even see the faces. We can't be sure it's them."

"It's them."

"Look at this video, Nolan. The lighting's terrible, and we don't even have a glimpse of the perp. Or an eyewitness description."

"Wouldn't help anyway. People can alter their appearance. And eyewitnesses aren't that reliable. What we've got here is ten times better."

"How?"

"Because." Nolan nodded at the screen. "Now we've got his vehicle."

The sun blazed overhead as Nolan returned to the park and made his way down the narrow road

188

jammed with emergency vehicles. While he'd been sidetracked at the police station, word had spread among local agencies about the new crime scene. The mix of vehicles now included sheriff's units, park district trucks, and cars belonging to Allen County Search and Rescue—although Nolan didn't really see what value an S-and-R team could add today. Everyone seemed to want a piece of the action.

Nolan parked his pickup on the shoulder and headed straight for the Delphi Center RV, nearly bumping into Aaron on his way out.

"Sara in there?" Nolan asked.

"Nope. Haven't seen her in a while."

Nolan scanned the chaotic scene. All the Delphi people wore blue coveralls, but Nolan didn't see a petite blonde in their midst giving orders. The two burial pits had been cordoned off with yellow scene tape. Brad Crowley stood off to the side, chatting with a young woman. She had long braids and wore a red ACSAR T-shirt.

Nolan walked over and interrupted them. "Either of you seen Sara Lockhart?"

Crowley looked around. "She was just here."

"She walked into the woods." The woman pointed. "That way."

"Why?"

"Dunno." She shrugged. "Bathroom break?"

Doubtful. Not with a luxury RV right there.

Nolan trekked past the burial site and into the

woods, following a hard-packed trail for mountain bikes. The path was hemmed in by cedar trees and mesquite bushes. Nolan heard a faint noise in the distance. He followed the sound of retching until he found Sara bent in half beside a boulder. She straightened and took a step, then swayed.

"Whoa." He rushed over and grabbed her arm just as she bent forward and threw up on his boot. She tried to tug her arm away, but he held it steady and pulled her hair back from her face.

For a moment, she was stock-still. Nolan pulled a folded bandanna from his back pocket and handed it to her.

"Sorry," she gasped, dabbing her mouth.

"You good?"

She nodded and stood up. Her green eyes were watery. "Sorry," she repeated as she wiped her chin. She glanced at his boots and closed her eyes. "God, how embarrassing."

"These are my crime-scene shoes. They've seen worse." Nolan glanced around, looking for any sign of bones or fresh graves. "What are you doing way back here?"

She laughed and folded his bandanna. "Who uses these anymore?"

Nolan just watched her. Her cheeks were pink—from heat and sunburn and probably embarrassment, too.

"Here, take a load off." Nolan guided her

to another big rock, and she leaned against it.

"I didn't want my team to see me puking my guts up," she said. "Not exactly good for morale."

"Is it the smell?"

She shook her head. "I'm immune to it now. I think maybe it's the heat. But this never happens to me. We've even got some shade today."

"Yeah, well, it's ninety-eight degrees, and you've been out here six hours. Those are tough working conditions. You should take a break in the air-conditioning."

She gave him a scowl, which let him know she was recovering. "Guatemala was tougher. And we had no AC anywhere."

Nolan didn't have a comeback for that, so he just watched her. Even with watery eyes and vomit-spattered coveralls, she looked beautiful. But he sensed she wouldn't appreciate a compliment right now.

"How's the excavation coming?" he asked.

"Good." She seemed grateful for a change of subject. "We've made steady progress on the two pits. Should be finished by evening."

"Today?"

"Yes."

"What can you tell me?" He held up his hand as she started to protest. "I know nothing's official yet, and I won't hold you to it. Just give me a sense of what it's looking like."

She took a deep breath. "Two individuals. Separate graves and different postmortem intervals."

"Any idea how long ago they were buried?"

"I have to run some tests—soil pH, that sort of thing. But my guesstimate is between one and two years ago."

"Both victims?"

"Yes. And so far, no obvious cause of death, such as bullet holes or blunt-force trauma to the skull," she said matter-of-factly.

"Okay, what about clothes or jewelry, anything personal that might help with gender or ID?"

"In one of the graves we found a small arrow-shaped pendant on a broken chain. I plan to check the database for it. No clothing in either."

"What, nothing?"

"Not even fabric remnants."

Nolan stared at her. Then he muttered a curse and turned away. He thought of that sick bastard out here dumping a naked woman into a shallow grave.

"Another thing, Nolan?"

He looked at Sara.

"They're young."

"You mean like teenagers or—"

"Probably early twenties."

Nolan's chest tightened as he watched her. She looked tired and defeated. Yes, she had been doing this a long time. And yes, she'd seen a lot. But clearly, this case was getting to her.

It was getting to him, too.

"What are you thinking?" Sara asked.

"This whole discovery reinforces my case theory." He nodded toward Sangria. "Kaylin liked to climb there. I think she was there when she witnessed something suspicious, and that's what made her a target for this unsub. I think the backpack in the other park was a decoy, meant to throw us off. But I think whoever buried these women here likely saw Kaylin and grabbed her. Maybe he took her someplace else, but this area is the original crime scene."

Sara sighed. "I wish that didn't make sense, but it does, unfortunately." She refolded his handkerchief and tucked it into her pocket. "I'll wash this for you."

"Don't worry about it."

She brushed her hair from her eyes, seeming self-conscious again. She didn't like him finding her in a private moment, and she was also probably worried about how it looked that they'd disappeared into the woods together.

Nolan checked his watch. "One of our officers is bringing subs for you guys. He should be here by now."

"Thank you. They'll appreciate that. I'll reimburse you."

"Get real."

She gazed up at him for a long moment. "I should get back."

"You should."

But she didn't move. She just stood there, staring up at him. He'd been about to leave, but the look in her eyes kept him rooted in place. Going with his intuition, he wrapped his arms around her. She rested her cheek against his chest, and relief rippled through him. At that moment, she needed him, and he was more than happy to hold her as long as she wanted.

She eased back.

"Sorry," she mumbled, smoothing her hair. "I'm a mess today."

"Don't apologize. Take all the time you need here. I'll keep an eye on the crime scene." He stepped back to give her some space.

"Wait." She put her hand on his arm. "I wanted to talk to you. About last night."

Damn it, he'd wondered if this was coming. She had that worry line between her brows now.

"You're mad I kissed you," he said.

"*No*. God. That part was good. I'm just . . ."

He stepped closer. "What? Just say it."

"I go back to San Marcos today."

He didn't respond.

"I live there, you live here. So what's the point of starting something?"

Nolan smiled slightly. "Does everything have to have a point?"

"Well . . . yes."

He shook his head.

"What's wrong with that?"

"Nothing at all." He gazed down at her. "Anything else?"

She looked confused. "No."

"Good. See you at the crime scene."

He left her there looking perplexed and headed back to civilization. She probably thought she'd talked him out of pursuing this thing, whatever it was. But she hadn't. Yeah, they lived in different places, but he liked her. More with every damn minute he spent with her, even when she was puking on his boots. There was something special about her, and he was determined to get her to give him a chance.

That part was good.

It was a small admission, but he'd take it.

Talia intercepted him on the edge of the clearing beside the scene tape. She looked over his shoulder, and her expression turned suspicious.

"What's going on?" she asked.

"Nothing."

"Biggs is here with sandwiches. Is Sara back there?"

"She's coming."

"Well, what does she say?"

"She doesn't know all the facts yet, but she will soon."

"And?" Talia looked up at him expectantly.

"And you need to brace yourself." Nolan put his hand on her shoulder. "This case is going to get a hell of a lot worse before it gets better."

CHAPTER 13

Sara scrolled through the photos of personal effects. The number of images was mind-numbing, and she'd already narrowed her search as much as possible by category.

She glanced at the small pendant in its clear plastic bag. She'd been thinking about it ever since she'd unearthed it at that first burial pit. She held the bag up to the light now and looked for any distinguishing marks, but, as before, there was nothing.

Aaron walked into the lab and placed a cardboard cup beside her computer. "Tall skinny latte, as requested."

She looked up at him blankly.

"I knew it." He slurped the foam off his icy concoction. "You don't remember, do you? On my way out the door, I asked if you wanted your usual, and you said, 'Yeah, sure,' without looking up."

"Sorry. I was distracted."

"No joke. You've been out of it all day."

Sara focused on her computer, trying not to react. She had been out of it not just today but yesterday and the day before that. Every day since she'd met Nolan, she'd been off-kilter. No, ever since she'd kissed him. Or since he'd kissed her. However it had happened, it had thrown everything off balance. How absurd that one little kiss could do this.

She shouldn't have let the time go. She should have had a rebound relationship by now, something to help her hit reset on her sex life. But her breakup with Patrick had been hard, and then one month had rolled into another and another. It had been two years since there had been a man in her life. And the weird thing was, she hadn't missed it. Sure, she'd missed the physical part sometimes. But she hadn't missed having a man around to sway her moods and steer her plans and edit her decisions. She liked her independence, and she didn't plan to give it up, ever again.

Anyway, this whole train of thought was pointless. She had too much work to do to get sidetracked with a romance that wasn't going anywhere. And it wasn't—no matter how much she liked talking with Nolan. Or kissing him. He was the lead detective on her most important case, and she needed to get their relationship back on a professional footing.

Aaron peered over her shoulder at the images on her screen. "You still stuck on that pendant from the burial site?"

"Yeah."

"Nothing similar in the system?"

"Not that I can find." She leaned back in her chair. "But I keep wondering if it has some personal significance that might help us in some way. What does an arrow symbolize?"

"Hmm, offhand? I don't know. Cupids? Native Americans? Sagittarius?"

She smiled. "I didn't realize you were into astrology."

He shrugged. "My birthday's in December. The zodiac symbol for Sagittarius is an archer."

"What are we talking about?" Kelsey asked as she walked in, also armed with a giant beverage, although Sara suspected hers was decaffeinated.

"Arrow symbolism," Sara said. "Any ideas?"

Kelsey walked over and looked at the pendant in the baggie beside Sara's computer.

"I don't know. Maybe she just picked it up at the mall or somewhere because it's pretty. I'd buy it." She leaned back against the counter and folded her arms. Like Sara, Kelsey wore her typical work attire of lab coat and jeans. Unlike Sara, her lab coat barely reached her knees because she was so tall.

"This isn't some cheap trinket, though," Sara said. "It's eighteen-karat gold. Which makes me think it's probably a gift."

"Hmm. Could be." Kelsey nodded at Sara's computer. "Where are we on identifications? Anything in the system?"

"Good news," Sara said. "We got a DNA hit on remains from the second burial pit."

"You're kidding."

Sara exited out of the personal effects page and pulled up the record. "Her name is Lisa Ryan. She's from Dallas."

"Holy crap," Aaron muttered. "I'm always amazed when it works."

"Me too," Kelsey said.

Their disbelief was understandable. Of the estimated forty thousand unidentified human remains being stored in morgues, crime labs, and police departments across the country, only a small fraction had been entered into NamUs. Most understaffed and underfunded agencies didn't have the resources to make entering records a priority, whether records of found remains or missing persons. Overworked cops, especially, were lax about entering their cases, and some didn't even know the system existed. Sara was committed to changing that by raising awareness, one cop at a time.

"I submitted her dental X-rays yesterday," Sara said. "We had a hit in no time."

Of course, some victims didn't have dental records. And some had never been fingerprinted, so even when investigators meant well, it wasn't always easy to upload useful information on a missing person.

"Age?" Kelsey asked.

"Twenty-one. She was last seen leaving work, possibly on her way to join some friends at a bar. The police in her case have always thought it was an abduction."

Kelsey studied Lisa Ryan's photo. She had brown hair, brown eyes, and a petite frame.

"Physically, she reminds me of those two victims in Tennessee," Kelsey commented.

"I think so, too," Sara said.

"She the one with the arrow pendant?"

"No, that was found in the other grave," Aaron said. "Hey, I thought of another one—Diana, goddess of the hunt, from mythology. She was an archer, wasn't she?"

Alex Lovell walked in with a computer bag in hand. She worked in the cybercrimes unit, where the standard uniform was jeans and flip-flops.

"Am I interrupting?" she asked.

"We were talking about mythology," Sara told her.

Alex wrinkled her nose. "Ew, freshman English. My teacher was a dick. Also, he was about a thousand years old."

"Yes, Diana was the archer," Kelsey said, getting the conversation back on track. "But I still don't think it has to mean anything, even if it's real gold. Maybe whoever bought it simply liked the design." She looked at Alex. "We're talking about a piece of jewelry found in one of the pits at White Falls Park."

"That's exactly what I'm here about. You have a minute?"

"Sure."

"Let's go to your office. I need to set up my laptop."

Sara led Alex into the small office she shared with her coworkers. Now that Kelsey had returned from vacation, it looked as cluttered as usual. Sara moved a stack of files off a chair and pulled it over to her desk.

Alex took the seat and quickly booted up her computer. "Okay, I've been investigating that drone footage you found online."

"*I* didn't find it. One of Kelsey's anthro students did."

"Well, whatever. I've been looking into it, and it's more interesting than I first thought."

"How so?" Sara sat down in the chair beside her. The image on Alex's screen showed the video clip that had presumably come from a drone camera high above their worksite.

"Whoever posted this started on Twitter. It came from two accounts. Then people saw it, and it went viral with users in this area."

"People who know White Falls Park."

"That probably accounts for a lot of them," Alex said. "And then when the media got hold of it, it was shared on a much larger scale."

"Okay. So?"

"So I've been looking into the original two

accounts, and a few things stand out. First, both accounts were created last Sunday morning." Alex leveled a look at her. "Think about that timing."

Sara thought back to Sunday. She'd spent Saturday night at the motel and gotten up early to meet Nolan at the park.

"What time Sunday morning?" she asked Alex.

"Shortly after eight. Both accounts."

Alex turned her computer to face Sara, showing her an account of someone named Goldilocks432. She opened another screen showing a second account, WondrGurl. No photo images on either account—only a generic silhouette.

"You're saying these accounts didn't exist before then?"

"That's what I'm saying. *And* this video is the only thing that was posted to them. In other words, they seem to have been set up for the express purpose of spreading this video. And then—even more peculiar—these two accounts were deleted."

"When?"

"Two days after the first video went up."

"Then how do you still have this?"

"I was tipped off before then and started my investigating, so I archived everything. You can't totally erase your tracks. There are still digital footprints."

Sara shook her head. "Don't you have to have followers to get people to see you?"

"Right. But there are some ways around that," Alex said. "For example, you can post things elsewhere that drive people to find you and look at your post, which is probably what happened here. And then, once other people start spreading the images on multiple platforms, it can take off."

Sara stared at the screenshot, a bird's-eye view of her team's dig site. The actual video footage was worse—a thirty-second clip that ended with a close-up view of the decomposed skull, complete with flesh and tufts of hair.

"I really hate that this video is out there," Sara said. "Can you imagine if this was your daughter? It's such a violation of this family's privacy, and they've already suffered a terrible loss."

"I know."

"And the way the camera closes in on her . . . it's almost voyeuristic."

"It *is* voyeuristic," Alex said. "And that's part of the reason I'm here. Whoever did this is sick, and he's getting off on this kind of attention."

Sara frowned. "What are you saying?"

"I'm *saying,* look at the timing. He knew about the excavation very early. Indicating he'd heard about it through the rumor mill versus the news, meaning he's probably local. And his purpose seems to be drawing attention, in particular, media attention, to this murder. *And* he went to a lot of trouble to cover his digital tracks."

"You're saying . . . you think he might be the killer?"

"Hey, I'm not a profiler," Alex said. "I'm just saying it's possible. It wouldn't hurt to talk to Mark in cybercrimes."

Sara looked at the screen. "I will. I'm seeing him this afternoon, actually. I've got a meeting with him and the detectives from Springville to go over what we know so far."

Alex lifted an eyebrow. "By 'Springville detectives,' I assume you mean Nolan Hess?"

"That's right. Nolan mentioned he knows you." Sara tried to keep her tone neutral, but she could see Alex's smirk. "What?"

"How is Nolan? I haven't talked to him in a while."

Sara's mind flashed to Nolan's intent brown eyes the moment before he kissed her.

"I don't know. Fine, I guess. Although I'm sure he's stressed by everything happening in his jurisdiction."

Alex studied her face, no doubt looking for more. "Nolan's a good guy," she said. "One of my favorite people, actually."

Sara nodded. "He seems nice."

"Nice? That's it?" Alex grinned.

"Okay, he's hot, too." She smiled as she felt her cheeks reddening. "What do you want me to say?"

"You don't have to say anything." She closed her laptop, still grinning. "I think the look on your face says it all."

Nolan surveyed the tall white columns as he mounted the Delphi Center's front steps. The building was bigger and more imposing than he'd expected, and he felt like he was entering the Supreme Court. He'd thought the place would be clearing out by Friday afternoon, but the lobby was busy with Delphi employees, as well as law-enforcement types like himself. Nolan went straight to the front desk, where he'd been told to get a visitor's badge.

"Nolan Hess," he said, showing his ID.

As the receptionist looked him up on the computer, he caught sight of Sara crossing the lobby. The last time he'd seen her, she was in dirty coveralls, standing in the center of a chaotic excavation site and dispensing orders to her team. She looked a lot more composed today in a crisp lab coat with her name embroidered on the front pocket.

She stopped in front of him. "Thanks for coming, Detective."

He lifted an eyebrow. "Detective?"

She turned to the receptionist. "Could I get a visitor's badge, please?" She glanced at Nolan. "Isn't Talia coming?"

"She's five minutes behind me."

Nolan clipped on his visitor's badge as Sara looked past him.

"Well, I don't see her, but she can find us." She turned to the receptionist. "We'll be in the first-floor conference room, so send her back, please." Another glance at Nolan. "Right this way."

He followed her, half amused, half irked by her formality.

She passed a coffee shop and a bank of elevators before turning down a corridor. Stopping at the first door, she knocked softly before entering. The windowless room had a conference table and an oversize whiteboard.

"I reserved the room starting at four, but looks like we're the first ones here." She pulled out the chair at the head of the table and set down an iPad.

"Who else are you expecting?"

"Mark Wolfe, who's in charge of cybercrimes."

Nolan took the chair to Sara's left, so he could keep an eye on the door. "Cybercrimes?"

"Cyber profiling, to be specific. He used to be in the FBI's Behavioral Analysis Unit. I hope you don't mind that I asked him to weigh in on the case."

"Sure, good idea."

"What is?" Talia asked as she walked in. She wore black pants today and had a visitor's badge clipped to her pale blue shirt.

"Talia, hi," Sara said. "I asked one of my colleagues to join us."

A tall man stepped into the room, and even without knowing his background, Nolan would have guessed he was a fed. He wore a suit and tie and gave a brisk nod as Sara made introductions.

Like Nolan, he took a chair on the far side of the table, facing the door. The seat put him opposite Talia, who seemed less than thrilled with his presence. She wasn't obvious about it, but Nolan had worked with her for years and knew all her tells.

"So, you used to be at Quantico, huh?" Talia pretended to be impressed. "How'd they lure you down to Texas?"

"My wife lured me," he said. "We met down here when we were working a case together."

Nolan was surprised by the candid answer.

"Is she with Delphi?" Talia asked.

"She's a detective in San Marcos."

Nolan could tell his answer scored points with Talia.

Nolan shifted his attention to Sara. "You said you had some news?"

"Several important developments." She tapped her iPad and brought the screen to life. A few more taps, and then she slid the tablet to the center of the table. Nolan recognized the photographs on display.

"We received confirmation this morning from

our cordage expert here at the lab," Sara said. "The bindings recovered on Sunday with the remains of Alicia Merino are made of the same twine that was used in two cold cases from Tennessee."

"The *same* twine?" Nolan asked. "Or do you mean the same *type?*"

"The same twine from the very same roll. Our expert was able to match the material through forensic fiber analysis."

"We're dealing with the same perp, then," Talia stated.

"In all probability, yes." Sara nodded at the tablet. "It looks like the same unidentified subject, or unsub, could be responsible. As you can see from the date stamps on these photographs, the bodies were recovered five years ago. The same purple twine used in all the bindings makes me think the roll is part of his murder kit."

"Damn." Talia looked at Nolan. "And you checked into this, right? The cops on these cases have no leads?"

"Nothing fresh," Nolan said. "I talked to them Wednesday, and they sent me some of their paperwork. No strong suspects. They had a persons-of-interest list they were working on at one point, but nothing came of it. And when I combed through, no one jumped out at me."

"You reran all the names?" Talia asked.

"Every one of them. No Texas connection that I could find."

"Another important piece of news," Sara said, "is the report from our tool-marks expert. After examining the vertebra, he believes a wire or garrote was used on Alicia Merino."

"Like the Tennessee cases," Nolan said. He'd been hoping the link wouldn't hold up to scrutiny.

"Wait, a *garrote*?" Talia looked from Sara to Nolan.

"It's a wire or cord with handles on the end."

"I know. I'm saying that's not your everyday murder weapon."

"It's unusual," Nolan agreed.

"And the last bit of news," Sara said. "We got an ID on one of the two victims from the burial site. Lisa Ryan. She was in the system, so we were able to get a quick turnaround."

"Which system?" Nolan asked.

"NamUs. This woman went missing fourteen months ago up in Dallas, last seen by a coworker as she was leaving the law office where she worked as a file clerk. At the time, her family provided a DNA sample and dental records, so we were able to get a quick hit." Sara's gaze settled on Nolan. "She went missing on April thirtieth."

"You're sure?" Nolan asked.

"I'm sure."

Talia looked at him. "What's the significance of April thirtieth?"

"That's a week before Kaylin Baird disappeared." Nolan sighed.

"You don't look surprised," Sara commented.

"I'm not. That date reinforces my case theory."

"And what is your case theory?" Mark asked, speaking up for the first time.

"I think Kaylin was in White Falls Park and witnessed a body being buried or some other criminal activity that made her a target," he said. "I think this unsub saw her and went after her, probably killed her right there or maybe grabbed her and took her elsewhere, then dropped her backpack in another park to throw off investigators."

Silence settled over the room, and Nolan looked at Sara. From the start of this thing, they'd been thinking along the same lines.

"What about the others?" Mark asked.

"They came later. Instead of burying those bodies, looks like he pulled into the park, made a quick turnoff, and dumped them off a cliff into a wooded ravine. So he changed his MO after Kaylin, probably decided that digging a grave, even a shallow one, was too risky. He had to find a quicker way to get rid of them."

"Do serial killers do that?" Talia looked at Mark. "Change things up like that? I thought they liked to stick to a script."

"Generally, it's more important to get away with their crimes, whether they stick to a script or not," Mark said. "These guys evolve, refine their technique. However, the killer's signature stays the same from one crime to the next."

"Explain the signature," Sara said. "I've never really understood how that's different from MO."

"The signature is about some emotional need that's satisfied from committing the crime, and it's the same every time," Mark said. "Maybe he needs to tie the victim up, control her, inflict pain before he takes her life—which is the ultimate act of control. The MO—the way he picks up his victim, where he takes her, where he disposes of the body—that can evolve over time as he gets better at his work."

"His work?" Talia shuddered. "That's messed up."

Mark nodded. "I don't disagree."

"What's wrong, Nolan? You seem skeptical," Sara said.

Nolan leaned back in his chair. "The five-year time gap bothers me. Serial killers don't just stop. Not unless they're dead or in prison."

"It might not be a gap in killing, just a gap in us knowing about it," Sara said. "For all we know, he left Tennessee and went to another state or down to Mexico for a while, then found his way back to Texas."

"Agreed," Nolan said. "But let's assume he

wasn't doing it somewhere else. Let's assume he was in prison. Maybe he got picked up for assault or burglary or, who the hell knows, check fraud. Point is, he might have done time."

"Which would mean we have his prints and DNA," Talia said.

"Exactly." Nolan looked at Sara. "Any word on that T-shirt you found the other night?"

"The lab's still working on it. It's at the front of the line, but it still takes time."

"What's the technician's name?" Nolan asked. "Maybe I'll check in after I finish here."

"Won't help. I already put a rush on it."

"Won't hurt, though, right?"

"Her name is Mia Voss, and she's in charge of the DNA lab," Sara said.

"Let's talk about the park," Mark said. "I think that's important. He seems attached to that location, which is why—even if your theory is true and Kaylin Baird witnessed him engaging in some sort of suspicious activity there—he continued to use the park as a site to dispose of his victims. The place is very much in his comfort zone."

"Maybe he's a park ranger or some other employee," Talia suggested. "Would that fit with your profile?"

"It's not a profile, really, because I haven't done a complete analysis," Mark said. "What I have is preliminary."

"Okay, your preliminary profile," Talia said.

Mark nodded. "I think the unsub is a white male in his thirties or forties."

Talia looked at Nolan. "Now, there's a surprise."

"He's physically active, probably engages in outdoor sports, such as hiking or climbing. He has a high school education but not beyond, although he has a fairly high IQ. I'd say he had an abusive relationship with his mother or another important female caregiver, based on the bindings and the sadism—"

"Sadism?" Nolan cut in.

"The cases in Tennessee," Sara said. "I don't know if you read the autopsy reports, but both bodies showed bruising and several bone fractures consistent with torture over a period of days or weeks."

"Weeks?" Talia leaned forward.

"The bone was fractured but then started to heal itself before death," Sara said. "He kept them alive for at least a week. I found evidence of the same sort of treatment in the case of Alicia Merino."

"That means he has to have a place to keep them," Nolan said.

"Somewhere remote," Mark agreed. "Or at least far enough from neighbors that he doesn't attract suspicion. Maybe a basement or a cabin somewhere."

"Weeks?" Talia repeated, looking at Nolan. "If he took that girl from Sixth Street, she might still be alive."

"What girl from Sixth Street?" Sara asked.

"Grace Murray," Nolan told her.

"Who's that?"

"She went missing from her cousin's bachelorette party last Friday," he said. "The lead detective thinks there's a connection."

"Based on what?" Mark asked.

"Nothing, except he's desperate," Talia said. "He's got no good leads, so he's basically grasping at straws. But if he's right and this guy *did* take her, then she might not be dead."

CHAPTER 14

Sara collected files from her desk and slid them into her computer bag. She kept meaning to catch up on paperwork, but she kept getting sidetracked with trips to Springville.

"Heading home?"

Nolan stood in her doorway, and Sara smiled before she could stop herself. She hadn't expected to see him again today.

He shook his head as he stepped into the room.

"What?" She walked around her desk.

"That look. You seem happy to see me now. I'm usually good at reading people, but you confuse me."

Sara didn't know what to say to that. She confused herself, too.

"Did you find Mia?" she asked.

"I did."

"Was she annoyed?"

"Some." He shrugged. "But she promised to have me something by tomorrow." He glanced around. "This is the anthro lab, huh?"

"Otherwise known as the Crypt. What brings you down here?"

He looked at her. "I wanted to see where you work."

The simple answer put a flutter in her stomach.

"Okay, well . . . let me give you the tour."

She led him into the adjacent autopsy suite, where five stainless steel tables filled the center of the room. All but one was occupied by bones recovered from Nolan's jurisdiction.

He walked to the nearest table and studied the remains.

"One of our two Jane Does," Sara told him. "Although I'm optimistic we'll get a name for her."

"Why?"

Stepping up to the table, Sara took a pencil from the pocket of her lab coat and pointed at one of the victim's molars. "She has some distinctive restorations. Also, her femur. See here?" She indicated a hairline fracture in the bone. "This is an old injury. It was properly set at the time, so there should be medical records somewhere. If we can get a lead on who she is, then it shouldn't be hard to confirm ID."

"That's where we come in."

By the tone of his voice, she knew the responsibility weighed heavily on his shoulders. He now had four victims—two still unidentified—in his community, along with a missing-persons case that was fourteen months old. Even with a task force working around the clock, the magnitude of the investigation was daunting.

Sara folded her arms over her chest. "How come you didn't tell me about the Austin woman?"

He looked like he'd been expecting the question. "I didn't know till Tuesday night when the detective tracked down Talia."

"You could have told me Wednesday at the gravesite."

"Would you have been able to work any faster?"

"No . . . But still. If this link is real, it adds a whole new urgency to what we're doing."

"I know."

He stepped over to a floor-to-ceiling shelf filled with animal bones.

"That's our reference collection," she said. "We get a lot of nonhuman specimens, mostly midsize mammals."

Nolan picked up a deer mandible and examined it. He glanced around the room, and his gaze lingered on the nearby table of bones. She liked that he didn't crack jokes or make irreverent comments. So many people didn't know what to make of her job or were put off by it. Patrick had been put off by it. He'd liked her working in the university setting, and when she started talking about how she missed forensics, he told her she'd be crazy to want to leave a good job in academia for grisly death scenes and midnight callouts.

Sara watched Nolan examining her workspace now, glad he'd made the effort to find her down here. He picked up a blue stress ball off the counter and squeezed it as he glanced around. She noticed his gaze land on the photo of her nieces, Ellie and Erin, building a sandcastle at Rehoboth Beach.

Nolan put down the stress ball and walked over to a pair of computer stations. Behind them was a bulletin board, where Sara had tacked photos of various artifacts she'd unearthed. The pictures showed a crumpled ticket stub, a dirt-caked watch, the arrow-shaped pendant she'd been fixated on for days.

"These are from crime scenes?" Nolan tapped the photo of the pendant. "I recognize this one."

"All those items are from unsolved cases. I keep them posted there as kind of a reminder."

He nodded. "Keeps them front of mind. I do the same but with mug shots."

"Like you said, sometimes it's the small things that break a case open."

He stepped over to her. "You're good at what you do," he said.

"So are you."

"Not lately."

"Don't be so pessimistic. You got some good leads today."

He didn't comment. It was hard to be optimistic

with the possibility of a new victim out there.

She held his gaze, and the moment stretched out. Sara's heart started to thud, and she knew what he was thinking even before he leaned down and kissed her.

His mouth was gentle this time. Not tentative but . . . seeking. It was a leisurely exploration, and his hands slid up her back, pulling her close. She let her body melt against him, unwilling to resist, even though they were at her *office* and anyone could walk in on them. She didn't care. She just wanted to kiss him and feel his arms around her. She wanted to feel something good for a change. His hair was silky between her fingers, and she loved the firm wall of his chest. But then he eased back, cupping the side of her face as he gazed down at her.

"What was that for?" she asked.

"You looked tense."

Her heart was hammering now, and she no longer felt tense but flustered. She should feel annoyed, too, but instead she was excited.

Smiling slightly, he eased back. "Looked like you were leaving. Want me to walk you out?"

"Sure."

Sara hung her lab coat, then grabbed her computer bag. Nerves flitted in her stomach as she followed him out the door and locked up.

They walked down the long corridor toward the elevator. They rode up without talking, and she resisted the urge to pelt him with questions. She wanted to know what he thought of the Delphi Center, her coworkers, her theories.

She wanted to know why he'd kissed her again and why he couldn't stay longer.

Nolan unclipped his visitor's badge and left it on the reception desk. The lobby was deserted except for the weekend security guard. They stepped outside into the warm breeze. The sun had dropped behind the trees, but they still had some daylight left. They started walking toward the parking lot, and Sara spotted his pickup in the front row right beside her Explorer.

She glanced at him. "So, what's next with the investigation? Do you have a plan?"

He smiled. "Of course. The plan is for Mia to get a DNA hit that magically solves the case."

"I'm serious."

His smile faded, and he looked down. "I've got a lead on a vehicle."

"Where?"

"Security cam picked it up at the bar where Alicia Merino went missing. It's a white Chevy Tahoe, about ten years old. No plate, but I've got make, model, and approximate year, so that's a solid lead."

They reached his pickup, and Sara thought of the last time they'd stood together beside his truck. She noticed his furrowed brow and the tense set of his jaw. The stress was weighing on him, and she wished the circumstances were different.

Maybe when everything died down . . . what? They'd go out for drinks together? Strike up a romance?

They didn't even live in the same town, and besides, he was married to his job. So was she. The chances of this going anywhere were non-existent.

But the thought of not seeing him anymore? That seemed wrong. Completely unacceptable.

His frown deepened.

"What?" she asked.

"I wish I had more time here." He eased closer, and her skin tingled again as he rested his hand on her shoulder. "But I have to get back."

"I know."

She wanted him to stay anyway.

"Keep me in the loop, Sara." He sounded all-business now as his hand dropped away.

"I will."

Grace thought about food. And water. She thought about tall, juicy hamburgers and fizzy Coke poured over chipped ice. She thought about apples, and peaches, and even pickles, which she hated. Anything to take her mind off the pain and the fear and the endless blackness.

He'd left behind a bottle of water and three small pouches of orange-flavored slime. Some kind of sports gel, she guessed, although sports gel was as foreign to her as monkey brains—which she would have gladly devoured this minute if given the chance.

The sticky little packets were just enough to keep her alive. Just enough to keep her from sliding into nothingness. Why hadn't he let her die already?

The answer was a sharp kick in her hollow stomach. *Because he's coming back.*

She had to think about food again. Anything, anything, anything besides the coming pain.

The last food she'd chewed had been a warm flour tortilla at the Mexican place on Sixth Street—which now felt like another planet in a galaxy far, far away. They'd ordered fajitas for the table, but Grace had passed, worried she wouldn't be able to zip herself into her dress for Bella's wedding.

Tears stung her eyes as she thought of her family. Had the wedding come and gone? Time was gray and shapeless, like smoke curling over a campfire, only there was no fire here, and everything was pitch-dark. Grace didn't know if it was day or night or how many hours she'd spent in this godforsaken tomb.

She tucked her knees to her chest to ward off the chill, but it didn't work. The floor of the cave was hard and damp, as were the walls. She squeezed her eyes shut and tried to think warm thoughts to keep her teeth from chattering.

Hot sand. Soft beach towel. Bright sunlight. She imagined a warm breeze and a bottle of water in her hand. She imagined guzzling it down in big, wet gulps that cooled her throat.

Grace whimpered, and the sound snapped her back to reality.

No warm beach. No thirst-quenching water. Just cold, empty darkness and the terror that never would end. Her stomach clenched as she pictured him looming over her.

He'd been back twice with a flashlight that made her blink and cower. He'd shoved her face into the dirt and raped her viciously. The first time, she'd struggled and fought him, only to feel his hands clamp around her neck, which introduced her to a whole new level of pain and panic. Turned out the survival instinct was strong. Her body wanted to breathe even more than her mind wanted to dissolve into blackness, letting the despair and the pain and the loneliness swallow her whole.

Miles above her, a high-pitched squeak, like fingernails on a chalkboard. And she remembered she *wasn't* alone. The bats were stirring. Soon the air around her would shift and churn as they left for their nightly hunt. It was her only hint of time passing.

Grace didn't trust herself to remember, so she'd peeled off the tip of a fingernail each time it happened. Six fingernails gone. Six days—although she had a sinking feeling she'd miscounted. Her mind felt fuzzy. Unreliable. The only thing she truly knew for certain was fear and pain.

The sharp claws in her stomach started digging again.

Maybe he'll be back soon.

She hated herself for thinking it.

She hated *him* for planting the poisonous seed in her mind.

If he *did* come back, she'd gouge out his eyes this time. She'd smash his face and take every morsel of food he had with him. She'd take his flashlight and bash his head in and knock his teeth out with it. She'd be ferocious. Wild. Savage.

If only she could get her wrists free, or her ankles. Or muster the energy to lift her head off the ground, or scream, or even talk.

A sob caught in her swollen throat, and she started to cry. Tears and snot leaked out, wasting her precious fluids, but she couldn't stop. The fear was back. She felt herself sliding deeper into the void, letting go of everything, all of it, even hope.

No, she told herself. She couldn't do it. She wouldn't give up. *No, no, no.*

CHAPTER 15

Talia pulled into Orr's Nursery and parked beside a sign advertising two-for-one bags of potting soil. She and Nolan were in an unmarked unit and had spent the entire afternoon working their way down the list of white Chevy Tahoes registered in Allen County.

"You been here before?" Nolan asked.

"Bought a rosebush here once."

"Thought you lived in an apartment?"

"It was for my mom." Talia cut the engine and surveyed the tables in front filled with daisies and marigolds.

"There's the vehicle," Nolan said, nodding at a row of cars beside the corrugated-metal building. A dusty white SUV with a bent rear bumper sat at the very end. The vehicle belonged to Chad Lindell, thirty-six. Lindell had done a year in lockup following an aggravated assault. Lindell had been one of the first names on their list, but his vehicle hadn't been at home, and Talia had had to track down his workplace through his parole officer.

Talia looked at Nolan, who had taken the lead

on all the previous stops. "I'm ready to switch. Mind if I do the talking this time?"

"He's all yours," Nolan said. "I'm not even here."

"What are you going to do?"

He smiled. "What do you think? Look for clues."

"What, like maybe he left a bloody murder weapon on the front seat?"

"Hey, you never know." Nolan pushed open his door. "You got this?"

"Absolutely."

They split up, Talia heading for the nursery entrance as Nolan strolled across the lot to casually check out the Tahoe. He wasn't exactly subtle, though. Even with his gun concealed under his leather jacket, Nolan looked like a cop. And any ex-con would spot their unmarked police unit a mile away.

A row of green wagons was parked at the nursery's entrance. Talia walked past them and was greeted by a smiling blond woman wearing a green apron.

"Help you this evening?"

"Chad Lindell. Where can I find him?"

The woman turned and pointed across the rows of shrubs in five-gallon containers. "At the side entrance there with that delivery guy."

"Thanks."

"Sure thing."

Talia took her time approaching the two men, who stood beside a tall stack of mulch bags. Chad also wore a green apron, and Talia recognized his shaved head from his booking photo. The man was short but stocky and probably outweighed Talia by a hundred pounds.

Chad signed something on a clipboard, then handed it back to the delivery guy, who nodded and walked off.

"Mr. Lindell?"

Chad turned around, instantly suspicious. His gaze went straight to Talia's badge.

"What do you want?"

"Detective Vazquez, Springville PD. I'd like to have a quick word."

He darted a look over her shoulder. "I'm working here."

"This won't take long."

He folded his arms over his chest.

"Would you prefer to talk at the station house?"

"No."

"All right. Sir, is that your vehicle out front there? The white Chevrolet Tahoe?"

"What about it?"

"The 2009?"

He frowned. "What about it?"

"A vehicle like that came up in connection with a crime recently."

"Hey." He stepped forward. "Some jackass backed into *me* and took off. I didn't even see it."

"When did this happen?"

" 'Bout a week ago. Why?"

"Did you file a report?"

"You think I have time to file reports? I'm working two damn jobs just trying to keep my head above water."

Talia nodded, pretending to be sympathetic. "Mr. Lindell, I noticed you received a speeding ticket in San Antonio last August."

The frown deepened. "I paid it."

"Do you get down there a lot, sir?"

"Come again?"

"San Antonio? How often do you go there?"

His gaze hardened. Obviously, she wasn't here about a crumpled bumper. "I don't know. Now and then. I've got friends there."

"When was the last time you visited San Antonio? Do you remember?"

"August. When I got the ticket. Why?"

"Are you sure?"

His glare intensified, but Talia stood her ground.

"I'm sure." He glanced over her shoulder again. "Anything else? I need to get back to work here."

She didn't say anything, just watched him, trying to read his expression.

"That it?"

"That's it, thanks."

He stalked off, and Talia watched him. He went right past several customers and disappeared into the corrugated-metal building.

Talia returned to her car, where Nolan stood waiting by the passenger door.

"How was he?"

"Hostile." She slid behind the wheel. "But not spooked. He lied about his Tahoe, though. Told me someone backed into him."

"How do you know he was lying?"

"I could tell."

"Okay. What about San Antonio?"

"He copped to the ticket in August. Said that's the last time he was there." Talia pulled out of the parking lot onto the highway.

"And?"

She glanced at Nolan.

"Do you believe him?" he asked.

She sighed. "I do, actually."

"At least you got him on record with that. Now, if we find out he was there October second when Alicia Merino disappeared, he's got a problem."

"I'll talk to his PO again. See if he knows anything about these friends in San Antonio."

"Not a bad idea," Nolan said.

"But I doubt if it matters. I don't think he's our guy."

"Why not?"

"Call it a hunch." She looked at Nolan. "How many left on that list?"

"Twenty-four."

"Seriously?" She slapped the steering wheel.

"We've been at this all day, and we've got shit to show for it."

Nolan shook his head. "Welcome to Homicide."

On impulse, Sara swung into the Walmart parking lot on her way into Springville. She passed through the rows of cars but saw no white Chevy Tahoes, old or otherwise. Across the street was a cinema, and Sara tried there, too, spotting a silver Tahoe parked at the end of a row. But besides being the wrong color, it was so new it had dealer plates.

Feeling foolish, Sara returned to the highway and cut across town to the motel. She didn't need to drive around town this evening. What she needed to do was catch up on paperwork and get a good night's sleep before tomorrow.

Her stomach growled, reminding her that she'd skipped lunch and it was almost six. Sara surveyed her options as she drew near the motel. Pizza Hut. Subway. The diner that the motel manager had recommended. And then there was the Dairy Queen where she'd gone with Nolan.

None of it sounded good, so she pulled a U-turn and made her way back toward White Falls Park. She'd noticed a Mexican place on Highway 12, and she had a sudden craving for chips and queso. She soon spotted the red neon sign for Flora's Tamale House. It was Sunday evening, and she took the packed parking lot as a good sign.

Entering the restaurant, Sara was greeted by Mexican music and the smell of fresh tortilla chips.

"Just one," she told the teenage hostess.

"Um, there's a fifteen-minute wait? Unless you care to eat in the bar?"

Sara glanced around, debating whether to wait for a table or risk being hit on. Hunger won out, and she claimed a stool at the bar as her phone dinged with a text message.

R U back in town?

Nolan.

Her nerves did a little dance as she responded: *Just got here.*

The screen showed him typing, but then he stopped. Sara bit her lip. Maybe she should have called him and asked him to meet her for dinner. She'd thought about it during her long drive but decided not to complicate things. The more time she spent with him, the harder it would be not to see him again after the case ended.

The bartender stopped by, and Sara requested a menu. She skimmed the choices, but she was thinking about Nolan. She shouldn't second-guess her decision not to call tonight, even if he took it as a brush-off. She was here for work.

"Hey, there."

She turned around, and there he was. Just the sight of him put a big goofy smile on her face.

"Hi. You found me."

"Saw your car out front."

He looked good—tall and broad-shouldered in a dark leather jacket that concealed the gun at his hip. He was wearing boots and those well-worn jeans she liked.

"You here for the night?" he asked.

"Yep. Back at the motel."

He nodded at the stool beside her. "All right if I—"

"Please. Sit down."

He took a seat as the bartender reappeared, this time with a smile for Nolan.

"What are you having?" Nolan asked Sara.

"I don't know. House margarita?"

"Rocks or frozen?" the bartender asked.

"Frozen, with salt."

"Nolan?" the woman asked, and Sara felt a dart of jealousy.

"Just a Coke."

Sara looked at him. Maybe he was still on duty.

"Anything to eat tonight, ma'am?"

She shifted her attention to the bartender, definitely catching a tone with the *ma'am.*

"Yes, I'll have the chicken enchiladas with a side of queso, please."

"You got it."

When the bartender left, Nolan turned to Sara. "Sorry, I can't stay," he said. "I've got a meeting."

"On a Sunday night?"

"The task force keeps weird hours. Plus, we've been in touch with Dax Harper from Austin, which is putting a fire under everyone."

"Does he really believe that teenager's abduction is connected?"

"He does. And we've got the FBI involved now."

"Who's the agent?" she asked.

"Rey Santos. You know him?"

"Not personally, but he worked a case with one of my colleagues back in the spring."

Sara glanced at the TV above the bar, which was playing a baseball game. She could feel Nolan watching her.

"So." She looked at him. "I was planning to call you tomorrow."

He lifted an eyebrow. "Is that right?"

"That's right." She leaned her elbow on the bar, trying to appear more comfortable than she felt. "Raul's meeting me at the park first thing in the morning."

"He bringing his dog?"

"Yes. I want to make sure we didn't miss anything at the burial site. And I wanted to update you on something."

The bartender was back with a Coke for Nolan and a margarita the size of a fishbowl.

"Good Lord," Sara said.

Nolan tapped his glass against hers. "Cheers."

"This thing is obscene."

"It's not as bad as it looks."

She picked it up with both hands and took a sip. It was cold and tart.

"How is it?"

"Perfect."

"Good." He smiled at her, and she felt a warm tingle that had nothing to do with the tequila. "What'd you want to update me about?" he asked.

She slid the fishbowl away and collected her thoughts. She was here to work, not flirt, and so was he.

"The victims who were buried," she said. "As you probably know, teeth and bone are the most durable parts of the human body, followed by hair and nails. We ran some tests on the victims' fingernails, and in both instances we recovered soil, grit, and fecal matter."

"Okay." His gaze narrowed. "Any chance this 'fecal matter' might have come from something like mulch?"

"Why do you ask?"

"Just thinking about something."

"I had one of our microbiologists analyze it. He tells me it's bat guano. And the grit is made up of cryogenic calcite crystals."

Nolan arched his eyebrows.

"Loose grains of calcite," she elaborated. "You know, mineral deposits. We think he keeps them somewhere isolated, right? So he can torture them for several days before he kills them."

"Think it could be a cave?"

"It's possible. Or maybe a pit." Sara tried to keep her voice even, although she was cringing inside. "What do you think?"

He ran a hand through his hair. "I think . . . damn. This thing keeps getting worse."

"You know of any cave systems around here? There was that small one in Rattlesnake Gorge, but we checked it out already."

"No." He heaved a sigh. "But I can talk to Tom. He knows the parks better than anyone."

"It might not be a park."

"Got to start somewhere."

Nolan looked up at the baseball game, but Sara could tell he wasn't really watching. He seemed distracted, and she hated that every time she saw him, he looked more and more stressed about the case.

He was good at his job, and it wasn't just a job to him. She liked the way he took the initiative. She liked the way he cared deeply about his community. So many investigators she'd met over the years had let cynicism or apathy take over as a survival mechanism. But Nolan had been in this field for almost fifteen years and managed to keep his heart intact.

She studied his strong profile as she took another sip of her margarita. Everything about him was intact. He was a handsome man, and not in that clean-shaven, business-suit way, but in jeans and work boots, with his scarred leather jacket and his two-day beard. She'd never realized how much she liked the rugged look until she met Nolan.

He looked over and caught her staring. The corner of his mouth lifted, as though he knew what she was thinking.

The bartender appeared with a steamy platter of enchiladas that she held with a napkin.

"Hot plate," she warned.

"Thanks." After she'd gone, Sara stared down at the massive amount of food.

Nolan smiled. "Hope you're hungry." He glanced at his watch, and the smile faded. "I wish I could stay, but I need to head out."

"It's fine."

He stole a chip and popped it into his mouth. "One of these days, I want us to have dinner together."

"We had dinner at Dairy Queen."

"That's not what I meant." His gaze locked with hers, and the look in his eyes made her nerves flutter.

He stood and reached for his wallet.

"I got it." Sara waved him off. "Don't be late to your meeting."

"Let's talk later."

"Sounds good."

He left, and Sara turned her attention to her food,

nearly burning her mouth on the molten cheese.

He wanted them to have dinner together. He wanted a *date*.

More than a date, if that look was any indication. He'd looked at her like that once before—in the park right after he'd kissed her.

Somehow she managed to eat most of her food and put a dent in the margarita. She left money on the bar and headed out to the parking lot, which was even fuller than before.

She slid behind the wheel and sat for a few moments, watching the traffic whisk by as the sun dipped low and colored the landscape gold. What should have been a tranquil Sunday evening was marred by images of a terrified young woman huddled in a cave or a pit somewhere. Sara couldn't shake the thoughts, and her stomach knotted as she pulled out of the lot.

The FBI was involved now, which was good and bad.

Good because they had resources and could cut through some of the red tape. Bad because their presence might increase competition among agencies, which could lead to people hoarding information. She had seen it happen before, and it wasn't pretty. Nolan was going to have to keep his eye on the other investigators, but he seemed up to the challenge. Having come from a big-city department, he was probably aware of the politics.

Let's talk later.

Later tonight later? Or did he mean tomorrow? And did he want to talk by phone, or was he planning to show up at her motel? She didn't know if she could resist the temptation to invite him inside.

Sara reached the turnoff for Main Street, but she kept going, focused on something Mark had talked about in the meeting. He'd analyzed the behavior of predators his entire career, first for the FBI and now for the Delphi Center. Even without creating a full profile, he'd sounded confident in his assessment, and his words kept coming back to her.

These guys evolve, refine their technique.

Was that happening right now, this instant? Was the killer off someplace—possibly someplace close by—thinking of ways to elude the task force that was now hot on his trail?

The park was done.

He had to know that.

Even if he literally lived under a rock and had somehow missed the news stories, he had to have noticed all the police vehicles streaming in and out of one of his favorite places.

White Falls Park was in his comfort zone. Sara hadn't needed a profiler to tell her that, and neither had Nolan. Two of the killer's first known victims had been found inside a park as well. They'd been dumped in water and had floated to the surface, possibly explaining why the killer had changed his MO by the time he reached Texas. But regardless of how the killer disposed of the bodies, parks were a common denominator. Was he a park ranger? A maintenance worker? A nature enthusiast?

She hoped the detectives were considering those possibilities and that they'd had more luck than the Tennessee cops who had pursued the same idea five years ago and come up empty.

These guys evolve.

Sara grabbed the map she'd left on the passenger seat and looked it over. She'd hit two nearby parks on her way into town. But both had been small, and neither had seemed like a suitable place to drop a body. There was another park on the southern side of the county, and she decided to swing by while she still had a bit of daylight left.

Her phone chimed, and she dug it from her purse. Aaron.

"Everything okay?" she asked.

"That's what I called to ask you. Kelsey said you've lined up Raul for tomorrow?"

"It's just a precaution, really. I want to make sure we haven't missed anything."

"Hmph."

"What does that mean?"

"Your 'precautions' keep resulting in excavations. Are you sure you aren't following some lead you're not sharing?"

"Really, I'm not. Just double-checking the area."

"Okay, well . . . if that changes, I'm available."

"I know."

"FYI, I spent most of the day in the lab trying to get a positive ID on that car-fire vic who came in yesterday."

"Any chance you saw Mia?"

"That's the other reason I called. I didn't see her, but she left a note on your desk about that T-shirt."

Sara's pulse picked up. "Did she get a hit?"

"She got something, apparently. The note said, 'Trace blood recovered. Analysis underway. Results TK.'"

"Damn, that's big. *Huge,* possibly, if the blood belongs to our killer."

"*Our* killer? You think you might be getting a little obsessed with this, Sara?"

"Not at all." Sara spied a gas-station sign and shifted into the right lane.

"Well, you seem very focused on it."

"Focused is different from obsessed."

"True. And how much of your personal money are you spending going to Springville? This is your third trip out there, and I'm sure you saw the director's memo about travel expenses."

Sara swung into the gas station and pulled up to

a pump. The fuel prices were attractive, but the gas station itself was a dump. The pumps looked ancient, and a hand-lettered sign in the window said NO BATHROOMS!!

"Listen, Aaron, I have to run."

"Nice dodge."

"What?"

"Forget it. I'll see you Monday. Unless something comes up, in which case you'd better call me."

"I will."

She hung up and got out. Grabbing a nozzle, she turned around to unscrew the gas cap. As she twisted the lid, her gaze landed on a white SUV pulling out of the lot.

CHAPTER 16

Sara stared after it.

"Holy crap. Holy *crap*." She spun around and slammed the nozzle back into place. It was a white Chevy Tahoe, around ten years old. She could tell from the vehicle's shape.

She twisted the gas cap back on and jumped behind the wheel. She hadn't gotten a look at the driver. Or the license plate. But she could follow it and get both.

Although, of course, it might not be *him*.

It probably wasn't, but . . . she had to follow up. She should at least get a plate number. She started her engine and shot a look at her glowing fuel light.

Screw it, she could gas up later. Nolan would want this lead. She whipped out of the lot as the white SUV became a dot in the distance.

Nolan would *not* want this lead. Not from her, not if it meant her chasing after a potential murder suspect.

Potential. That was the key word.

Really, what were the odds? Investigators were looking for an old white Tahoe somewhere near

Springville. This area was the killer's comfort zone. Not only that, but Sara was on her way to a park where she suspected the killer might be scoping out a new dump site for his next victim.

She grabbed her phone and found Nolan's number. Damn it, he was probably in his meeting by now. She called and waited for his voice mail, but instead he picked up.

"It's me," she said quickly. "I just spotted a white Tahoe that fits your description at the gas station on Highway 194 near Stony Creek Park."

Silence.

"Nolan?"

"What are you doing at Stony Creek Park?"

"I'm not there yet. I'm on my way. I pulled in for gas and saw this Tahoe. It's the right color, age, everything—"

"Where are you now?"

"About a hundred yards behind it."

"Pull over."

"*What?*"

"Pull the hell over. Don't follow him."

"Don't you at least want a plate number?"

"Not if it means you getting hurt."

"*Nolan.*"

"Seriously, Sara, pull over."

"Don't be ridiculous. I can get a plate number. He's *right* in front of me."

"Sara."

She pressed the gas, gaining on the SUV. She

was closer now, but a black pickup pulled onto the highway, blocking her view.

"Shit."

"Sara? Are you pulling over?"

"I will, but I want to get a license plate, in case it's him. It's a strange coincidence that he's out here in a remote part of the county near Stony Creek Park, don't you think?"

"Sara, pull over now."

"I'm about to be close enough to read the plate."

"Would you listen to me—"

"Hanging up now. Bye."

She tossed the phone away and grabbed the camera bag off the seat beside her. Dragging it onto her lap, she steered with one hand as she fumbled with the camera.

"Come on, move it," she muttered as she maneuvered around the black truck. There he was. After a few moments, she eased into the right lane.

The Tahoe was in front of her, but still not close enough to read the license place. She lifted the camera, pressed the zoom button, and took a few quick shots.

She rested the camera on her lap as she leaned forward and peered through the windshield. Distance wasn't the only problem—the license plate was brown with grime.

Sara's heartbeat thrummed. She studied the

silhouette through the back window, but the glass was tinted, and she couldn't discern much about the driver. Based on the shape, it looked like a man behind the wheel.

The road curved right. She passed hillsides covered with thick brush. The landscape here was untamed, wild, and she hadn't seen a house in miles. The SUV picked up speed. Sara's pulse picked up, too. Had he seen her?

Her phone chimed, but she ignored it.

The road curved right again. And *again* he picked up speed. He'd noticed her. Why else would he speed up?

And why would he speed up at all, unless he had something to hide right now, something incriminating?

Another call. She snatched up the phone.

"What?"

"I've got a unit heading your way, so you can pull over."

She put the call on speaker and dropped the phone into the cupholder.

"If I do that, I'll lose him. He just sped up, and I think he's trying to shake me."

"Jesus, Sara."

The road curved left, and Sara tapped the brakes. After another curve, she reached a straightaway.

"Damn, where'd he go?"

The road ahead of her was empty.

"He turned off somewhere, Nolan. Damn it, he ditched me! How's that for suspicious? He has to be hiding something."

Sara pressed the accelerator, but the nearest car was a blue sedan several hundred yards ahead.

"Give me your exact location," Nolan said.

"About half a mile west of Stony Creek Park, maybe more. You know, his license plate was all smeared with dirt. I couldn't even get a digit."

"Was it a Texas plate?"

"I think so, yeah. But I can't be sure. I really couldn't see."

"Okay, Crowley's on his way."

Sara glanced in the rearview mirror. Her heart jumped into her throat at the sight of a white Tahoe.

"He can get your statement and—"

"He's back."

"What?"

Her chest squeezed. "He's behind me, Nolan. Right now. He's speeding up."

"You're sure it's the same vehicle?"

"Yes."

"Okay, slow down. See if he passes. Maybe you ticked him off, and he's messing with you."

Sara moved the camera to the seat beside her. She took her foot off the gas, trying to keep an eye on him and on the road at the same time. Her heart hammered as the big silver grille moved right behind her.

"He's not passing me."

"Shit. Okay, listen. He's probably just trying to intimidate you."

"It's working." Sara gripped the wheel, watching the reflection in her mirror. He had a cap pulled low over his face, casting a shadow, but she could see his hands on the steering wheel.

"He's Caucasian, and he's wearing a blue ball cap," she said. "That's about all I can tell."

"The sheriff's office is about six miles away. When you reach Tillman Road, you're going to take a right turn."

A sign ahead indicated an S-curve coming soon. She looked around, panicked. She was going too fast, but she didn't want to brake and get rear-ended.

"Sara?"

He was right on her bumper now. She nudged up her speed, but then the road curved, and she gripped the wheel.

"I have to slow down," she said, taking her foot off the gas. The road made another bend, and she struggled to keep control.

Boom!

Sara's head snapped backward. She careened onto the shoulder. Her stomach clenched as the tires hit gravel, and then she was spinning,

spinning, spinning—a blur of trees and sky and rock. She gripped the wheel, and her stomach did a free fall. She glanced at the rearview mirror as she sailed backward into a wall of trees.

CHAPTER 17

Sara's neck hurt. Her chest hurt. She blinked her eyes open, and everything was gray and blurry.

She struggled to breathe and reached for the door handle. Pain zinged up her side.

Seat belt.

She jabbed the button with her thumb, again and again, until finally it released. She reached for the handle again, less surprised by the jolt of pain this time as she struggled to push open the door.

Sky.

But it was dimmer than she remembered. How long had she been out? *Had* she been out?

Grabbing onto the door, she leaned forward and managed to lever herself out, yelping when her shin met with something sharp. A splintered tree branch jutted up from the ground. The entire limb had been shorn off.

Had she done that? She glanced around. Her Explorer had plowed through some small trees, it looked like, before landing backward in a ditch at the base of a rock wall. She was probably lucky the trees had cushioned her fall, or the impact would have been worse.

Sara's foot snagged on something, and she stumbled, catching herself on the trunk of a tree. The light was gray and hazy. Or maybe her brain was hazy. She felt nauseated. Disoriented.

The rumble of an engine snapped her to attention, and she whirled around. A truck. The roar got louder and louder, until it was right on top of her. She flattened herself against her Explorer as the truck barreled past in a cloud of dust and exhaust.

Sara bent over, coughing and gasping, trying to catch her breath. Her gaze fell on a tear in her black yoga pants. Blood oozed out, trickling down her leg.

Another engine approaching—this time from the other direction. Why hadn't anyone stopped? Glancing around, she saw that the front of her Explorer was mostly concealed by foliage. She ducked around limbs to check out the back. The bumper and side panel were crumpled, and one of her taillights was broken.

Images flashed through her brain. The curve in the road, the spin, the trees coming at her.

The big silver grille in her rearview mirror.

Sara's heart skittered, and she looked around. Where the hell was he? Had he taken off?

Leaves rustled behind her. Sara jerked her head around, sending pain shooting down her spine.

She scanned the area, gripped by the sudden certainty that she wasn't alone.

Go.

Go go go.

She rushed back to her Explorer and grabbed the phone from the cupholder, then stumbled away from the wreck. Swiping at the leaves and branches, she climbed from the ditch. Her foot slipped, and she ended up palms-down on the gravel, her phone in the dirt as she stared at the pavement just inches from her nose.

Scrambling to her feet, she stepped clear of the highway and looked around. The lanes were empty, and relief washed over her. If there had been a car coming, she could have been killed.

Her relief evaporated as she did a slow turn and realized there wasn't anyone in sight who might help her.

Where was the man who'd rammed into her? She saw no sign of him, but fear took hold as she pictured him lurking nearby.

Sara scooped up her phone. Her fingers trembled as she tapped the emergency call button.

No service.

Frustration burned her throat as she stared down at the screen. She cursed and looked around. No cars. No people. Dusk was falling, and she felt an urgent need to get away from the accident scene.

Accident. Yeah, right. She'd been run off the road.

Noise in the distance. A car, or maybe a truck, by the sound of it. She stepped up to the highway and prepared to flag it down.

Then she thought better of it. Maybe it was him.The engine grew louder. Panic took hold of her as she glanced around. She was out here unarmed. Defenseless. She was a sitting duck. She should hide, and then at least she could see who it was before they saw her.

Sara plunged into the woods.

Nolan swerved onto the shoulder and jammed to a halt beside Crowley's patrol car. Sara's Explorer was about ten yards up, ass-first in a ditch.

Nolan jumped out. "Where is she?"

Crowley held up a finger, telling him to wait as he finished a radio transmission.

Nolan jogged to the Explorer. No one inside. He whipped his phone from his pocket as he looked around. For the fourth time, he called her, and for the fourth time, he got kicked straight to voice mail.

"God *damn* it!" Nolan rounded the SUV, checking out the dented back panel.

His gaze swept over the ground, but he saw no footprints, no blood trails.

"Maybe she flagged a ride."

He glanced up at Crowley. "No way."

"Well, I just talked to dispatch," Crowley said.

"They took a call eight minutes ago about the accident."

"Was it her?"

"No. Some passing car." Crowley looked up and down the road. "No sign of a driver at the scene, so they didn't stop."

Nolan was back at the door, leaning into the front seat. Sara's phone was nowhere. A camera sat on the floor alongside her purse. Her wallet and a lipstick had spilled out.

"Fuck!"

"You think she caught a ride?" Crowley asked from behind him.

"Not without her purse."

Nolan went around to the other side, slipping on the ditch and catching himself on a tree limb. He glanced down and spotted a gouge in the dirt where someone else had recently pulled the same move. Looking around, he still didn't see any footprints, but something on a leaf caught his eye.

Blood.

Nolan's heart lurched. He knelt for a closer look and saw more dark droplets on some weeds.

"Damn, is that a blood trail?" Crowley asked.

Nolan pushed past him, plowing through the brush. The trees and shrubs hugged the hillside, but then the road curved up ahead, and the wall of rock gave way to a tangle of bushes and trees.

"Sara!" Nolan jogged along the shoulder, darting his gaze everywhere at once.

She hadn't taken her purse. Why the hell had she left her vehicle without her purse?

Maybe she wasn't thinking clearly. Maybe she was injured. Obviously, she was injured. There was blood leading away from the wreck.

Nolan's chest tightened. He couldn't breathe. Ever since her call had dropped, he'd felt like his lungs wouldn't work. He scanned the highway now, desperate for any sign of her.

"Sara!"

Nolan reached the curve. No more blood trail that he could see. He headed down into the ravine, fighting his way through the thorny brush.

Someone had been behind her, trying to run her off the road. Or maybe she'd skidded off the road. Either way, she was scared. Maybe she'd decided to hide.

Kaylin Baird's faced flashed into his mind, and Nolan's heart squeezed.

Always too late. Always too late, and he had no idea what the *fuck* was happening.

"Sara!"

He skidded down a slope, grabbing a branch as he almost fell.

"Nolan."

He whipped around.

"Nolan."

He caught a flash of white through the trees. He

ran toward it, batting the branches out of his way.

Sara sat on a rotten tree trunk holding her hand to her forehead. Blood streamed down her face.

Nolan's heart missed a beat, and he rushed over.

"Are you okay?"

She looked up, her eyes wide with fear. "Is he gone?"

CHAPTER 18

Sara leaned against the back of the police cruiser and watched the tow truck back up to her Explorer. The piercing *beep beep beep* made her head feel like it was about to explode. She closed her eyes. Her ribs ached. Her mouth tasted sour. She still felt queasy, and a layer of dust coated the back of her throat.

She stuffed the bloody wet wipe into her pocket and looked up the road at Nolan and Brad Crowley talking in low voices. Crowley kept glancing back at her, looking more and more nervous by the minute as he and Nolan swapped info.

Sara turned her attention to the tow-truck driver. Nolan knew him—big surprise. Nolan knew everyone. After attaching a winch to the front of her SUV, the man had slowly pulled it from the ditch. The back end was crumpled, but the rest looked okay.

Sara closed her eyes and rubbed the bridge of her nose. She ached everywhere, even her teeth. She needed an aspirin. Or better yet, a stiff drink.

The tow-truck driver slid behind the wheel of

her Explorer. It started right up. Sara walked over as he revved the engine a few times.

"Thanks for getting me out of there," she said.

"No problem. Your tires are okay, and your engine sounds fine."

Nolan walked over. "You sure about that, Al?"

Al looked at Sara. "We can take it in and run some diagnostics if you're worried about it."

"That won't be necessary, but thanks," she told him. Then she walked around to the passenger side and retrieved her wallet from the floor. She dug out a credit card and handed it to the driver. He walked back to his rig.

Nolan gazed down at her. "How's the head?"

"Better."

"You dizzy?"

"A little."

"I can take you to the ER to get checked out."

"I'll be fine."

She touched the tender spot above her temple and bent down to check it in the side mirror. She didn't remember hitting her head, but there was definitely a bump there. Most likely, she'd conked it when she slipped in the ditch before fleeing into the woods.

She straightened, and Nolan was watching her with a furrowed brow.

The tow-truck driver returned with her card and a receipt. "Come by the shop if you'd like a free estimate on the body work, ma'am."

"I will, thank you."

Nolan shook his hand. "Thanks, man."

Sara watched him walk away.

"You shouldn't be behind the wheel right now," Nolan told her. "Let me drive you."

She sighed because she knew he was right. "Fine."

She opened the passenger door and gingerly slid into the seat. Nolan eased her door shut, then walked around and climbed in on the driver's side. He adjusted the seat back and gave her a worried look as she carefully fastened her seat belt. Her ribs were bruised but not broken, and her main concern was the two-inch gash on her left shin.

"Sure you don't want to hit the ER?"

"Yes."

"How about the firehouse? I know the paramedics there, and they could see if you need stitches."

"It's just a few scrapes. All I need is a first-aid kit."

He said something under his breath as he pulled onto the highway.

"What's that?"

"Nothing."

"I'm sorry you missed your task force meeting," she said. "You really didn't need to come all the way here."

He shot her a look.

"Any chance you can still make it?"

"Talia can fill me in."

Sara gazed out the window as the dusky landscape whisked by. She'd spent almost an hour out here on the highway dealing with this mess.

"What were you doing at Stony Creek Park?"

She glanced at him. "I wanted to have a look."

"What did you think you'd find?" His voice had an edge now, and her defenses went up.

"We all seem to agree this area is the killer's comfort zone," she said. "We know he needs a new place to dispose of bodies now that his favorite park's crawling with cops. And according to your APD contact, there's a chance he has a victim with him as we speak."

Nolan kept his gaze on the road, but the muscles on the side of his jaw tensed.

"What's the problem with taking a look around?" she asked.

"You should leave that to the investigators."

"*I'm* an investigator, thank you very much."

"The police investigators. You work in a lab."

"I work in a lot of places." She folded her arms over her chest, annoyed with him for things that definitely weren't his fault. He'd come out here to help her. Logically, she knew that, but she couldn't help feeling shaken. And bitchy. And out of sorts.

She glanced at him, and the sight of his hand on

her steering wheel made her feel better for some reason.

She had to be losing it.

Sara looked out the window. "What do you think the odds are it was him back there?"

Nolan kept his gaze on the road and didn't answer.

"Nolan?"

"I don't know. We have ninety-seven white Tahoes from that date range in this county and the surrounding three counties alone. So it could have been a lot of people."

"Yes, but this particular white Tahoe ran me off the highway."

"You were tailgating him, so he could have been responding to that."

"If that's all it was, he could have flipped me off. Instead, he tried to end my life. Clearly, he didn't like someone following him. Maybe he didn't want someone to see where he was going. Or maybe he didn't want me getting his license plate—which was conveniently unreadable, by the way. I snapped a few photos, but they all turned out blurry."

Nolan didn't comment.

"He stopped to watch me after the crash. Doesn't that sound strange to you?"

He looked at her. "You said you didn't see him."

"I didn't."

"How do you know he stopped to watch?"

"I don't, for sure. I just . . ."

"What?"

"I had a feeling about it. When I stumbled away from the wreck. It felt like someone was watching me."

Felt like. Listen to her. She sounded paranoid.

Sara stared out the window at the dark landscape punctuated by the occasional glow of houses. They were still on the outskirts of Springville.

Nolan didn't talk. Neither did she. The only sounds were the hum of the engine and the faint murmur of the radio.

Nolan reached Main Street but kept going. The shops were closed, and most still had all their red-white-and-blue decorations on proud display. They passed the Baptist church and turned left into a neighborhood. Sara's pulse picked up as she looked around. It was a tree-lined street of clapboard houses with wide front porches.

Nolan swung into a driveway and parked.

"What are we doing?" she asked.

"You said you wanted a first-aid kit. You can use mine."

She stared at him in the dimness. Then she looked at the porch. A yellow light glowed beside the door. Curiosity sparked inside her. And something else she didn't want to put a label on.

Before she could change her mind, she grabbed

her purse off the floor and slid from the SUV. Nolan locked it with a *chirp,* and Sara joined him on the stone path leading to his front door.

She looked around, taking in the oak trees, the porch swings, the neatly kept lawns. Everything had a sort of storybook feel to it, and the street could have been a movie set in Anytown, USA.

Sara followed him up the front steps. A red-lidded Tupperware container sat on the doormat. Nolan picked it up, then opened the screen door with a squeak.

"What's that?" she asked.

"Not sure." He unlocked the door. "M&M cookies, if I had to guess."

"Nice. Your mother drop by?"

With a small smile, he ushered her inside and flipped on a light. "My elderly neighbor across the street. I changed some light bulbs for her the other day."

Nolan's house smelled like him—something subtle and masculine that made Sara picture him stepping out of the shower and wrapping a towel around his lean hips. She ignored the cascade of nerves as she glanced around. Two big brown sofas dominated the living room. He had an old-looking area rug and a coffee table, as well as the obligatory wall-mounted TV, but that was about it for the furnishings.

He led her into the kitchen, where he set the

Tupperware on a granite bar. Much like hers, the bar was piled with junk mail and paperwork. Sara scanned the room. Beside the back door were several pairs of Nikes that clearly had some miles on them.

"I was wondering about that."

He glanced up from a drawer he was rummaging through. "About what?"

"You're a runner."

He opened the freezer and filled a baggie with ice cubes. "I do it when I can. Which isn't as much as I should." He pulled open another drawer and took out a hammer. "You run?"

She snorted. "No."

He set the bag of ice on the counter and gave it a few quick taps. He stepped over and handed her the ice pack. "For your head."

"Thank you."

She couldn't explain the sudden lump in her throat as he gazed down at her with those expressive brown eyes.

"I'll be right back. Help yourself to anything."

He walked out, leaving her alone in his kitchen. She leaned back against the counter and pressed the bag to the side of her head.

What was she doing here? Her nerves started up again, and she stepped over to the sink to wash her hands. She found some paper towels in the cabinet and was dabbing the cuts on her palms when he returned with a tackle box. He'd gotten rid of his leather jacket, and his badge and holster had disappeared.

"I still think you should get checked out."

She didn't reply as he opened the box.

"That's a serious first-aid kit," she said.

"Never hurts to be prepared."

He took out an antiseptic wipe and tore it open, and her pulse picked up as he gently took her head in his hands.

"I can do it."

"Let me." He smiled slightly. "Gives me an excuse to touch you." He tipped her head back with one hand and used the other to dab the cut. "Does it sting?"

"No."

"You're a really bad liar, you know that?" He dropped the antiseptic wipe on the counter and dug a Band-Aid from the box. Nolan peeled it open and carefully applied it to her forehead.

His gaze met hers, and her pulse picked up again.

She moved away from him and shifted her attention to the tackle box. She poked through the contents, looking for ointment for the cut on her leg.

Nolan turned and opened the fridge. "Can I ask you something?"

She shot him a wary look. "Maybe."

He popped open a Sprite and set it beside her,

then leaned back against the counter and watched her.

"Why are you nervous around me?"

"I'm not."

His eyebrows tipped up.

"I'm not nervous, I'm just . . . I don't know. Worried, I guess."

"About what?"

"I don't know." She tried to select the right words. "I don't want to give you the wrong impression."

"What's the wrong impression?"

Her throat felt dry, and she reached for the Sprite. It tasted cold and sweet, but he was still watching her and waiting for an answer.

"I don't want you to think . . ."

"Think what?"

"That I want to start something right now. A relationship."

He smiled. "And you think I do?"

Her stomach knotted. Damn, this was awkward. She was so out of practice with dating.

"Sorry," she said. "I shouldn't make assumptions."

"Hey, I'm not denying it." He stepped closer, and her skin suddenly felt hot. "But why are you so worried about giving me the wrong impression?"

"Because." She cleared her throat. "You seem like a stand-up guy, and I want to be up-front with you."

"A stand-up guy?" He sounded amused now. "That's what you think?"

"I don't know."

But she *did* know. He was totally a stand-up guy. He was practically a Boy Scout. He did chores for his neighbors and rendered first aid and looked out for everyone in his town. He had roots here. He was a freaking pillar of the community, and he had to be one of the most eligible bachelors in Springville.

Her stomach did a little dance. To distract herself, she found a tube of ointment and several bandages and took them to the breakfast table. Sinking into a chair, she tugged up the leg of her pants.

"Damn, Sara."

"It's fine," she said, cleaning the gash. It was long but not terribly deep.

He stepped over, and her heart thrummed as she felt him watching her movements. He knelt in front of her.

"That looks bad," he said, and all the amusement was gone from his voice.

"It's not."

He gently took her ankle and straightened her leg. Then he tore open a new wipe with his teeth and started carefully brushing dirt from the cut. The wound stung, but she was too focused on his hands to care. His gaze met hers. He opened a bandage and applied it to

266

her shin, and she slid the torn pant leg over it.

"Thanks."

He didn't respond. He kept his eyes on hers as he knelt there in front of her. Slowly, he reached up and feathered her hair away from the cut on her face. Her heart was thudding wildly now. Her chest felt tight. He was kneeling between her legs, watching her with that look again, and there was something so carnal about it she could hardly breathe.

"Relax," he whispered.

"I can't—"

He leaned in and kissed her.

Every nerve in her body sparked. He moved into her, sliding his palms over her thighs and resting them on her hips. She kissed him back, and he tasted just like she remembered. She combed her fingers through his soft hair as she tangled her tongue with his.

She'd missed him. Which made no sense, because he'd only kissed her twice. But she'd been thinking about it, craving his taste and his scent and his hands.

Taking her hips, he slid her to the edge of the chair, parting her thighs with his body, and she gripped his sides with her knees. He was so warm and solid, and she felt like she was falling into him as he pulled her against him. Sliding his fingers under her T-shirt, he tugged it up over her head and tossed it away. His heated gaze landed on her black lace bra. She didn't want him to notice her bruises, so she dragged him close for another kiss, brushing her fingertips over the stubble along his jaw.

Dipping his head down, he trailed kisses over her throat as he reached around for her bra clasp. He deftly unhooked it, then slid his hand around to cup her breast. He looked up at her as his mouth closed over her nipple, and she nearly shot off the chair.

Sara arched against him, moaning. This was crazy. They were in his kitchen, practically on the floor, but all she could do was tip her head back and enjoy the intoxicating heat of his mouth on her skin. Just a moment ago, she'd called him a stand-up guy, but he flatly rejected that, and now he was on his knees in front of her, proving her wrong. He was setting her on fire with his mouth and his hands, banishing every worry, every logical reason not to do this, as he slipped her bra from her arms and dropped it to the floor.

He kissed her neck. "Mmm. You smell good."

"I do?"

"Always."

His breath felt warm against her skin as he slid his lips to her collarbone, and she shivered. Everything he did was so sensual, so hot. And it had been so, so long since she'd felt anything like this. His palm glided over her knee and came to rest at the top of her thigh, and she squirmed closer.

"Nolan." She clamped her knees against his hips and pulled his head up to kiss her.

He eased back, and desire flashed in his eyes. "Can we—"

"Yes."

He stood and pulled her to her feet, and she glanced down to see half her clothes on the floor. She started to reach for them, but he slid his arms around her, wrapping her in his amazing scent. She rested her head against his chest.

"Come on." He took her hand and led her—topless—through his living room and into a dim hallway toward the back of the house. She couldn't believe she was *doing this*. It was exhilarating. The air was cool against her skin, and she felt a heady mix of nerves and anticipation as he pulled her into his dark bedroom. She couldn't see, but her leg brushed against something, and she knew they were standing beside his bed as he kissed her again. She savored the taste of him, loving his fingers on her bare arms and back.

She pulled away and watched him as she sank onto the bed and scooted back. Her eyes adjusted to the dimness as he bent down and took his boots off. Then the mattress creaked as he stretched out beside her.

"This better?" he asked.

"Yes."

He eased on top of her, and she yelped.

"What?" He pulled back. "What'd I do?"

"Nothing. Just my rib."

He switched on the lamp. "Jesus, Sara."

She blinked down at her torso, where a red-purple bruise stretched from her sternum to her hip.

"It's from the seat belt. It's nothing."

His eyebrows shot up. "Nothing? Are you crazy? You're all banged up."

"I'm fine."

He reached a finger out, trailing it down her body, barely grazing her skin. He looked at her. "We don't have to do this right now."

She scooted over on the bed. "Lie down."

"Sara."

"Lie *down,*" she said with command in her voice. She wasn't going to let this moment slip away.

He didn't move for a few seconds, but then he finally stretched out on his side, facing her. He picked up her hand and kissed her knuckles, and the gesture was so sweet it made her throat tighten.

"I don't want to hurt you," he said.

"You won't."

She pulled her hand loose and nudged him onto his back. She got on her knees beside him and tugged at the hem of his T-shirt. He sat forward and pulled it over his head, then tossed it away. The muscles in his torso rippled as he leaned back on his elbows to watch what she did. She pushed her yoga pants down her legs, hopefully distracting him from her bruises, because all she had on now was a pair of black bikini panties.

"Sara . . ."

"Shh." She straddled his lap, resting her weight on the hard ridge of his erection.

He groaned and closed his eyes. "You're going to kill me."

"How?" She leaned forward, kissing him ever so lightly as her nipples brushed against his chest.

"You are so sexy. Everything you do. I've been thinking about this."

A thrill went through her. "What have you been thinking about?"

He sat forward to cup her breast, and the hard pull of his mouth sent a jolt of heat straight to her core. She combed her fingers into his hair. He was so good at everything he did, as though he knew just what she wanted and how she wanted it, and she felt a rush of excitement about what was coming. She brought his head up for another kiss, tracing her fingertips over his stubble. Then she shifted her position, grinding against him, and he made a low sound in his throat.

She loved the way he kissed her and touched her. She loved being in charge. And she loved the intense look in his eyes when he watched her. He slid his hands around her and kissed her deeper, harder, and she rocked against him as the kiss went on, until her body throbbed and she felt dizzy with need.

Sara moved off him and looked him over, taking in his perfectly sculpted chest. She'd always known he looked good in jeans, but he looked especially good in *just* jeans. She trailed her finger down his muscular body and let it rest on the snap.

He lifted a brow. "Need help?"

"No."

Heat flared in his eyes as she traced her finger farther down, then back up again.

"Sara . . ."

"What?"

He swung his legs off the bed and stood up, watching her as he stripped off his jeans and his briefs and lay back on the bed.

Sara's heart skipped a beat.

"Hey." He took her hand. "Don't look at me like that."

"Like what?"

He pulled her in for a kiss that went on and on until her heart thrummed wildly and her skin felt hot. And suddenly, it hit her that it had been two long years since she'd done this, and she needed to slow things down.

He seemed to sense her hesitation, even if he couldn't possibly know what it was about. He stroked his hands softly over her arms. And then his fingers were at her hips, tugging the thin straps. She sat back so he could slide her panties off and toss them away. His gaze moved slowly over her, following the path of his hand over her calf, her knee, her thigh, to finally settle at her bare hip.

"You are so beautiful."

Her skin flushed at the words. Maybe he'd said it to put her at ease, but it worked. She braced a hand against his shoulder and straddled him again, then closed her eyes and kissed him.

He tasted so good, and she lost herself in the kiss, pressing her body against him and running her hands over his strong arms. He started to ease back, and she brought her hands to his face.

"Don't stop," she whispered against his mouth, tracing her fingertips over his jaw, his neck, his shoulders. She loved everything about touching him and feeling his hard, powerful body beneath her.

She kept kissing him and kissing him, and she heard the drawer beside her open and close and the tear of paper. Then he guided her down on top of him, and she gripped his shoulder as she felt pressure, followed by pain. Then he shifted her hips, and the pain turned to shocked pleasure as he filled her completely and every nerve in her body sang.

For a moment, she didn't move or even breathe.

But then the warm stroke of his hands down her back made her relax, and she started moving against him. He held her by the hips and let her set the rhythm, and everything felt so amazingly, intensely *good* she never wanted it to end. His body was so strong and powerful, and she felt his energy rocking into her with every move.

"Sara?"

"Hmm."

"Babe, look at me."

She opened her eyes, and the raw need on his face made it better. Stronger. Brighter—if that was even possible. She kissed him deeply and felt like she was burning from the inside out, and she surged against him again and again until their skin was slick with sweat and she couldn't wait anymore.

"Nolan, please."

"Come on."

"Please."

He thrust into her, reaching a place so deep that she cried out and came apart. And then his hips bucked hard, and he pulled her even tighter against him as he came, too. For an endless moment, they were fused together, and he held her tightly through the aftershocks.

Her head fell against his shoulder. His skin was hot. Damp. For a moment, she didn't move, she just absorbed the feeling of his arms around her as her mind reeled.

She eased back, panting, and he brushed the hair from her eyes and looked at her.

"You okay?"

She smiled.

"Did I hurt your ribs?"

"No." She leaned back, trailing her hand down his chest. She shifted up and off him, then flopped back on the bed, closing her eyes. The bedspread was cool against her skin, and the room seemed like it was spinning.

"Be right back," he said gruffly.

She didn't move. She felt lax. Liquidy. Like if she drifted off right now, she might never wake up.

Everything dimmed as he switched off the lamp, and then the mattress sank as he stretched out beside her. He smelled so good. His skin. His bed. His room. She wanted to stay here all night, but she couldn't. Sleeping here would contradict all that she'd told him about not wanting to start something.

Of course, everything she'd just done contradicted that.

A sharp noise had her bolting upright. "What's that?"

He sighed heavily. "Someone's at the door." He snagged his jeans off the floor and pulled them on. He picked up his T-shirt and pulled it over his head as he walked out.

Sara looked around and spotted the clock on

the nightstand. Ten fifteen. She leaned close to the window and parted the blinds. But the window faced a fence, and she couldn't see the street.

Sara listened. The front door opened and closed. A moment later, he was back. She watched his shadowy silhouette as he got rid of his clothes again.

"Who was it?"

"Brad dropping off my truck."

"By himself?"

"Talia brought him."

He stretched out beside her as she propped up on her elbows.

"So . . . they know I'm here?"

"I'm guessing they noticed your car."

She fell back against the bed and sighed.

He stroked a hand over her hip. She moved closer and rested her head against his chest. It was easier to be beside him without eye contact. He caressed her hip, his fingers sending warm ripples over her skin.

Two years.

No, two years, one week, and . . . four days.

She wondered what he'd think if he knew she'd just broken a long streak of celibacy. Maybe he did know. It might have been obvious when she'd practically begged him not to stop.

Sara rested her hand on his chest. His skin was warm, and she nestled closer, because even now, even in his bed, she still couldn't get enough of him.

What was she doing? She hadn't planned this. Fantasized, yes, but she hadn't *planned* what would happen if she threw caution out the window and had sex with him, even though this couldn't go anywhere, and she didn't want a relationship.

Hey, I'm not denying it.

She'd been right. He'd basically told her he wanted to start something, something she was sure would get thorny and complicated. It was already complicated. His coworkers knew she was here.

She pulled her hand back and sighed.

"Sara." He took her hand and put it back on his chest. "Stop worrying."

"I can't."

She felt the vibration in his chest as he laughed softly.

"What?" She sat up on her elbow, and he was smiling at her, looking infuriatingly sexy with his perfect chest and his mussed hair. "What are you laughing at?"

"You. Who cares who knows you're here?"

"I do."

"Come here." He pulled her down and rolled her onto her side so her back was facing him. Then he slid her hips against him.

"What—"

"Shh." His warm hands glided over her shoulders, and he started massaging them.

At first, she tensed. But as his strong thumbs kneaded her muscles, she felt the tension draining away. He gathered her hair and shifted it over her shoulder, making room for his skilled fingers as he massaged away her stress. She felt herself caving into him—into his warmth, his humor, his affection—and the touch was so intimate it brought tears to her eyes. He had no idea—none—how long it had been since a man had touched her like this, with caring and tenderness and a desire to make her problems go away. She forced the tears back and ignored the lump in her throat and tried to enjoy the moment for what it was. A moment. A fleeting snippet of time when she could block the world out and just *be*.

After a few blissful minutes, he kissed the back of her neck. "Better?"

"Um-hmm." She nestled back against him, trying not to think about anything at all besides the heat of his body and the weight of his arm on her waist. She wouldn't think about tomorrow. Not tonight. Tomorrow and all its problems would come soon enough.

CHAPTER 19

Sara picked up her shirt off the floor and pulled it on as she crept to the window. Peering out, she was relieved to see Nolan's pickup parked in front instead of in the driveway, blocking her in. She unlocked the door and opened it. Holding her breath, she slowly pushed the screen door open and slipped outside, easing shut the front door and then the rusty screen.

Sara started down the steps, halting when a skinny gray dog rushed up to her. She reached down so it could sniff her fingers with its damp nose.

"Hi," she whispered. "Where'd you come from?"

She glanced across the driveway at the glow coming from the window of the neighbors' kitchen. They were up early, too.

Sara hurried across the lawn, waiting until she was right beside the Explorer to pop the locks with a too-loud *chirp*. She tossed her purse onto the passenger seat, and the dog watched from the grass, tail wagging, as she slid behind the wheel and backed out.

Sara let out a sigh as she passed the little white church on the corner. It looked misty and ethereal in the predawn light. She combed a hand through her messy hair. Then she turned up the radio and tried to find news, traffic, weather—anything to distract her from what she was doing.

It didn't work, and she thought about Nolan all the way across town, particularly when she passed the familiar gas station where the shop-keeper she'd met was flipping the CLOSED sign to OPEN.

She focused on the road and made her way through two more empty stoplights to the motel. Now that the holiday had passed, it was no longer crowded, and the space right in front of Sara's room was open. She parked and gathered her things, making a mental to-do list as she dug the key card from her purse.

First, she had to check her email and voice mail. Then shower and dress. Then she had to grab some coffee before heading to White Falls Park, where she was meeting Raul. She slid from her SUV, and the smell of bacon hit her as she crossed the sidewalk.

And she had to get something to eat. Food was a must if she was going to be any use at all today, which was already looking doubtful.

She let herself into her room and found it just as musty-smelling as when she'd checked in yesterday. Eyeing her computer bag on the bed, she decided to shower first. The second she logged in, it would be far too easy to get distracted and delayed.

She turned on the shower and stripped off her clothes. Avoiding her reflection in the mirror, she stepped into the tub and ducked her head under the spray. The hot water sluiced over her skin, and finally, *finally,* she let her thoughts flow.

She thought of Nolan's body, his hands, his skin. She thought of his mouth in the darkness when he'd kissed her awake and kept her up half the night.

Since she'd first met him on that rocky path, she'd been wondering what it would be like to sleep with him. And now she knew. It was amazing. Incredible. Mind-blowing.

So . . . box checked. Curiosity satisfied.

No, even after all those hours in the dark, her curiosity *wasn't* satisfied, and she had a whole new flurry of unanswered questions swirling through her head.

She hated this. She felt tense and edgy, and her stomach was in knots as she remembered sneaking out on him.

What was so bad about it? People did it all the time. She never had, but it certainly happened. She didn't need to feel guilty.

A sharp rap on the door made her freeze. She turned off the water and listened. It couldn't be him.

Could it?

She darted a look at her cell phone sitting by the sink, but she had no new messages. She grabbed a towel and dried off. The rapping came again, louder this time. It was insistent and confident. And definitely male-sounding. Wrapping the tiny towel around her, she crossed the room and looked through the peephole.

A police officer stood there. She'd seen him before, but damned if she could remember a name.

She tugged up her towel. "Who is it?"

"Officer Biggs, Springville Police Department."

"May I help you?"

"Could you open the door, ma'am?"

Sara engaged the security latch and cracked the door a few inches, keeping her body shielded as she looked through the gap.

"Sorry to bother you, ma'am. Is this your vehicle parked here? The black Explorer?"

"Yes."

His gaze dropped to her bare shoulders, and his cheeks colored. He cleared his throat. "Ma'am, are you Sara Lockhart, from the Delphi Center Crime Lab?"

"Yes. What's the problem, Officer?"

"I thought I recognized the vehicle. I was doing a routine patrol when I noticed your window busted out."

"Excuse me?"

"The front window on the passenger side. It's busted out, and there's glass all over the pavement there."

"Hold on."

Sara closed the door. She rushed to the bed and dug some clothes from her duffel bag. She twisted her wet hair into a knot and slid her feet into flip-flops before grabbing her phone off the sink.

Biggs was on the sidewalk now, his back to the door as she opened it. She strode over to her SUV, where a pile of glass glinted like ice chips in the morning sun.

"What the—? When did this happen?"

He looked her over. "That's what I need to get from you. Did you hear any disturbances outside your room overnight?"

"I wasn't here overnight. I just pulled in"— she checked her phone—"about twenty minutes ago. It must have happened while I was in the shower."

"I see." He cast a glance over his shoulder at the black-and-white police unit that was double-parked behind several cars. "Wait here. Don't touch anything."

He walked off, and Sara stepped to the window, leaning close to get a look at the interior of her Explorer. The glove compartment was open. No visible damage to the steering column. She walked around to the back, and the cargo door and bumper looked just as hideous as yesterday. Sara cupped her hand over the window and peered inside. Her evidence kit and tools were there.

"Step away from the vehicle, please." Biggs was back with a clipboard. "Our CSI is on his way. He'll want to check for fingerprints."

"That won't be necessary. I'm a CSI, and I'm happy to handle it."

"That's all right, we'll handle it," Biggs said. "They're already on the way."

Sara bit back a curse. *They?*

Biggs started filling out paperwork, no doubt creating a report that was going to derail her morning. She went back into her room. By the time she had a cup of coffee brewed, another police unit was turning into the motel parking lot.

Sara watched, guzzling coffee to wake herself up as the officers huddled together. The new guy was a uniform, but judging by his hefty evidence box, she guessed he was also a licensed CSI. Cops in small departments often wore multiple hats.

Sara set her coffee down and walked up to him. "May I borrow some gloves, please?"

"Ma'am?" He shot a questioning look at Biggs.

"I need to open the back."

After a nod from Biggs, the officer crouched down to open his kit and handed Sara a pair of blue gloves. She tugged them on and carefully opened the cargo door. She stared at the space for several long moments and opened each of the other doors to do a thorough inspection. Then she peeled off the gloves and stepped onto the sidewalk to give Biggs her statement, complete with every detail she had noticed about the parking lot when she'd arrived this morning.

As they were finishing up, a white pickup pulled into the lot. Nolan looped around the row of cars and slid into an empty space at the end.

"Ma'am?"

She looked at Biggs. "Yes?"

"I said, anything else besides those two items?"

"No."

Nolan wore a tie today, along with slacks and dress shoes, and Sara's nerves fluttered as he walked toward her. His hair was damp from the shower, and he'd shaved in the brief time since she'd last seen him.

He stopped in front of her. "You all right?"

She nodded.

He turned to Biggs. "What happened?"

"At approximately six thirty-five A.M., I was driving through the parking lot behind the diner there when I decided to swing through the motel. I noticed broken glass in the parking space beside the Explorer, and then I noticed the broken window." He nodded at Sara. "I thought I recognized the vehicle, so after notifying the manager, I knocked on Ms. Lockhart's door to let her know."

"It's Dr. Lockhart," Nolan said.

Biggs darted a look at her. "Sorry. I, uh, let Dr. Lockhart know about the break-in, and she took a look through the vehicle and advised me that her Nikon camera was missing, as well as her phone charger that had been plugged into the dash there."

Nolan looked at Sara. "Anything else?"

"I don't think so."

Nolan walked past her and joined the CSI examining her shattered window. They crouched beside the glass shards and talked in low voices as Sara looked on, a ball of dread forming in her stomach.

Biggs flipped through his papers and asked her to sign a few places. With a crisp nod, he headed for his car, and Sara turned her attention to Nolan, who was still talking to the CSI.

She'd left his house this morning without even saying good-bye, and yet he seemed totally normal. No sulking. No attitude. He gave no indication whatsoever that there was anything personal or contentious between them.

And maybe there wasn't.

He walked back over, and she searched his eyes for any sign of resentment.

"You sure there's nothing else?" he asked matter-of-factly. "Just the camera and the charger?"

"I'm sure."

He nodded at her SUV. "Looks like someone used a crowbar or a tire iron to break the glass, so I wouldn't bet on us getting any prints. And the motel doesn't have security cams."

"Yeah, I noticed that."

"What was on that Nikon?" he asked.

"Not much. It had a new memory card, so just those few blurry photos from last night."

"The Tahoe?"

"Yeah."

"What about your room?" he asked.

"What about it?"

"Any chance someone was in there?"

Sara's blood ran cold. "How? I mean, my door was locked."

"You're sure?"

"Well . . . yeah. I mean, it locks automatically."

No way someone had been in her room. They would have had to tamper with the lock, and she'd seen no sign of that. She walked over to the door to check, just to make sure. With Nolan at her side, she examined the doorframe and locking mechanism but saw no evidence of any damage.

"I don't see anything," she said.

Nolan checked his watch. "What time are you meeting Raul?"

"Seven thirty. I'm already running late."

"Biggs is going with you."

"What? Why?"

"Because I asked him to."

"That's ridiculous! *Why* would you ask him to?"

Anger flared in his eyes—his first hint of emotion this morning. "Because someone ran you off the road last night, Sara. Because someone just broke into your car. And because until we know more about what happened, you shouldn't be walking around a crime scene unescorted."

"I'll be with Raul."

"Raul isn't armed. Biggs is."

She took a deep breath, trying to rein in her temper. "Nolan, come on. You guys are short-staffed. I couldn't possibly ask one of your officers to waste his time babysitting me—"

"You're not asking, and it's not your call. You're working in *my* jurisdiction, and you need security." Another look at his watch. "I'd do it myself, but I have a deposition at eight."

Sara gritted her teeth and stared up at him. He was determined—she could see it in his eyes.

"Biggs has supplies in his trunk," he told her. "He'll help you get a trash bag taped over your window until you can get it fixed, along with everything else."

Biggs walked over and stopped short, as if sensing an argument. He looked from Nolan to Sara.

"Here's a copy of the report," he said, handing it to her.

She folded it in half. "Thank you, Officer." She turned to Nolan with a fake smile. "And thank you, too, Detective. I appreciate your time this morning."

"Don't mention it."

Talia followed the highway's sharp curve, tapping the brakes when she spotted Nolan's pickup. She rolled past it, then pulled onto the shoulder and parked. Grabbing her backpack off the passenger seat, she got out.

Nolan stood beside his truck, rummaging through the chrome toolbox mounted behind the cab. He wore slacks and a dress shirt with the sleeves rolled up, and she knew he'd been at the courthouse earlier.

He glanced up as she approached. "You bring the camera?"

"Yup."

Nolan grabbed a heavy-duty flashlight and led her down the dusty shoulder to a pair of orange traffic cones. He kept a crapload of emergency equipment in his personal vehicle and encouraged other officers to do the same. You never knew when you might come upon someone with car trouble, and his motto was *Be prepared.*

Talia looked around at the empty lanes. The afternoon sun had dipped behind the hills, leaving this stretch of highway in shadows.

"This where Sara went off the road?" Talia asked.

"About thirty yards back."

Talia crouched beside him. She unzipped her backpack and pulled out the camera she'd checked out of the equipment room. It was worth more than a week's pay, and she was careful as she handed it over.

"Thanks." Nolan checked the settings. Then he set up the ruler for scale and handed her the flashlight. "Aim the light right over the tread mark."

Talia positioned the beam so all the ridges in the dirt stood out. The effect would have been better at night, but the extra light still helped. Nolan snapped a few shots.

"He pulled off the road after he hit her?" Talia asked.

"Sara thinks he did."

"How do we know this is his tire track?"

"We don't." Nolan crouched closer to the ground and took a few more shots. "But I combed this whole stretch, both sides, and this is the only track out here."

"What about the emergency responders last night?"

"They parked north."

Talia looked around. This wasn't a heavily traveled highway, but still this didn't seem conclusive enough. Almost twenty hours had passed since the incident, and anyone could have pulled over. All this forensic work seemed like a waste of time, but he'd insisted she meet him out here with the camera.

Nolan returned to his truck for a container of quick-dry dental stone. He added a bottle of water to the jug and gave it a shake, then carefully poured the goop over the tread mark.

"Where'd you learn that?" she asked. "I must have missed that day at the academy."

He didn't look up. "I've had some seminars over the years."

"I should do that."

Nolan didn't comment. Talia watched him, noticing the tight set of his jaw as he poured the plaster. Sweat beaded at his temples, and he had to be hating the heat in those stuffy clothes.

"How is she?"

He knew she was asking about Sara, and he didn't look up. He finished pouring and set the jug aside. "Don't know."

Talia tried to read his expression. She'd been sure Nolan and Sara had a thing going, especially with her car at his house last night. Maybe she was wrong. Even if he and Sara *didn't* have a thing going, he had to be worried about someone rear-ending her last night and then the break-in this morning. It hadn't taken long for the details of both incidents to spread through the department grapevine.

"You're pretty fixated on finding this Tahoe," Talia said.

"I am."

"And it's not personal?"

He looked up at her.

"I'm just pointing out this is a lot of effort to track down a vehicle if we don't even know for sure it's our guy," she said.

"It's our guy."

"You're sure?"

"Yes."

Talia watched him work. He seemed tense, and she had a strong suspicion it had more to do with Sara than the case.

"So . . . Sara went back to San Marcos, I take it?"

"Yeah."

"Does she know about Michelle?"

His look darkened. "No. Why?"

"Just wondering."

Nolan never talked about his ex-girlfriend or the reasons he'd left Austin PD. At least, he never discussed it in Talia's presence. She'd had to discreetly ask around to learn that he'd left his job after the cop he was dating was investigated by IA for corruption. She'd lost her job over it. Officially, Nolan's name had been cleared, but he'd left the force anyway. Talia had never figured out whether it was the breakup or the blowback from his coworkers that ultimately made him want to leave.

"If you like her, you should tell her about Michelle," Talia said. "It'd be better coming from you."

"I know."

He got quiet again, clearly wanting a change of subject. Maybe she shouldn't have said anything personal, but she liked Nolan and didn't want to see him blow it with Sara. Men could be so clueless when it came to relationships.

Nolan glanced at his watch. "Fifteen minutes to dry." He looked at her. "I talked to Biggs this afternoon. Nothing new at the park."

Talia stood up and folded her arms. Nolan stood, too, and they gazed down at the drying plaster. She glanced up and down the highway. Not a single vehicle had driven past since she'd parked. This was a quiet backroad.

"This unsub feels local to me," she said. "He knows this area. I feel like this is right in his backyard."

Nolan grabbed the jug and walked back to his truck. "That's the chief's take, too," he said, putting the jug in his toolbox.

"What? That the killer's from here?"

"He thinks he started in Tennessee, but maybe he's from here originally, or at least he's lived here a while."

"What about you? You think he's from here?"

"Looks that way." Nolan checked his watch again.

"I'm not sure why you're bothering with that cast when it doesn't prove anything," she said. "Even if the tread mark is his, no way it's admissible at trial."

"Something you should learn: the best three leads to follow are vehicles, fingerprints, DNA. In that order."

"Says who?"

"Me. And anyone else who's been on the job a few years."

"I'd think DNA would come first."

"Yeah, well, DNA's slow. So if you're talking about a trial, DNA's great. In terms of an active investigation, the other two are faster. Vehicles are tough to hide and easy to trace. They're easy to link to people. And if a vehicle you're looking for is a crime scene, you find it, and you've got a treasure trove of physical evidence. So trust me, we're not wasting our time here."

Talia did trust him, even if he could be a little arrogant at times. Nolan was smart, experienced, and dedicated to the job. But he was also impatient.

"You'll see what I mean when we get our hands on the vehicle," he said. "We'll have this guy cold."

"*When,* not *if?* You sound confident."

"You're not?"

"No, sure. But I'm a realist, too," she said. "We've got some good leads, but somehow this guy's managed to elude police in multiple states for at least five years."

"Doesn't matter, he's got us now." Nolan slammed shut the toolbox. "One way or another, we're going to nail him."

Sara hunched over the big map, trying to understand all the codes and symbols. She traced her finger over the line that paralleled Highway 12 and then made a snaking connection to Rattlesnake Gorge. The line looked like a creek, but she hadn't seen it on any other maps, so maybe it had dried up long ago. The reference librarian had warned her this map was forty years old.

Frustrated, Sara slid the map aside and checked her watch. Damn it, she'd been here two hours already. She'd come to the library on her lunch hour, and she'd lost track of time. It was easy to get immersed surrounded by the silent stacks and the musty smell of books.

She grabbed the next map on the pile. This one showed detailed topographical features of Allen and the surrounding counties. This map was newer, and she studied landmarks, trying to locate White Falls Park. She found the highway and traced her finger along it, looking for the turnoff.

The chime of her phone shattered the quiet.

Sara stood up, pushing her chair back with a screech as she reached for her purse. The phone chimed again as she dug it out and read the number on the screen.

"Hello?" she answered eagerly.

"Uh, I'm looking for Sara Lockhart?"

"This is she. Is this Will Merritt?"

Students glared up at her from the surrounding tables.

Sorry, she mouthed, grabbing her bag.

"Yeah, I got your message from the other day. Sorry it's taken a while. I've been off the grid."

Sara hurried past rows of bookshelves.

"Hello?"

"I'm here," she said. "Thanks for returning my call."

A librarian shot her a death scowl as Sara strode past the reference desk and pushed through the turnstile.

"Your message said something about an article on caving," he said. "Who do you write for again?"

"I don't." Sara plowed through the glass door and into the sunlight, and the heat slapped her like a wet towel. "I wanted to talk about *your* article. The one that appeared in *Outside*."

"Yeah, well, it's been a while," Will said. "That was back, let's see, two summers ago."

Sara swiped at her phone, looking for the bookmarked article. It was all about caving, and the photographs showed caverns as big as cathedrals, with jagged stalactites dripping down from the top. "Actually, it was last March, I believe." Sara stepped into some shade beside the library and dug a notepad from her purse. "You wrote about various caves in the Texas Hill Country, and I'm particularly interested in the ones near Springville."

"Springville, Texas."

"That's correct. We're conducting an investigation here into a missing-persons case, and—"

"Wait, *who* did you say you write for?"

"I don't write for anybody." Sara took a deep breath, annoyed that he hadn't really listened to her message. "Let me back up. I'm a forensic anthropologist with the Delphi Center Crime Lab. One of my cases involves some bones discovered in a gorge not far from the caves you featured in your article. I wanted to know—"

"White Falls Park."

"Correct." She slumped against the building. "You remember it?"

"Yeah, I was back down there a couple months ago for some mountain biking. Did a piece for my blog, *High Life*."

"Yes, I read it, as a matter of fact. Anyway, these remains were found within the park boundaries, and in your article, you mention that the caves you toured were *near* White Falls Park, and I wanted to understand where exactly. I'm having trouble locating any maps of the local caves."

"I'm not sure there are any. Least, not that I've ever seen."

Sweat trickled down Sara's back, and she glanced at her watch again. She needed to get back to the lab.

"So, how did you learn about the caves?" she asked.

"Some of my biking buddies told me about them. Word of mouth, you know. They're on private property, so you can't get to them from the park."

"Oh, yeah?" Sara jotted the details in her notepad. "How did you get to them?"

"Some locals drove me out there on an old dirt road."

"Well, do you have GPS coordinates?"

"No."

"How about landmarks?"

"Yeah, I've got some of that recorded on my phone."

Sara's pulse sped up. *Finally,* a lead on the caves.

"I'd have to go back and listen. I do everything audio when I'm climbing or biking. Keeps my hands free."

"I understand. Would you mind checking? We could really use the help pinpointing a few things. You remember offhand what any of the landmarks were?"

He sighed. "You know, it's been a while. I remember a couple of those bobbing oil wells."

"Pumpjacks?"

"Yeah, but they weren't moving and looked abandoned. And I think we went over a low-water bridge and passed some grazing black-and-white cows. I remember because my girlfriend called them Oreo cows."

"Your girlfriend was with you?"

"She took the photos they ran with the piece."

Pumpjacks and Oreo cows. Sara would have much rather had GPS coordinates, but at least it was something.

A call beeped in, and Sara checked the number. Nolan. She hadn't talked to him since Monday, and it was Wednesday now.

"I might have more in my notes," Will said. "I can listen and get back to you."

"Call me anytime, as soon as you find anything. I'd appreciate it."

"Sure, no problem."

Sara clicked off with the writer and stared down at her phone, debating whether to pick up. Before she could decide, Nolan's call went to voice mail.

Sara leaned back against the building. She took a deep breath and pressed play on the call. She'd been hoping for it and dreading it for days.

"Hey, it's me," he said, and just the sound of his voice made Sara's chest ache. "I wanted to get back to you on those fingerprints from your break-in. CSI didn't lift anything usable, like we thought. Same for the door to your motel room."

She closed her eyes. They'd known it was a long shot.

"We're still working your case, but no suspects so far, and the timing bothers me. You should stay vigilant about your personal safety." He paused. "I know I don't need to tell you that, but . . . be careful, Sara."

CHAPTER 20

Nolan was having a crap week. And not just because he'd spent most of it chasing down dead-end leads on the phantom white Tahoe.

Nolan hadn't seen or spoken to Sara since Monday morning, when he'd left her in the motel parking lot with Biggs. Since then, three full workdays had gone by without a word. She hadn't responded to his message, and he hadn't called again.

He was giving her the space she wanted, showing her he didn't want to pressure her into starting something just because they'd spent the night together.

She didn't want a relationship. She'd made that clear. He definitely would have preferred it the other way, but he could respect what she'd told him.

Problem was, respecting it meant keeping his distance, which meant he had no idea when or even *if* he would see her again. And his desire to see her again had started to dominate his thoughts.

The timing was bad. He needed to be focused

on the case with everything he had. Nolan had put in two straight eighteen-hour days and gone to bed dead tired, only to discover he couldn't sleep because his bed smelled like her. He probably should have thrown his sheets in the wash, but he was too tired even to do that—which just showed how rational he was. Lack of sleep was messing with his head.

It was messing with his work, too. He'd been snipping at everyone, including Talia, who'd opted to work on her own this afternoon rather than ride in a car with him. She'd been tactful about it, pointing out that they'd cover more ground with a divide-and-conquer strategy.

Nolan didn't blame her. He knew she was right. With no new developments in days, the investigation was stalled, and they needed any and every lead they could turn up at this point.

Nolan neared a mailbox and slowed to check the number. The name on the box said HANSEN, and Nolan followed the driveway to a weathered wooden house surrounded by a chain-link fence. On the east side of the house stood a tall pecan tree with a green Volkswagen parked under it. On the house's west side was a dilapidated shed that looked like it might blow over in the next storm.

Nolan got out of his car, eyeing the fence and searching for a dog. He spotted it at the open front door, confined behind the screen. The dog was big and brown, and it started barking as Nolan opened the gate.

"Lucy! Cut that out!"

Nolan turned to see a woman stepping out of the shed. She wore a blue apron over her clothes and had silver curls piled in a bun on top of her head. The dog started going crazy as she walked toward Nolan.

"Lucy, stop!"

Lucy didn't stop, and the woman rolled her eyes.

"Elaine Hansen?"

"That's me." She smiled. "Sorry about her. She gets excited for visitors."

"Nolan Hess, Springville PD."

"I know who you are. I went to school with your dad." She took a rag from her apron pocket and started wiping her hands. "What can I do for you, Detective?"

"I'm here about your late husband, Todd. Specifically, I have some questions about his car."

She looked surprised. "The Mustang?"

"He drove a Mustang?"

She laughed. "Drove? No." She waved a hand. "That thing was up on cinder blocks the last twelve years. Todd could never get it to run."

"I'm here about the SUV. Our records show a 2005 Chevy Tahoe registered to his name."

"That one wasn't much better." She tucked the

towel into her pocket and fisted a hand on her hip. "It *ran,* don't get me wrong. But the transmission conked out, and after Todd was gone, I didn't want to fool with it, not when my Jetta works fine."

"So what did you do with the Tahoe?"

"Donated it to the church for a tax write-off. And for charity, of course, but you know what I mean."

Nolan gritted his teeth as he took out his notebook. This was a complication he didn't need today. If the church had sold it, it could be anywhere. "Which church is that, ma'am?"

"Second Baptist over on Oak Street."

"Do you remember when you sold it?"

She looked down and shook her head. "Let me see. Last November? December? Seems like it was before the holidays. Come on in, I'll check." She started toward the shed, and the dog's barks grew frantic.

" 'Scuse the mess," she said, ushering Nolan inside. "I'm making my mud pies, as Todd liked to call them. Keeps me busy."

Nolan had to duck his head to get through the door. The shed turned out to be a workroom with a potter's wheel at the center. Shelves filled with unfinished creations lined the walls—bowls, mugs, vases. Elaine crossed the room to a table overflowing with tools and paperwork. She picked up a bright blue mug and shuffled through some papers beneath it. "Let's see . . . I know it was before Christmas."

Nolan's phone vibrated with a text, and he pulled it from his pocket to check the screen. It was Crowley.

"I think it's inside. Sorry." She brushed past him, leading him back into the yard. "This isn't about the Baird case, is it?" she asked over her shoulder.

"Why do you ask?"

"Well, you're our best officer, so I figure that's your case, isn't it? Unless this is about those bones they found in the park last weekend."

She mounted the porch steps, and Nolan followed her, keeping an eye on the dog.

"It's a case out of San Antonio, actually. We're following up on something."

"Lucy, *sit!*"

The dog sat, to Nolan's surprise. She watched from her spot by the door as Elaine led Nolan into the den, where a rolltop desk covered in paperwork sat in the corner. She started combing through stacks as Nolan glanced around. The space was small and cluttered, with sagging furniture and towers of books everywhere.

"You really have to feel for the Bairds."

"What's that?" Nolan looked at her.

"Sam and Kathy? Kaylin's parents?" She shook her head. "Of course, Sam drinks too much. And he was always hard on those kids, but can you

305

blame him? What would you do if your daughter started taking up with those druggies?"

"You're talking about Kaylin's friends?"

"Those kids are bad news. Especially her boyfriend, the Sharp boy."

"Kaylin's boyfriend?"

"Yes, what's his name, Tristan?" She stopped rummaging. "I once saw him and Kaylin buying drugs at the movie theater. Right there in the parking lot in broad daylight, bold as you please." She shook her head and resumed her search. "I swear, that boy's got a lot of nerve."

Nolan watched her comb through her desk, wondering if she had firsthand information or gossip.

Another text message, and Nolan took out his phone. Crowley again, and Nolan swiped the screen to read it: *CALL ME ASAP.*

"Well, I must have misplaced it, but it was right before Christmas. I know that for sure. And the church has a record of it. I can give them a call."

"I'll handle it," Nolan said, slipping his phone into his pocket. "Who'd you talk to over there?"

"Reverend Cook. He was in the office when I brought in the title, signed the receipt himself."

"I'll talk to him." Nolan took out a business card. "Meantime, if you find it or remember the date of the transaction—"

"I'll give you a call."

"Appreciate it."

She ushered him out, and the barking started up as soon as he stepped through the door. Nolan dialed Crowley as he walked to his car.

"I got your message," Nolan said. "What's up?"

"Talia asked me to call you."

He slid behind the wheel. "Why didn't she call me?"

"She's got her hands full with something. You know that vehicle you're looking for? The white Tahoe?"

"What about it?"

"She found it."

Nolan tracked Talia down at her parents' place, where the gravel driveway was choked with cars and pickups. Following the lead of several people, he found an empty patch of lawn and parked at an angle so he wouldn't get blocked in.

Nolan peeled off his shades as he got out. Someone had set up a slip-and-slide in the front yard, and he recognized several of Talia's nieces and nephews. One of the little girls gave him an excited wave before taking a running leap onto the plastic.

The air smelled of barbecue, and through the screen door Nolan heard a baseball game playing. He stepped inside, and people yelled and jumped to their feet as someone hit a homer.

"Nolan!" Talia's mother walked up to him. "So glad you could come. She's in back." She wiped her hands on a dish towel and shooed him toward the kitchen. "Go right through."

"Thank you."

Nolan made his way through the kitchen, nodding and greeting Talia's sisters as he went. Every bit of stove space and counter space was occupied with food, and a big white sheet cake sat in the center of the kitchen table.

Nolan stepped onto the enclosed back porch as Talia came inside.

"Hey! Finally." She held up a beer bottle. "Want one?"

"I'm good."

"Crowley caught you." She held the back door open as a dark-haired man stepped inside holding a tray of barbecued ribs. "Nolan, you remember my dad?"

"Diego, good to see you. Is it your birthday?"

"My pop's. You staying for dinner this time?"

" 'Fraid I can't."

Diego shook his head, and Talia gestured for Nolan to follow her out.

Nolan stepped into the yard, where another relative stood beside a giant barbecue pit. Talia led Nolan away from the smoke to a wooden picnic table. She hopped on top of it and smiled at him.

"You found the Tahoe?" Nolan asked.

"Almost."

He crossed his arms. "What does that mean?"

"I almost found the Tahoe that ran Sara off the road, *and* I almost found the driver." She took a swig of her beer and set the bottle down. "Sure you don't want one?"

"Yes. Talk."

"Okay, so I read Sara's statement. She first spotted the Tahoe when she pulled in for gas at that place on Highway 194."

"Arnie's, I know. I interviewed the clerk already," he said. "Nothing. And they don't have surveillance cams."

"You interviewed *a* clerk."

Nolan frowned.

"The clerk on duty that day was in the back when you stopped in for an interview."

Nolan's phone buzzed in his pocket, but he ignored it. "You talked to him?"

"Took some doing, but yeah." She rolled her eyes. "I had to sweet-talk Arnie—gag—but I knew he was full of shit because he hires people off the books, and I knew he probably had someone else working who didn't want to get mixed up with police."

Nolan tamped down his annoyance. He hated being lied to, but it came with the job. "Okay, what'd you get?"

"The clerk—Manuel Gomez, forty-eight, no rap sheet, by the way—remembers the vehicle. Says the guy comes in from time to time."

"What's that mean?"

"Every few weeks or so. Always buys twenty dollars cash of the cheapest unleaded."

"He have a description?"

"Yes."

Nolan watched her, rubbing his jaw. Talia's eyes danced with enthusiasm over this supposedly great lead.

"Why aren't you excited?" she asked. "Haven't you been saying the fact that this *particular* Tahoe ran Sara off the road means this *particular* Tahoe is our unsub? I mean, he's clearly from around here. He stops at this place on a regular basis."

"It's circumstantial."

"God! Nolan, come on! Don't you even want a description?"

"Let's hear it."

"White guy, thirties. Medium height, medium build, brown hair."

"You've got to be fucking kidding me."

"And he has a scar on his forehead above his right eye."

"That's better, but not by much."

She tipped her head to the side. "You're really pissing me off here."

"Sorry. I'm frustrated." He blew out a sigh. "I've spent the last three days running down crap that hasn't gotten us anywhere." He ran his hand through his hair. "Okay. We need to get this guy with a sketch artist."

She nodded. "I agree. But we have to get one who speaks Spanish, or else I need to sit in and translate. And besides a sketch, there's also the possibility we could stake out the gas station and wait for him to come in."

"Yeah, with all our unlimited manpower and resources."

Nolan's phone buzzed, and this time he looked. It was Springville PD, and he'd also missed a call from the Delphi Center.

"One sec." Nolan stepped away from Talia and called the Delphi Center back. Maybe it was Sara.

"Detective Hess, I just left you a message."

He recognized the voice as Mia Voss from the DNA lab.

"Sorry I missed your call."

"Good news," she told him.

"I could use some."

"I finished my work on that T-shirt you submitted and corroborated my findings. In addition to the victim's DNA, we found a second sample."

"Okay. And?"

"We've got a forensic hit."

The darkness seemed endless, but Grace refused to let it take over her mind. She was going by the bat clock now, tracking her days and nights with the animals' nocturnal movements. All but a few of them had left for the nighttime feeding,

311

and Grace had a break from the squeaks, which meant she could focus.

Her bindings were some kind of synthetic twine. The bindings around her wrists were attached to the wall with something metal that *clinked* when she moved her arms. Was it a chain? Several carabiners linked together? Grace didn't know. But it was short, giving her just enough room to have one place to sleep and one place to pee. She was like a dog on a very short leash. A pit bull someone kept chained in the front yard to growl and look menacing.

Why hadn't he replaced the twine with something stronger by now, like handcuffs? Maybe he thought she was weak. Dehydrated. Depleted. And she was.

Maybe he thought that even if she *did* manage to free herself, she would have no idea how to get out of this pitch-black cavern. Maybe he thought she was too injured to go anywhere. Maybe he was just fucking with her.

Grace lay on the cold floor of the cave, sawing away at her bindings. It was her only option. She'd tried over and over to pull the chain from the wall. But it was in there good, and all she'd managed to do was rub her skin raw until her wrists were on fire. The pain was excruciating. And she'd once thought her blisters from Bella's sandals were bad.

Thinking of her family put a clench in her

chest. She couldn't think about her mom and dad right now. Or her aunts and uncles. Or the friends she was supposed to share an apartment with in the fall.

Focus, she told herself as she continued her effort. The bindings were tight. He was good at knots. But Grace had discovered a flake of stone, and if she held it just right, between her index and middle finger, she was able to saw at the twine.

Grace's fingers cramped, and the rock slid from her grasp. *Shit.* Pressing her cheek to the hard ground, she felt around for it. Finally, she found it. Using her tongue, she managed to get the rock into her mouth. Pain zinged up her side as she scooted forward and carefully maneuvered it back into her hand.

Slowly, steadily, she worked. She had no fingernails left to peel now. It had been eleven days. The last time he'd come back, she'd been still and lifeless. A dying mouse.

He hadn't liked that. It was her one flicker of triumph since she'd walked into this nightmare, and she'd paid for it with a smashed cheek and a bloody lip. It was worth it.

On his way out, he'd torn open a gel packet and tossed it at her. Only one, and no water.

When he was gone, she'd sucked down every ounce of sustenance and gone back to working like a dog. She was a pit bull, not a mouse.

She wasn't dead, but dangerous.

CHAPTER 21

Unlike the Crypt where Sara worked, the Delphi Center's DNA lab had a prime location on the building's top floor.

"Nice view," Nolan said as he followed Mia down the hallway where windows overlooked acres of rolling hills.

"We like it." She glanced at him over her shoulder. "You ever been here before?"

"Just downstairs."

Nolan pictured Sara in the cramped office where he'd kissed her. He hadn't talked to her in days, and her SUV hadn't been in the parking lot when he arrived.

Mia opened a door and led him into a spacious laboratory where several white-coated scientists hunched over microscopes. He followed her past an industrial-size refrigerator, which he guessed contained rape kits and other biological evidence. She stopped at a long slate table and nodded at the evidence bags Nolan carried.

"Before we get to the test results, let's see what you brought me," she said.

"Sure."

Mia tugged a wide strip of butcher paper from a roll and covered the table. She pulled her strawberry-blond hair into a ponytail, which made her look even younger than she already did. Nolan still couldn't get over the fact that a woman who probably got carded trying to buy alcohol was one of the nation's top DNA experts.

"Okay, big package first," she said. "What's in it?"

"A backpack belonging to a hiker who went missing in White Falls Park fourteen months ago," Nolan said. "Kaylin Baird, age nineteen."

Mia pulled on a pair of gloves, then handed him some. "White Falls Park, the same location where the four victims were recovered?"

"That's right. So we obviously think there's a connection between the cases, but we have nothing to prove it conclusively. I'm hoping you can do that."

She nodded. "I assume you already ran all this evidence before?"

"The state crime lab checked for prints, blood, whatever. No blood, and the only prints they found belonged to Kaylin."

"What about the smaller envelope?" she asked.

"That's Kaylin's phone."

Mia smiled. "I was hoping you'd say that. We like phones."

"It was checked for prints, too, but they found nothing."

"Nothing at all?"

"*Nada*. And that supports my case theory," Nolan said.

She folded her arms over her chest. "Walk me through your case theory."

"Kaylin doesn't fit the killer's pattern. He's been known to abduct women, often from bars or other public places at night. After he kills them, he dumps them in remote parks. So far, we know of two victims in Tennessee and four here in Texas."

"And Kaylin? What happened with her?"

"She was last seen hiking in White Falls Park early on a Saturday morning. She was supposed to meet a ride later in the morning, but she didn't show. Her backpack was recovered at a different park twenty miles away, cell phone inside."

Mia took a utility knife from her lab coat pocket and sliced through the seal on the smaller evidence envelope. She carefully removed a slender iPhone.

"I don't think the unsub selected Kaylin like he did the others," Nolan said. "I think he happened onto her at some point, probably when she witnessed him getting rid of one of the bodies. One of the victims disappeared the week before Kaylin, and her body was found buried near Kaylin's favorite hiking spot. You follow?"

Mia nodded. "Was this phone on or off when it was recovered?"

"Off. Which doesn't make sense if she was meeting up with friends. I think he turned the phone off before he put it in that backpack and dumped it in a different park."

"Where he hoped it would throw off investigators?" Mia asked.

"Or at least distract us. Which it did. We spent a lot of time scouring that park and came up with nothing."

"So, you believe your unsub handled this phone, and yet it's clean of any fingerprints. That's very good news."

Nolan gave her a questioning look.

"Well, he probably wiped the phone down because he handled it without gloves," Mia said. "That fits in with your scenario that he didn't plan his interaction with this woman, that it was a spur-of-the-moment thing prompted when she witnessed something suspicious in the park."

"Why is that good?"

"The good part for us is that criminals often make bad decisions when they're in a hurry or amped up. You know the most common item used to wipe prints off something? A shirttail." She smiled, and Nolan felt a ray of hope. "And a shirttail is loaded with DNA. So, if your scenario is accurate—"

"He wiped his prints and left his DNA behind."

"Let's hope." She replaced the phone in the

envelope. "Now, are you ready to hear about the other item you sent in?"

"You said you got a forensic hit. That means a hit on evidence, not a person, right? Which means he's not a convicted felon with a DNA sample in the system."

"Let's back up," she said. "You submitted a T-shirt recovered from Little Rattler Gorge. We tested it and found DNA from the victim all over it—sweat, blood, tears."

"Tears? You can tell that?"

"The saline-like substance was found on her shirtsleeve, probably when she wiped her eyes."

Nolan bit back a curse.

"Along with the victim's biological fluids, we also recovered a tiny spatter of blood belonging to someone else, probably resulting from a physical struggle. Maybe she hit him or scratched him. We ran *that* profile through the system and got a hit on the crime-scene index. In other words, the profile matches an unidentified DNA profile recovered at a separate crime scene."

"What do we know about this crime scene?"

"It's in Texas, for one," Mia said. "I'll put you in touch with the submitting agency. You ever been to Maverick?"

"No."

"There's not much there. A motel and a few gas stations. It's mainly a stop-off for tourists on their way to visit Big Bend Park."

Nolan's pulse picked up. "Parks again."

"That's right."

"And where did this DNA come from?"

"The police there can tell you more, but when I spoke to them earlier, they said it's an abduction case. A woman went missing from the motel there. Her car was found, driver's-side door open, purse and keys inside. A small droplet of blood on the armrest of the door is what yielded this profile, and it isn't the victim's blood. So police believe it belongs to her abductor."

Nolan stared at her, unable to believe how strong this lead was. It fit the pattern in so many ways.

"I understand there's a task force," Mia said. "Has anyone been checking out this parks connection?"

"The feds," Nolan told her. "It's easier for them to access databases across state lines, so we've been having them do it. They've been running down criminal records on former park employees in both states. We need to double down on the effort."

"Starting with Big Bend."

"Damn. This is a good lead."

She nodded. "Happy to help. I hear it's been a tough case." Her expression darkened. "Any word on the Austin woman who went missing from Sixth Street?"

"Grace Murray. Nothing new as of this morning, and it's been twelve days."

"I'm guessing the task force is frustrated."

"Extremely. Every new lead feels like one step forward, two steps back."

"That's how it always is." Mia peeled off her gloves. "You can't lose heart."

Sara turned to the sheriff's deputy squeezed into her guest chair and tapped her pencil on the computer screen. The X-ray showed the fractured humerus of six-year-old Bradley Benson, who had been reported missing eight months ago.

"The X-rays are very clear," she said. "See that line there?"

"You're talking about the arm bone?" The deputy leaned closer, and Sara got a whiff of the onions he must have had for lunch.

"It's a spiral fracture. I'm sure you've seen this type of injury before."

He nodded. "But you're saying this was earlier? Before the head injury?"

"That's correct. The spiral fracture, the wrist fracture, and the two rib fractures occurred months before death."

The man stared at her screen, his brow furrowed with concentration. He seemed reluctant to accept these autopsy results. It was a lot to absorb, and this deputy was a bit on the green side.

"Have you interviewed any suspects yet?" Sara asked him.

He seemed to snap out of it. "Suspects?"

"That's right."

He cleared his throat. "I'm not at liberty to discuss that at this point."

Was he for real?

"Well, do you know who filed the missing-persons report?" she asked.

"I can't discuss that, either."

"Do you know if it was a parent?"

"I'm not at liberty to discuss specifics."

Sara rolled her eyes. "I'm not a reporter, you know. We're on the same team here."

He had the decency to look embarrassed. "Irregardless . . ."

Sara waited for him to finish the thought. He didn't, and she was done tiptoeing around his ego.

"Well, *I'm* at liberty to discuss specifics, so let me tell you what *I* know after ten years of dealing with these sorts of cases. I know this child was abused. Severely, and over a period of years. I know this child's mother and father, along with any stepfather or boyfriend at this kid's house, should *all* top your list of suspects in his murder. And I know that if the mom didn't do it, then at the very least, she's complicit in this crime."

The deputy gave a skeptical frown.

Sara turned to her computer and clicked open

a photo of a tattered Winnie-the-Pooh blanket. It had come zipped inside the pouch with the boy's remains, which had been found in a culvert less than two miles from his home.

Sara tapped the screen. "This child came to us wrapped in a blanket, Deputy. You know who does that? A mother feeling remorse."

The deputy looked at her but didn't say anything.

"This mom *knows* what happened to her son," Sara told him. "Get her to talk to you."

"Easier said than done."

"She's the key to your case."

He nodded and stood up, collecting his hat, along with the autopsy report Sara had completed early this morning. "Appreciate the input." He tucked the report under his arm. "Thank you for the quick turnaround."

"Absolutely."

Sara watched him leave with an ache in the pit of her stomach. Would he listen to her advice? Or was she talking to a wall? Sometimes Sara wished she had a badge instead of a damn lab coat.

She propped her elbows on her desk and rubbed her temples. Her headache was back with a vengeance. It had started making regular appearances every day around six.

Sara clenched her teeth and tried to will it away. But of course, that didn't work. Lack of sleep wasn't helping. Neither was the steady barrage of cases—three new ones in the last two days. Frustration churned inside her. She felt powerless and exhausted and, with each day that ticked by, more depressed by the world around her. She swiped the tears from her cheeks and stood up. Enough. She needed to get out of here. She needed to go home and take a break and think about something besides death and suffering.

She hung her lab coat on the door and grabbed her purse. Poking her head into the autopsy suite, she saw Aaron bent over his microscope.

"It's ten to six," she said.

"Give me fifteen minutes."

"No hurry. I'll wait upstairs."

He glanced up. "You okay?"

"Fine. I'll meet you in the lobby."

She ignored his look of concern and headed out the door into the long windowless corridor. Most days, she liked the solitude of working down here, but every now and then, it made her want to tear her hair out.

The elevator *dinged,* and she darted around the corner to catch it, nearly smacking into someone. She jumped back.

"Whoa." Nolan gazed down at her, and she felt a flood of relief. She wanted to hug him, but she kept her hands to herself.

His brow furrowed. "What's wrong?"

"Nothing." Her pulse was racing suddenly. "What brings you down here?"

"Had a meeting with Mia. Thought I'd stop in and say hi. You all right?"

"You know, shit day." She waved off his concern. "You don't want to hear about it."

"Well, can I give you a ride home?"

She tipped her head to the side. "How'd you know I needed a ride home?"

"You're here. Your car isn't. I figure it's in the shop?"

"It is."

"Then let me take you home."

Sara gazed up at him, still shocked at seeing him. He looked good. He wore jeans and his leather jacket, and he had the five o'clock shadow going. And suddenly, a ride with Nolan was exactly what she needed.

"I'd like that. Let me tell Aaron." She pulled out her phone and sent a message as they walked to the elevator.

"Thanks for the offer," she said when they stepped inside.

"Sure." He looked her up and down. "Does your shit day have anything to do with the Clarke County deputy I passed on my way down here?"

"Yes," she said, but didn't elaborate. She didn't want to dump all her problems on him.

They reached the lobby, which was busy with Delphi staffers heading home for the night, probably to spouses and children and adoring pets.

Sara was going home to an empty refrigerator and a stack of unpaid bills.

She looked at Nolan. "So, what's up with Mia?" she asked, trying for cheerful.

He held open the door for her as she stepped into the warm evening air. "She has DNA results from the T-shirt we found."

"I thought she already finished with that. She confirmed the DNA belonged to the victim."

"She found a second DNA profile and turned up a forensic hit," he said.

"You mean the crime-scene index?"

"Yep."

"So it's a link to another crime," she said, "but not a specific person."

"Yep."

Nolan sounded disappointed, and she knew he'd been hoping their unsub might have served time and be in the system already. It was a lot easier to find someone who had a track record with the police.

They walked to his pickup, which was even dustier than the last time she'd seen it. What had he been doing this week? She reached for the door before he could open it and slid inside.

His truck had a masculine smell that was becoming familiar, and she leaned back to enjoy it as he slid behind the wheel. He shot her a curious look as he backed out of the space. They exited the parking lot, and he turned east on the highway toward San Marcos.

He looked at her. "Where to?"

"Market Street and Elm," she said. "I'm next door to the bakery."

"The old paper factory."

"You know it?"

"Yeah."

Sara watched the scenery whisk by, feeling her tension drain as she got some distance between herself and work. She and Aaron had come in early and stayed late for the past three days.

"You want to tell me about it?" Nolan asked.

Sara looked at him.

"Whatever that deputy did to make you cry."

"He didn't make me *cry*."

Nolan shot her a look.

"Okay, fine, I'm upset." She sighed. "It's this case we got yesterday. A child's remains found wrapped in a blanket."

"The Benson boy."

"You know the case?"

He nodded.

She should have figured he'd know about it. "I did the autopsy last night. Based on my findings, we're talking about a six-year-old who weighed thirty-four pounds at the time of death. He was forty inches tall."

"Malnourished."

She nodded, looking away as the tears welled

326

up again. *Children who aren't loved don't grow.* It was a simple fact she'd learned from Underwood in the early days of her career.

"I'm sorry."

She scoffed. "Why on earth are *you* sorry?"

"I hate that you have to see stuff like that."

"You've seen it, too. I'm guessing that's one reason you left Austin PD for a smaller town."

"You see that stuff everywhere, which is why it sucks." He cast a wary look at her. "And that's not why I left APD."

Silence settled over them as Sara studied his profile. She didn't want to push, but she had the sudden urge to know. In some ways, they'd been as intimate as two people could be. In other ways, she felt like she hardly knew him.

"What happened there?" she asked. "You mentioned a 'cloud of suspicion,' but that doesn't really tell me much."

He was silent, and she figured she'd overstepped her bounds.

"I was with someone." He cleared his throat. "Michelle. We were partners. Turned out she wasn't the person I thought she was."

"Partners as in—"

"We worked together. And later, after she transferred to Vice, we had a personal relationship, too. She got caught up in some stuff." He shook his head. "I guess sometimes you never really know people."

Sara watched his expression, trying to fill in the gaps. Had she taken bribes? Planted evidence? "What exactly—"

"There were some guys shaking down suspects while they were being collared for drug offenses. They had a ring going, you know, taking kickbacks to cut people loose. She got involved."

Without asking, Sara knew with absolute certainty that he'd had no idea. His integrity was as much a part of him as his eye color.

"How did you find out?" she asked.

"Nathan. I didn't believe him at first. We were at a bar when he told me, and I thought he was messing around. When I realized he was serious, I took a swing at him, damn near broke his nose."

"You *punched* Nathan?" Sara tried to imagine it.

"Wasn't much of a punch, but yeah."

"Jeez, Nolan. And you're still friends?" She recalled Alex's words. *Nolan's a good guy. One of my favorite people.* She'd said that about a man who had punched her husband at a bar.

"I apologized. We're good now."

Sara took a deep breath and blew it out. What an ordeal for him, both professionally and personally.

"Did you leave the department on bad terms?" she asked.

"Officially, no. It was never tied back to me,

but there was still blowback. Some people had doubts, and I could feel it every time I came to work. I didn't think I could be effective if even a handful of my coworkers didn't have faith in me, so I made a move."

"Are you glad?"

"Nothing about it makes me *glad,* really, but I think it's for the better. I like what I'm doing now, I like being in a place where I know folks personally. It's a smaller department, so I *am* able to have a bigger impact—that wasn't just bullshit." He glanced at her. "You asked me about this before, the night we went out for beers."

That night seemed like ages ago now. So much had happened. They'd become friends, and more. Sara didn't have a label for the more part, and she was too overwhelmed right now to think about it. She didn't need one more iota of stress today.

She leaned her head back, letting the hum of Nolan's truck soothe her. She suddenly felt exhausted, and she didn't want to talk about work anymore. Nolan seemed to take the hint, and the minutes ticked quietly by as they neared downtown San Marcos. Most of the shops had closed for the day, but the restaurants were just starting to fill up.

Nolan neared Sara's vintage brick building.

"Thank you for the ride," she said.

"No problem. You want to have dinner?"

She looked at him. He sounded so casual, but she sensed he cared about her answer, and she felt a flood of nerves. She didn't want to lead him on, didn't want him to think this was the start of something serious. But she didn't want to let him go, either.

"There's a pasta place on the corner that's pretty good," she said. "Leonardo's? It's the red awning just down from my building."

"That works."

Nolan neared the restaurant and smoothly parallel-parked in front of a meter. He cut the engine and looked at her. Before she could lose her nerve, she grabbed her purse and slid from the truck.

The aroma of garlic bread hit her, and she felt a rush of anticipation. Only some of it had to do with food. Nolan joined her on the sidewalk, and she noted the clusters of people milling outside the restaurant holding pagers. Beneath the red awning, every patio table was full.

Sara's head started to throb. She didn't want to wait in line tonight, or be around crowds, or make small talk. Her emotions felt too fragile today.

Nolan was watching her with those sharp brown eyes. "What is it?"

"Let's not do this."

He steered her away from the crowd. "What's wrong?"

"I'd rather be at my place. Let's get takeout. You mind?"

He rested his hand on her shoulder. "I want to spend time with you, Sara. I don't give a damn where."

CHAPTER 22

Sara's nerves started up again as she unlocked her door with Nolan at her side. She didn't know where this was going. No, she *did* know. It was going nowhere. She probably wouldn't see him after the case ended, so she was digging a deeper hole for herself by spending all this time with him. She should make an excuse and head this off now, but instead, she was doing the exact opposite.

She stepped into her apartment, and the instant she switched on the light, she remembered just how messy it was. She'd rushed off to work this morning without even making the bed.

Nolan paused to look around, then set the bag of food on the bar.

"Good windows," he said, zeroing in on her favorite feature besides the wood floors. He walked over to check out the view, and Sara took the opportunity to snatch her bathrobe off the sofa arm and scoop up several pairs of flip-flops. She opened the utility closet, dumped everything onto the washer, and shut the door.

Nolan looked amused. "Don't clean up for me."

"Oh, don't worry."

Clean was a pipe dream. A basket of clothes perched on her breakfast table, optimistically waiting to be folded. Sara grabbed several mugs off the coffee table and took them to the sink. The dishwasher was full, so there wasn't anywhere to stash them.

Nolan shrugged out of his jacket and tossed it onto the armchair. He turned to examine her bookshelves, and she admired his wide shoulders as he reached for a framed photo.

"Machu Picchu?" he asked.

"You know it?"

"I spent a summer in South America after college."

"Where?" she asked, surprised.

"Santiago. It was an immersion program. I was trying to learn Spanish. Thought it would be useful for work."

"Is it?"

"I'm not great, but I get by," he said.

She didn't know why she was so surprised. Nolan traveled and read and cared about other cultures. She remembered her crack about Tolkien and realized she'd been too quick to judge him. One of her dad's sayings popped into her head: *Small-town doesn't mean small-minded.*

Nolan replaced the photo and picked up another one showing her with several friends on a ledge overlooking Peru's Sacred Valley. She hadn't taken notice of whether Nolan kept photos in his house or who was in them. It was a missed opportunity, and she'd missed it on purpose. She hadn't wanted to get emotionally involved. And yet here she was, inviting him into her home and feeling anxious about what he thought. She wanted him to like it. She wanted him to see her as a successful, independent woman who'd built a life for herself in a new place. She didn't know why she wanted so badly for him to see her that way, but she did.

She walked closer and sat on the back of the sofa. "Thank you for not giving me crap the other day."

He set down the picture frame. "About what?"

"The way I slipped out without saying good-bye."

"You didn't 'slip.' I felt you get out of bed."

"Oh."

Guilt needled at her, and she wasn't sure why. They weren't in a relationship.

And yet he'd come to her motel when he heard about the burglary. And he'd left her a message with an update about the fingerprints. And he'd stopped by the lab to check on her. He'd been totally decent to her, and she'd been avoiding him because she was afraid. All these conflicting feelings swirled inside her, and she hadn't planned on any of this.

Her plan had been to establish herself at her new job and make friends and focus on her career path. Her plan had *not* been to fall headlong into another serious relationship, especially a long-distance one that would force her to compromise.

She'd been trying to protect herself from getting too involved. But when she was around Nolan, the attraction took over, and all her logic and planning seemed to evaporate.

She stepped closer, and his gaze heated as she reached up to touch the stubble along his jaw.

"I'm glad you came and found me today," she said.

He watched her intently as she brushed her hand down his shirt and traced her fingers over his gold detective's shield. It represented so many hours and months and years of hard work and commitment, and she admired that.

He didn't move a muscle as she trailed her fingertips over the grip of his gun and the holster that was warm from his body heat. Her fingers moved to his belt buckle. She glanced up. The intensity in his eyes sent a flurry of nerves through her, so she focused on his belt and getting it undone without looking clumsy. She unfastened the buckle, and he took over, pulling his belt and holster off with smooth efficiency. He set them on the coffee table and added handcuffs and car keys to the pile.

He took her wrist and pulled her close, then bent his head to kiss her, taking her mouth with raw need he didn't bother to hide. His kiss was deep and hard, and she could practically taste his pent-up frustration with her as he melded her against him and went after her mouth. His teeth nicked her lip.

"Sorry," he muttered.

"No, I like it."

Groaning, he clutched her against him and walked her backward to the couch, then lowered her over the arm. He eased down on top of her as she pulled at his shirt, impatient to get her hands on his bare skin. He worked the buttons of her blouse, and one popped off, skittering across the wood floor.

"Shit."

She pushed his hands away and hurriedly undid the buttons, then wrestled her arms free. He swooped down to kiss her breast through the thin white bra, and she wished she'd worn something even remotely sexy. But she hadn't expected to see him today, much less bring him home with her.

His mouth was hot and hungry, and she stroked her fingers through his hair. He slid his hand behind her, once again deftly unhooking her bra, and he pushed it up and out of his way. He took her nipple into his mouth, and she cried out, arching against him as she tipped her head back.

She loved his weight on her and the rasp of his beard against her skin. He kissed her and teased her with his mouth as the need built and burned inside her.

"Nolan."

He moved up to her lips, and she slid her hands under his shirt, loving his lean waist and the valley at the base of his spine. She remembered the way their bodies fit together so perfectly and felt a giddy surge of anticipation. She wanted to be skin to skin.

She pulled away. *"Bed."*

He paused to look at her. Then he pushed up and in one smooth motion scooped her off the couch, making her gasp when he stumbled over a stray shoe on the floor. He went straight for the bed and dropped her unceremoniously on the rumpled sheets. Sara untangled herself from her bra as he took his shirt off and tossed it away. He rested his knee beside her, and the bedframe squeaked under his weight.

He stretched out over her, resting his weight on his palms. "I've been dying to kiss you."

"Then kiss me," she said, hooking her leg around his hip. Instead, he hovered over her, looking down at her yellowing bruises.

"How are your ribs?"

"Fine." She brought his head down to kiss him, shifting her hips until she had him right where she wanted him. But then he pulled back and

stood up, stripping off his clothes as she watched from the bed.

Sara kicked off her sandals and unfastened her jeans, and his gaze heated as she pulled down the zipper. He took her cuffs and gave a sharp tug, then whisked the jeans off and dropped them to the floor. The bed creaked again as he stretched over her.

Slowly, he kissed his way down her body, sliding his hand between her legs as she pressed against him. She'd missed him, and he knew it. There was no point in pretending otherwise as he stroked his palms over her. He knew just how to touch her, just how to make her hot and needy. She writhed under him as he brought her right to the edge. But then he backed away, and she whimpered with frustration as he moved off the bed and rummaged through his jeans on the floor.

"Hurry."

He tore open the condom with his teeth and got it on, and then he knelt between her thighs. She looked into his eyes as he shifted her hips and pushed inside her.

He felt so good, so amazingly *right,* and she couldn't believe she'd been hiding from him all week. She clutched him to her, and their bodies moved together. The metal bedframe squeaked and squealed, and she had a fleeting worry about her downstairs neighbors.

Nolan pushed up on his hands. "Damn, that's loud."

"Sorry," she gasped. "I haven't done this here."

He laughed. "What, in *bed?*"

"This bed, this apartment."

He froze.

"Nolan, *please* don't stop."

He moved his hips again, thrusting into her over and over, until her entire body burned and quaked and felt like it would come apart. She ran her hands over his shoulders, his arms, his rippling back. She pulled him in tight, tipping her head back as he drove into her.

"Nolan . . . that's so good. Oh, my God."

He moved faster, harder, and she felt his muscles bunching under her hands.

"Babe, come on."

She opened her eyes, and the look on his face as he struggled for control magnified everything she was feeling. She clutched him against her and shattered. He gripped her leg and gave a powerful thrust that smacked the headboard against the wall as he came, too.

He collapsed on top of her, and she lay flattened beneath him, limp and sated. She couldn't breathe, though, and she was about to mention it when he rolled onto his back.

"Holy shit." He looked at her, his eyes wary. "Are you okay?"

Instead of answering, she scooted against him and rested her head on his damp chest.

"Sara?"

She sighed and fell asleep.

The lobby of APD headquarters was busy with plainclothes cops, uniforms, and a good number of desperate-looking people here either for questioning or to bail someone out. Talia walked to the directory on the wall and scanned the list of departments.

"Talia?"

She turned around to see Dax Harper standing behind her. He wore a black Spurs jersey and ripped jeans, and his hair was sticking up like he'd just crawled out of bed. His badge dangled from a lanyard around his neck.

"You're a hard man to get hold of," she said.

"I meant to call you."

She crossed her arms and stared up at him.

"I've been busy all day," he added.

"Well, hey, if you're not busy now, how about I catch you up on a few things about your case?"

Dax shook his head, smiling slightly. "I knew you'd bust my chops when I didn't call you back."

"I'm not busting anything. Let's talk."

He looked her over for a moment and glanced around. "This way."

He walked to a door and tapped a code into a

keypad. He held the door open and then led her down a long corridor and into a break room. It had a table and chairs, a vending machine, and an ancient-looking Mr. Coffee.

"Want anything?" he asked, taking out his wallet.

"I'm fine."

Dax fed a bill into the machine and tapped a selection. "I was working undercover all day."

"That explains the hair gel."

He patted his hair self-consciously as she leaned back against the counter.

"The Grace Murray case?"

He retrieved his drink and twisted off the top. "Nah, this was something else, something top priority."

Talia couldn't imagine working in a department where a recent kidnapping wasn't considered top priority. But then, she'd never worked for a big urban department.

He took a swig of his Mountain Dew.

"You know that has, like, eighty grams of sugar, right?"

"Still busting my chops." He set the bottle on the counter beside him. "Tell me what's up."

"I think we've got a witness."

His eyebrows tipped up.

"Chevy Tahoe, description matches up. One of our investigators spotted it leaving a local gas station. She followed him and tried to take a picture of his plate, and the driver flipped out. First he tried to lose her, and then he ran her off the road. Next morning, her vehicle was burglarized, and the camera was stolen."

"Seriously?"

"Seriously."

"That's a little suspicious."

"No joke." Talia didn't mention that the "investigator" wasn't exactly a police officer. Talia knew Sara Lockhart was credible, but Dax didn't.

"I interviewed the gas-station clerk," Talia continued. "He said this guy comes in from time to time, always pays cash. We've got a bilingual sketch artist lined up to do a drawing tomorrow morning. Once we have a sketch, I thought you could flash it around here, see if anyone recognizes this guy from the area where Grace Murray disappeared. We'll show it around our area, see if anyone knows him."

Dax didn't say anything. He rubbed his hand over his plastered hair, seeming to think about it.

"Well?"

"Well, what?" he asked.

"Well, what do you think? You told us a white Tahoe was spotted near the bar where Grace was around the time of her abduction. You think it might be worth showing a sketch around, see if anyone got a look at the driver?"

"Yeah, and we're a step ahead of you." Dax checked his watch.

"How are you a step ahead of me?"

"You have some time right now?"

"Time for what?"

"Come with me."

CHAPTER 23

It was dark when Sara opened her eyes. She glanced at the clock. Ten twenty. She lay there for a moment, disoriented, and then reality snapped back. She got up and found Nolan—jeans, no shirt—standing in the light of her open refrigerator, and she felt a pang of yearning so strong it made her breath catch.

He glanced up.

"You hungry?" she asked, tying the sash of her robe.

He looked her over, and his gaze lingered on the thin white silk.

"Starving," he said. "Thirsty, too."

She walked over and opened the door wider. "I've got beer, Diet Coke, hard lemonade."

He winced.

"Water?"

"I'll have a beer."

She grabbed a Corona for each of them and popped off the tops. She noticed his phone on the bar beside a notepad filled with scrawled handwriting. So while she'd been in a sex-induced slumber, he'd been working. He worked a lot, she'd noticed. Possibly as much as she did.

Sara handed him the beer. "I see you've been busy. Any developments?"

"Just checking in with Agent Santos. He's following up on those background checks."

"Park employees?"

"Yeah." He swigged the beer. "Texas and Tennessee, mostly. We may expand it tomorrow if the leads he's got so far don't pan out. He has something on a guy near Big Bend."

"Sounds promising."

"Maybe." He combed a hand through his mussed hair. "I feel like he's closer. Like right in my backyard."

"What does Santos think?"

"I don't know. We'll talk later."

As in tonight? Tomorrow? Sara didn't want to ask.

The paper bag of carryout sat right where they'd left it when they came in, and Sara reached inside to feel the cardboard containers. Room temperature.

"We can microwave this," she said, opening a cabinet. She took out some plates as Nolan unpacked the food.

"You had ravioli," he said.

"Yeah?"

"They mixed up our order. This is two fettuccine alfredos."

She stepped over to look. "Can you deal with

345

fettuccine? If you want to go back, I can throw on some clothes."

"Please don't." He gave her a heated look as he took the plates from her hands. "I'm good with fettuccine."

Nolan took over serving the food, and Sara pulled out a bar stool and sat. She sipped her beer, enjoying the view as he moved around her kitchen, randomly opening drawers. He had muscular shoulders and defined abs. He was tan, too, so she could tell he must run with his shirt off sometimes.

There was no denying it. Nolan was amazingly hot and amazingly *nice,* and she couldn't believe he was in her kitchen, shirtless, making dinner.

He got the microwave going and looked up. "What?"

"Nothing."

He watched her as he took a sip of beer. Then he nodded at the photo taped to her fridge. It was a shot of her excavation team in front of their tent.

"Where was this?"

"Guatemala. That was our 'mobile housing unit,'" she said.

"You lived in a tent for a year? I'm impressed."

"It was pretty nice, actually. Kind of like *M*A*S*H*."

He leaned back against the counter. "Were you

running to something or away from something when you went down there?"

"Who says I was running?"

He raised an eyebrow.

"Away from something." She sipped her beer. "My engagement ended abruptly, and I needed a change of scenery."

"Hmm. Sounds like there's a story to that."

"Not a very interesting one."

The microwave *dinged,* and he set his beer down to get the food. "This 'abrupt end.' Did you leave him at the altar?"

She bristled. "Why would you assume I left *him?*"

Nolan scooped pasta onto a plate. "Otherwise, he would have been the one running to Guatemala." He put a fork on the plate and slid it over.

Sara turned her bottle on the counter. It was time to get this conversation out of the way. He leaned back and watched her, waiting patiently for her to open up.

"It was two months before the wedding," she said. "I got cold feet and started to panic. So we broke up. I canceled all the plans and paid every-one back their security deposits. It was a mess. And then three weeks later, I got on a plane."

Mess was an understatement. The invitations hadn't gone out yet, but they were printed. Her mom's friends had already given her a bridal shower, so she had returned all the gifts and written notes. It was awful. If she ever decided to get married again, she was going to a court-house.

The bigger mess was Patrick. He'd been furious and humiliated. And his anger wasn't the worst part, because underneath all that, she knew he was badly hurt.

Nolan brought his plate over and took the stool beside her. She tried to read his expression.

"Sounds like a rough time for you."

"Me?" She laughed. "What about him? I'm the bitch who hurt and embarrassed him in front of everyone he knows."

"You're not a bitch."

She let the words hang there, not sure how much more she wanted to share. She didn't talk about this a lot, but she felt obligated to tell Nolan. After all, he'd told her about Michelle, even though the topic clearly made him uncom-fortable.

"My dad called me a flake," she said, surprised the word still stung after two years. "My mom said I'm shortsighted—which is basically code for 'You're going to regret it one day that you didn't snag a husband.' My brother said I have a mean streak." She twirled pasta around her fork. "I guess I shouldn't be surprised he took Patrick's side. They were friends from college. That's how we met in the first place."

"Is your brother married?" Nolan asked.

"Yeah. Why?" Sara scooped up a bite.

"I'm trying to understand where he's coming from. Why would he want you to go through with it when you weren't sure?"

She watched Nolan as he twirled pasta. They had the same fork-spinning method, only his bites were bigger.

"He's been married six years and has two kids," she said. "He seems happy, but we're not all that close, so who knows? His wife's a life coach." She rolled her eyes. "She actually gave me her business card after I called off the wedding. Like I need a card if I want to call my sister-in-law." Sara shook her head. "*Why* are we talking about this, anyway?"

"Because I want to get to know you."

She met his gaze. Those brown eyes were so serious, and she felt a flutter of nerves.

"Nolan . . . this thing with us . . ." She trailed off, not sure what she wanted to say.

"We don't need to label it."

"I tried to warn you, I'm bad at relationships."

He laughed. "Says who?"

"My ex-fiancé, for one."

"Yeah, well, he may be biased."

"The same thing happened in college when I had a two-year boyfriend. I'm not good at commitments. I start to feel . . . trapped."

He lifted an eyebrow. "Claustrophobic, maybe?"

"You're making light of it, but I'm bad at follow-through."

"Bullshit."

It was her turn to laugh. "How can you say 'bullshit' when you don't know me that well?"

"I know enough." He sipped his beer, watching her. He placed the bottle on the counter. "I know you spent six years getting a PhD. That takes follow-through. You spent a year on a humanitarian dig, when most people would have lasted a week. You applied for and landed a job at one of the top crime labs in the freaking *world*. You follow up on cold cases and victims everyone else has forgotten about. You work like a maniac, giving up most of your weekends." He paused. "When something matters to you, you commit."

His words filled her with a tingling sense of disbelief.

He got up and carried his plate to the sink, then turned and leaned back against the counter, smiling.

"I bet Patrick was all wrong for you, anyway."

She shook her head. "You never even met him."

"Don't need to. I bet I could guess what he's like."

"Now your arrogance is showing."

He folded his arms over his chest. "Let me take a stab at it." He rubbed his chin and looked at her. "Private college. Maybe grad school but no doctorate. You're more educated than he is, so he's probably threatened by you."

"Go on."

"I'm guessing he's a rules type. Law and order. And you were living near Washington, so . . ." He gave her a squinty look. "FBI agent, D.C. office."

Her mouth dropped open.

"Am I right?"

"No." She cleared her throat. "U.S. Attorney's Office, Alexandria, Virginia."

"Sorry, I'm way off."

No, he'd pretty much nailed it. Sara just stared at him, too shocked to speak.

"I bet he's pretty shrewd, too," Nolan said, "so when he realized you weren't going to marry him, he said a bunch of shitty things to you to give you a complex and keep you from moving on."

That hit a little too close to home. Every word Patrick had said to her had been stuck in her head for two years on a continuous loop.

You're a selfish bitch, Sara.

I'm a bitch because I want to talk about this?

You think you can just jerk people around? If you do this now, that's it. We're done, and I can tell you right now, you're going to end up alone.

Sara took her plate to the sink. "You don't need to be my shrink."

He shrugged. "Fine. But *you* brought this topic up twice now, trying to scare me off. I'm

351

just pointing out you've got a hang-up about something, and I don't think you should."

"I'm not trying to scare you off."

"No?"

"No."

What was she trying to do? She wasn't sure, and that was part of the problem. She'd been involved in two long-term relationships, and both had failed. She didn't want to go there again, at least not right now. Now was supposed to be her time to focus on herself and her career, to be the strong, independent woman she'd always wanted to be.

She turned to look at Nolan, and he smiled slightly as he gazed down at her with those deep brown eyes. How had this happened? She'd taken so many precautions, and still she could feel herself being pulled in. She wanted to trust him. She wanted to give in to this intoxicating feeling of being with him, even though she'd perfected being alone. She had it down to a science, really—going through her life without letting people close. She had her job, her friends. But she didn't have intimacy. She was terrified of it.

Nolan watched her with that perceptive look of his, and she felt like he could read her thoughts.

His phone beeped with a text, and he stepped over to check it. He was probably getting a call-out, meaning he would have to leave after this weirdly open conversation.

But he read the message and put the phone down. He came back and stood beside her as she rinsed the plates.

Was he getting ready to leave? Nerves flitted through her stomach. She didn't want him to go yet. She wanted him to spend the night, but he obviously still had his head wrapped up in his case. He might even be waiting for a call from Santos. Maybe he was looking forward to ducking out of here, just to even the score from the other night. Although a move like that seemed too vindictive for him.

She shut off the faucet and turned to face him, bracing herself for a tactful departure.

Nolan eased closer, resting his hand at her waist, and she felt the warmth of his fingers through the thin silk. Sara's pulse started to thrum. He was gazing down at her with that simmering look she recognized.

"I don't want to be your shrink, Sara." He brushed his hand over her shoulder, dipping his finger under the fabric behind her neck and making her shiver. "I don't want to be your life coach, either." He pulled her close.

"What do you want?"

The corner of his mouth curved up. "For now? I want to be the guy who makes your bed squeak." He kissed her forehead. "And eats pasta with you"—his mouth moved to her temple—"naked in the middle of the night."

She slid her arms around his neck. She loved the way he felt against her. She loved the solid heat of his body and the way he made her forget all her hang-ups and get lost in the moment.

He pulled her tightly against him.

"We're not naked," she whispered.

"Not yet."

They rode in the unmarked SUV Dax had used for his undercover work, and Talia was impressed. It had a crack in the windshield and fabric sagging down from the ceiling.

"I think this car's older than I am," she said.

Dax glanced at her. "You could be right."

They turned onto Sixth Street, and she looked around. Partygoers spilled out of the bars and clustered on street corners. Chalkboard signs advertised musical acts and cover charges. Talia took it all in. Thursday was a big night, evidently. Or maybe this was every night. She didn't hang out in Austin's bar district.

A pedicab swerved in front of them, and Dax slammed on the brakes. The driver shot him the bird.

"You been here lately?" Dax looked at her.

"I haven't."

"Neighborhood's changed a lot. More hotels, restaurants. Everything's gotten pricier."

He continued down the street, passing clusters of young people milling outside bars.

"So, tell me about your TO."

Talia looked at him. "Who?"

"Nolan Hess. He's your training officer, isn't he?"

Dax had been doing his homework.

"More or less," she said. "What about him?"

"You like him?"

She narrowed her gaze. "Why?"

"I'm wondering what his rep is. He used to work for us, you know."

Obviously, he'd heard the rumors about why Nolan left APD. Talia had heard, too, and she knew they were crap.

"Nolan's solid," she said simply, and left it at that.

Dax hung a right into a narrow alley, then turned right again. Graffiti covered the walls on either side of them. He reached a corner and rolled to a stop. Looking down the side street, Talia spotted a blue neon sign on the corner.

"Blue Brew," she said.

"You been there?"

"No, but I've heard of it."

He looked at her.

"I like blues music," she said. "I keep up."

Why did she feel the need to back up her claim? Maybe because she didn't want him to think she was limited just because she lived in a town where the nightlife consisted of a two-screen movie theater.

Talia turned her attention to the bar, where a line of people waited out front.

"She was seen there by the bouncer?" she asked.

"That's right. Around eleven thirty."

Dax continued down the narrow alley. He passed a Dumpster, and Talia clutched her door as he missed it by maybe half an inch. At the corner, he hung another right and pulled over in a no-parking zone. They'd made a loop and were facing Sixth Street again.

"Bouncer at Blue Brew wouldn't let her in," Dax said. "Didn't like her ID."

"It was fake."

"Right. And it wasn't even hers. Belonged to one of her friends. But *that* bouncer wasn't the last to see her. Bouncer at *this* place"—Dax pointed through the windshield—"Sullivan's Pub, he claims he saw her walking *away* from Blue Brew toward the hotel where she was staying. He said a white Tahoe pulled over, and she got inside."

"He said that? She just 'got inside'?"

"He said that's what it looked like. They had a short conversation, and she got into the vehicle."

Talia shook her head. "That's the part I don't understand. Why would she get a ride with some random guy?"

"Happens all the time."

"Yeah, but we're talking about a college

356

student. She's smart, supposedly. And she's not from here, so you'd think she'd be cautious, not just hop into a car with some stranger."

"You did."

She looked at him.

"You barely know me."

She scoffed. "I'm armed."

"So am I."

"And I'm a black belt in tae kwon do. I could take you out in a heartbeat."

He smiled. "You think so?"

"I know so."

He shook his head. "My point is, I'm a cop, so you think you can trust me, but that's all it takes to get you in my car."

"What's all it takes?"

"Some bullshit reason to trust someone."

Talia looked across the street, disconcerted by the whole conversation. A giant slab of a man stood outside Sullivan's Pub checking IDs.

"Is he the one?" Talia asked.

"No, the guy's off tonight."

"And Grace was standing on that corner there?"

"Yeah, right across the street. He remembers both the driver *and* Grace."

"And this bouncer is sure it was her? You interviewed him?"

"Yeah, you know, I thought I might, since he's a witness in my case and all."

She ignored the sarcasm. "After we get our

sketch tomorrow, I'll send you a picture. You can run it past your guy and see if it matches the Tahoe driver he saw with Grace."

"No need. We've already got a sketch."

"You do?"

"Witness sat down with a forensic artist this afternoon and came up with a picture. It's good, too. Lot of detail."

"You're kidding me."

"Nope. Not kidding," he said. "As of five o'clock today, we have a sketch of the unsub, and you're welcome to it."

CHAPTER 24

Grace was living on anger, raw and pure.

She sawed the twine, ignoring the warm ooze of blood sliding down her arm. Blood was good. It meant she was alive. Her heart was still beating, so she hadn't died and started to decompose in this godforsaken pit.

Scritch scratch scratch.

Grace strained against the bindings.

Scritch scratch scratch.

She gritted her teeth and pulled.

Scritch scratch scratch.

She rested her cheek in the dirt, struggling not to cry as she grasped for the strength to keep going, to keep making little, tiny scratches. The effort left her exhausted. Worn-out. Drained of even the slightest drop of energy.

He can't win.

She took a breath and tried to make her fingers move again, tiny cuts with the flake of rock, but she couldn't seem to move. It felt like an eternity since she'd started scratching at this damn twine. It felt like even longer since she'd eaten. Or had a sip of water. Just the thought of food made her stomach clench. And then it filled with hot, churning rage.

Don't let him win.

She gripped the flake of rock again.

Scritch scratch scratch.

No food, no water. Had he forgotten her here? Had he left her to suffer a slow, wasting death? The prospect filled her with panic. She imagined her skin rotting. She imagined ants and rats and dung beetles swarming over her and feeding on her flesh.

Scritch scratch—

Movement.

Grace pulled her wrists, straining against the twine.

Scritch scratch scratch.

She pulled again, and suddenly—*whoosh!*

Her hands were free. She pulled the twine away and moved her arms, flailing them in disbelief. She jerked the gag from her mouth and pulled it over her chin. Her mouth was bone-dry, but she spat angrily at the ground, desperate to be rid of the taste.

She was *free.*

Grace sat up and instantly fell back, conking her head on the hard ground. She felt dizzy. Breathless. Just that one effort seemed to sap her energy.

Rolling onto her side, she tried again, slowly pushing herself up onto her sore elbow.

She'd done it. She'd really done it. Her hands were free. Her arms were free. Her mouth was free.

Grace's heart raced as she groped around the floor of the cave. *Think.* She'd had a plan. She'd had one. She tried to clear the cobwebs from her brain as she struggled to get it back.

Her hand encountered a torn gel packet, and she snatched it up, licking it desperately, even though she knew it was empty.

Nothing.

She flung the packet away, and her plan came back to her. She had to get out of here. *That* was the plan.

He always approached on her right side, so the entrance to this cave or pit or cavern, or whatever it was, was in that direction. She shifted her body and tried to stand, but her legs quivered, and pain shot up from her hip.

Crawling, then. She could crawl.

She forced herself to her hands and knees and managed a short lurch forward. And another. And another. She groped through the darkness, reaching her hand in front of her for any obstacles. After she shuffled along for a few feet, she encountered the cool wall of the cave. She brushed her fingertips over it, taking in the bumpy texture. She used it for a guide as she crawled along the floor. Rock bit into her knees, but it felt good. And terrifying. She was moving, finally, after days and days and days of being cemented in one place.

Something brushed her shoulder, and she jerked back.

A spiderweb? A spider?

She felt the wall and decided to try to stand again. Slowly, carefully, she got to her feet, leaning her hands against the wall for support. Her legs felt feeble, but they seemed to work. Nothing broken. Keeping her palm against the cool stone, she made her way through the blackness.

Icy tentacles of fear slithered through her body and curled around her heart. She couldn't see a thing. She longed for a flashlight or a candle or even a matchstick. Just a brief flare of light would mean hope. But there was nothing, only inky darkness.

Grace concentrated on her breathing as she shuffled forward. In. Out. In. Out. The ground beneath her bare feet was cool and hard and damp in some spots, probably from dew or ground-water dripping down from above. This had to be a cave. And it had to have an opening. She only hoped she'd picked the right direction when she set out. What if she hadn't? What if she'd taken the wrong path? What if she fell into a pit? What if she was moving deeper and deeper into an endless cavern, and she got lost and never found her way out?

Shut up, Grace. Just shut the fuck up and move.

She shuffled along, and the ground seemed to be sloping down. Gravity helping her. Or maybe her quivery legs were working better as she got her circulation going.

What would happen when she reached the opening? It was nighttime. She knew that. The bats were out now, hunting for food. Grace peered into the blackness, wishing for the slightest glimmer of moon or stars—anything to guide her.

Snick.

She halted. The hair on the back of her neck prickled as she listened. Was it a bat? A predator?

Him?

She listened closely, but there was only silence. She waited a long moment, then started moving again, feeling her way.

Closing her eyes, she said a silent prayer. *Our Father, who art in heaven, get me out of this hellhole. Show me the way. Our Father, who art in heaven, get me out of this hellhole. Show me the way.*

Grace stopped. She felt something. The air was different here. Not as still and stagnant. It smelled like . . . cedar. Or juniper. She didn't know exactly, but it was trees or grass, something fresh. Hope surged through her, and she hurried her steps.

Our Father, who art—

Her foot slipped. She lurched forward, trying to

catch herself. She expected the ground to hit her. But it never came, and she instantly knew she'd picked the wrong way.

A rusty scream tore from her throat as she fell into the void.

CHAPTER 25

Sara awoke slowly to the sound of a phone. It wasn't hers.

She shook off the fog and looked across the room to see Nolan's leather jacket draped over the armchair. He was here. In the shower, from the sound of it.

She pulled on her robe and padded to the kitchen. She needed caffeine to clear the haze. As she measured out coffee grounds, she thought about everything that had happened.

She'd invited Nolan home with her.

He'd spent the night.

For the first time in years, she'd let her guard down with a man and delved way too deep into stuff from her past. She should probably feel self-conscious or maybe regretful, but she didn't feel either of those things. She felt . . . light.

His phone beeped again, and she eyed it on the counter. The shower went off. Then the bathroom door opened and closed, and she heard him moving around but resisted the temptation to watch him dress. A minute later, he appeared in the living room shirtless and barefoot, jeans unsnapped. He snagged his shirt off the floor and glanced at her as he slid his arms into the sleeves.

"Someone's pinging you," she said. "Coffee?"

"Yeah." He walked over, buttoning up. "I borrowed your razor."

She smiled, picturing him using her dainty pink razor. "No problem. Cream? Sugar?"

"You don't have cream."

"I don't?" She checked the fridge and discovered he was right.

She poured two mugs and handed him one. He kissed her forehead before taking a sip.

"I'm running late," he said. "I can drive you to work, but it needs to be soon."

"I'm supposed to pick up my car at nine. Kelsey said she'd take me."

His phone beeped again, and he walked over to check it, tucking in his shirttail as he read. He frowned and muttered a curse.

"What's wrong?"

"Nothing." He shook his head. "The case is heating up."

"What's that mean?"

He scrolled through a text, then looked over at her. "Austin's come through with something. A possible sketch of our suspect."

"Really?"

"This happened last night." He kept scrolling. "Talia's bringing it to the task force meeting."

"I want to see it."

"Huh?" He glanced up.

"The suspect sketch."

"I'll send it to you."

He crossed the room and picked up his shoes and socks from the floor. He sank onto an armchair and quickly put them on. Clearly, he was late for something important, and this was exactly the scenario she'd worried about: his work needed him, and he was with her, a hundred miles away.

He grabbed his belt and holster off the coffee table. As he threaded the belt through the loops, she remembered unbuckling it last night. He picked up the handcuffs off the table and looked at her as he tucked them into place.

"You working this weekend?" he asked.

"Probably. Why?"

He walked over and slid his hand around her waist, sending a ripple of heat through her. "I'm slammed, but I'd like to see you. I don't know when, though. Feels like things are coming to a head." He released her and grabbed his jacket. "Can I call you when I know my timing?"

"Yeah." Nerves tightened her stomach as she followed him to the door and flipped the latch. "Or even if you don't." She paused awkwardly. "Call me anyway."

He bent down and kissed her. "I will."

When he was gone, Sara returned to the kitchen

and picked up her coffee. She sipped it absently as she replayed their rushed conversation.

Thing were heating up, coming to a head. There was a suspect sketch.

He was slammed with work, and still he wanted to see her.

She looked at her rumpled bed and pictured Nolan in it. The two pillows were bunched together in the middle because they'd spent the night curled up together.

And it hit her.

There was no heading this off. It had already happened. Whatever this was, she was in it.

Her downstairs buzzer sounded, and she looked at the intercom. Was he back? He wouldn't come back—he was late. Maybe he'd forgotten something.

She crossed to the intercom and pressed the button. "Yes?"

"Hi, it's Alex. Can I come up?"

"Uh, sure." Sara checked her watch and buzzed her in. What would Alex be doing here at eight in the morning? Sara threw on some clothes and smoothed her hair as she opened the door.

Alex was striding down the hallway. She wore her usual jeans and T-shirt and had her computer bag on her shoulder.

"Sorry to bug you so early, but this couldn't wait."

"No problem."

She stopped in front of Sara and gave her a puzzled look. "Weirdest thing, I could have sworn I just saw Nolan's truck on your street."

Sara opened her mouth to say something but couldn't think of a thing.

"Oh, my God. Was he *here?*"

"He just left." Sara ushered her inside. "You want some coffee?" Before Alex could answer, Sara went into the kitchen and started pouring a mug.

Alex's grin faded as she set her computer bag on the counter. "Well, that's interesting."

Sara slid the mug across the counter. "It is." She took a deep breath. "I think I just did something stupid."

Alex laughed. "I bet it was worth it."

"No, the sex part definitely was, but I think . . ." She rubbed her forehead. "I think I might have just started a relationship."

"Hmm. And?"

"*And* . . . and he's a workaholic cop who lives nowhere near me! This will never work out." She combed her hands into her hair. "And he's an unbelievably *good* man, and one of us is going to end up disappointed. What the hell am I doing, Alex?"

She gave Sara a sympathetic look.

"Forget it. Let's not talk about me." Sara held up her hands. "Let's talk about whatever you have that couldn't wait."

Alex unzipped her computer bag. "I've been investigating that drone footage, and I found something interesting." She took out her laptop and powered it up. "After tracing the digital footprints of the user who set up these two Twitter accounts, I'm more convinced than ever that he's our unsub."

"Why?"

"He's got some disturbing tastes in porn. This goes beyond the run-of-the-mill BDSM stuff. He frequents sites that serve up violence and snuff films."

"As in people being murdered?"

"Correct."

"Can we identify him?"

"I'm working on it. I've got Laney working on it, too, because she specializes in the dark web. But in the meantime, I wanted to show you this."

Sara leaned closer for a better view.

"Digging around, I found another video clip," Alex said. "This one is longer than the others."

"Okay."

"It's only a few more seconds of footage—twelve, to be exact—but it reveals something interesting."

Alex clicked open a file of video footage. This clip started low to the ground, near some mesquite trees.

"There." She hit pause. "See that?"

Sara leaned closer. "What?"

"That black glove. That's his hand in the shot. See? He's standing right there."

Sara saw that there was, indeed, a gloved hand on the edge of the picture.

Alex resumed the clip, and the camera lifted into the air, giving more of a bird's-eye view. The ground below whisked by as the drone swooped over parched land dotted with scrub trees. Suddenly, the land dropped away, and Sara recognized Rattlesnake Gorge. A few moments later, the blue tent came into view, and from there all the footage was familiar.

"This longer clip shows the drone actually being launched," Alex said. "Thing is, that property it was launched from? It's not part of the park. It's private property, and I checked out the satellite images. Whoever owns the land has livestock, along with some oil and gas wells. It's all gated and fenced."

Livestock. Oil and gas wells. Sara thought of her conversation with Will Merritt about the location of the caves he'd visited.

"Do you know if there are any caves on this property?" she asked Alex.

"Caves?"

"It's a theory we're investigating. We know he kept some of the victims captive somewhere, and trace evidence suggests it could have been a cave."

"I don't know."

"And the thing about the gates," Sara said. "How can you tell all that from the drone footage?"

"You can't. I called a friend of mine in the Allen County sheriff's office and asked him to do a drive-by. He said the place is locked up. Tall game fence, heavy-duty locks on the gates. You can't just wander in there and launch a drone."

"But he did, so you're saying . . ."

"I think whoever launched this drone camera is the unsub. And I bet he owns this property or knows who does."

Grace's eyes drifted open. A blade of sunlight cut into her skull. She closed her eyes and tried to turn away, but her head seemed to explode.

She sucked in a breath and felt razors slicing into her side.

She'd fallen. She'd broken . . . something. At least a few ribs. She tried to move her legs. After a moment's resistance, she was able to drag them over the gravel.

She could move her legs.

She was in sunlight.

She turned her head, ignoring the pain as she drank in her surroundings. She was in a pit, surrounded by rock walls. The floor of the pit was shadowed, but a shaft of sunlight fell over her face.

Sun.

Grace tried to push up. But pain tore through her shoulder, and she collapsed. She looked at her wrists, filthy and black and oozing with pus. The wounds were disgusting, the result of days and days of tight bindings.

But the bindings were gone now. She was free. She'd stumbled into a pit, and now she had to get herself out before he discovered she was gone and came looking.

Grace's eyes burned with tears. They were tears of relief, as well as of terror at the thought of him finding her *now* when she was so close to escape.

She took a shallow breath. And another. And another. Bracing herself for the pain, she used her good arm to push herself up. Then she tested her legs. They felt heavy and sore, but with the twine gone, she could move them. She pushed to her knees and leaned on her palm as pain rocketed through her skull and her vision blurred. She probably had a concussion. But that was the least of her problems if she didn't get out of here.

She took another breath and crawled toward the wall of the pit. Slowly. Painfully. An inch at a time across the uneven floor. Puddles of milky water reflected the sky above her—*blue sky.* Her throat felt parched, but she couldn't drink. Not yet. She didn't have time to be sick and puking from contaminated water. She had to get out of here.

He was coming back.

Pebbles cut into her knees as she inched toward the wall. When she finally reached it, she pressed her hand against the stone. It was cool and damp. She slumped against the rock, dizzy from exertion.

Looking up, Grace saw clear blue sky. But it seemed miles away. Light-years.

She wiped the tears from her cheeks. After another shallow breath, she pushed herself to her knees. Her thighs quivered. Grace gripped the stone and pulled herself up.

Nolan shot backward out of his driveway. He was going to be late, but he'd needed to stop home and change. He couldn't show up for work in the shirt he'd worn yesterday, which had obviously spent the night on somebody's floor.

Cruising down his street, he thought of Sara. Her last relationship had done a number on her. Her jilted fiancé had made her feel guilty for following her instincts and planted the idea in her head that she was bad at relationships. Now she questioned her own judgment—which Nolan recognized, because he'd done the same after Michelle. Sara was wary, and Nolan didn't want to push. But he wanted to show her she could trust him.

It was ironic, really. Being with someone deceitful had made Nolan more determined to listen to his instincts when it came to people. His instincts told him Sara was special and they were special together. He just hoped *she* realized it eventually and didn't put her guard up again.

Nolan wanted to see her tonight. Or at least talk to her. Seeing her was definitely better, but he had the distinct feeling his day was going to go sideways.

Nolan neared the church on the corner and spotted Reverend Cook in the parking lot. He had been trying to reach the man since Wednesday. Nolan glanced at his watch and cursed, then whipped into the parking lot and pulled into a space. Cook paused on the sidewalk as Nolan hopped out.

"Detective Hess." Cook offered him a handshake.

"Morning, Reverend. I've been trying to reach you. Left a couple of messages with your staff?"

"Oh." He made a face. "Sorry about that. Betsy's getting a little . . . forgetful. It's become a bit of a dilemma for us."

Nolan nodded. "Got it. Listen, I need to touch base on something. I was talking to Elaine Hansen, and I had a question about her donation last year."

"Todd Hansen's widow?"

"That's right. She mentioned she donated Todd's car after he died. A white Chevy Tahoe. I need to find out where it went from here."

"Here?"

"After she donated it to you guys."

"*Elaine* Hansen?"

"That's right."

The reverend shook his head. "We got a sofa from Elaine. And a few bags of clothes, if I recall, but she didn't donate a vehicle."

"You sure? You want to check your records or—"

"I'm quite sure. We don't get many vehicle donations, as you can imagine. Now, the sofa I remember quite vividly. We put it in our recreation hall, where our youth group meets."

Nolan just looked at him. "You're sure Elaine Hansen never donated a white SUV?"

He smiled. "I'm positive."

"Thank you for your time."

Nolan got back into his truck. Why had she lied? And what else had she lied about? Something gnawed at him, a detail he'd meant to follow up on but hadn't. It hadn't seemed important until now. And maybe it wasn't.

He scrolled through his phone and found his list of witnesses in the Kaylin Baird case. He called Maisy Raines.

"Hello?"

"Maisy, this is Detective Hess. You got a minute?"

The cramped lobby smelled of tires, and Sara eyed the clock as she left yet another message for Will Merritt. Why hadn't he called her back? She'd sent him two urgent emails and left a voice mail, but he still hadn't responded. Maybe he'd dropped off the grid again.

She checked her watch and cast an impatient glance into the service bay. Her Explorer looked ready to go, but she was still waiting for the paperwork.

Sara sank into a plastic chair and pulled up the article she'd bookmarked from *Outside* magazine. She clicked Will's name, hoping to be taken to an alternative email address or maybe a social-media link. Instead, she was taken to a list of his articles: "*Big Walls in Big Bend, Mountain Biking Ramps Up, Caves of Central Texas.*"

Sara went still. She skimmed the list, which included articles dating back six years.

"*Free Soloing in Tennessee.*"

Her blood turned cold. She scanned the list again. Big Bend, Central Texas, Tennessee.

"Oh, my *God.*"

Sara jumped to her feet.

Nolan scanned the cars in the parking lot. He'd expected every member of the task force to have beaten him here, but the lot was almost empty.

His phone beeped, and he looked down to see a text from Talia.

On my way in. Task force mtg nixed.

Yeah, no kidding. Where the hell was everyone?

Nolan started to reply, but he got an incoming call from Sara. He picked up.

"Hey, can I call you back?"

"No, listen." Her voice sounded breathless. "Remember the blogger I told you about?"

"No."

"Will Merritt. He writes this blog called *High Life*, and he freelances for *Outside* magazine."

"Okay, yeah. What about him?"

"I was going through his archives, Nolan, reading up on caving. Turns out he's written about dozens of parks in the past six years, including Rocky Shoals in Tennessee plus Big Bend and White Falls in Texas."

Nolan didn't say anything.

"Nolan? You there?"

"Yeah."

"Don't you think that's a bizarre coincidence? I mean, like, too bizarre to even *be* a coincidence?"

"It's interesting."

"That's it? That's all you have to say?"

"Six years is a long time. How many blogs and articles has he written?"

"I don't know. Fifty or sixty that I could find. But *three* of them feature a park where one or more of these victims was discovered or went missing."

"Yeah, and fifty-plus don't. And the West Texas woman didn't go missing from inside a park. She was near one."

"Come on. You need to look into this."

He sighed and checked his watch. "Where are you?" he asked. "It sounds like you're driving."

"I'm headed to Springville. I want to show you the notes from my conversation with this guy. Nolan, I think he's our unsub. He said he was 'off the grid' a few days ago, which is why it took him a while to call me back, and now he's dodging my calls again. I think he might be with Grace!"

"Will Merritt, two *t*'s?"

"*Yes*. He has a blog about extreme outdoor sports, and he works freelance for *Outside* magazine. He fits the profile perfectly, Nolan."

"I'll check him out. Send me the dates on those articles."

"I'll pull over and do it now. Listen, there's something else, too. Alex Lovell stopped by my place this morning with a new lead on the drone footage. You remember from the recovery site?"

"What about it?"

"She thinks the drone was launched from private property adjacent to the park. She thinks the property owner could be our unsub, or maybe he knows the guy and gave him access to the property."

This lead sounded a lot more promising than the blogger.

"You have the address?" Nolan asked.

"I can send it," Sara said. "A sheriff's deputy

did a drive-by, but as far as I know, no one's really checked this out."

"I'll handle it. How far out are you?"

"I don't know. Forty-five minutes, maybe."

"When you get in, go to the police station, all right? I'll meet you over there."

"Okay."

He ended the call.

Sideways, just like he'd thought. He had too much to do to waste his morning waiting around for people, so he got on the highway and called Talia.

"Where are you?" he asked.

"Good morning to you, too."

"How come everyone bagged the meeting?"

"I don't know about everyone," she said. "But Dax Harper is in Austin, Rey Santos got tied up with something in San Antonio, and I'm at Arnie's getting gas."

"Where's the chief?"

"No idea."

Nolan gritted his teeth. "Well, did you interview that clerk?"

"Yes, and he confirms the guy in the Austin police sketch is the same guy he saw."

"Hey, that's great."

"Yeah, what's not great is that APD wants to release this."

"What do you mean?"

"They want to put it on the news and set up a

hotline," she said. "See if we can get an ID from the public."

"What the fuck? That's the fastest way to tip this guy off. We need to circulate this thing locally, see if we can get an ID on him, and then close in on his location before he figures out we're on to him and has a chance to bolt."

"I know. I told them that."

"Damn it. Call Hank. Fill him in on the situation. He's friends with a couple of lieutenants there. Maybe he can convince them to wait."

"That's a good idea. I'll do it."

"And I also need you to call Rey Santos and ask him if he's come across the name Will Merritt anywhere. That's spelled with two *t*'s."

"Who's that?" she asked.

"A magazine writer who did some work in this area. Sara thinks he might be a suspect, and we need to see if he has a sheet."

"Okay, but why don't you call Santos?"

"I'm driving. I'm heading out to the Hansen place to interview the widow again. Everything she told me in our interview is crap, and I want to know why she lied to me."

"You think she's protecting someone?"

"If she is, I'll find out," he said. "And send me that sketch, would you? If he's local, I might recognize him."

"I didn't."

"I've lived here longer than you have."

"Okay, let me get Hank to lean on APD, then I'll work on the rest."

They clicked off, and Nolan trained his gaze on the road. His pulse was thrumming like it did when a case started to come together.

The unsub regularly bought gas at Arnie's, which meant he probably lived nearby. It was a stronger lead than the magazine writer, but he'd promised Sara he'd look into it, along with the lead about the ranch near the park. But first he needed to follow his gut, and at the moment his gut was telling him there was something extremely off about this thing with the widow.

Elaine Hansen had lied about donating an SUV to her church. She'd lied about having a receipt from Cook. And if Maisy Raines was to be believed, she'd lied about seeing Kaylin Baird at the movies with her "boyfriend" Tristan Sharp. Maisy swore Kaylin and Tristan had never been a couple.

Nolan tried to recall what he knew about the Hansens, but it wasn't much. Todd Hansen had died last year, and he remembered they had a daughter, but she would have been ahead of him in school.

The Hansen place was on the outskirts of town, where the houses sat fairly far apart. Still, people tended to know their neighbors. Nolan hung a right at the mailbox and scanned the driveway, half expecting the phantom white SUV to be parked there. It wasn't. Neither was the green VW. He eyed the garage, which he had assumed was used for the Mustang Todd kept on cinder blocks.

He parked and got out. Glancing at the shed and then the house, he decided to try the shed first. The flimsy door stood ajar.

"Mrs. Hansen?" He tapped lightly on the door with the back of his knuckles, and it swung open. "Elaine?"

He stepped inside the makeshift studio, which was hot and stuffy. The potter's wheel sat silently in the center. A low creaking noise drew his attention to a kiln in the corner. A glowing red light indicated the kiln was on, accounting for the heat. Nolan's gaze landed on some blocks of clay wrapped in plastic along the wall. Several of the bags were tied with purple twine.

Nolan stared at the bags, then looked around the room at the stool, the workbench, and the shelf lined with potter's tools. Someone had tacked pegs into the wall, and from one of them dangled a twisted wire with wooden handles on the ends.

Nolan's pulse pounded as he stepped closer. The thick wire was kinked from use. The wooden handles were smooth and rounded and smeared with dried clay. In strong hands, the wire could slice through a block of clay like butter.

He imagined what it could do to human flesh.

Nolan slid his phone from his pocket and dialed Dispatch. In a low voice, he relayed the situation and requested backup, then switched his ringer to silent.

Unsnapping his holster, he left the shed and approached the house. With his hand on the butt of his gun, he scanned the bushes and trees, then checked the windows for any sign of movement. As he mounted the steps to the front porch, muffled barks erupted behind the door. Lucy's face appeared at the window as she barked and pawed at the glass.

His phone vibrated, and he checked the screen before answering.

"It's too late," Talia said.

"What's too late?"

"Hank called, but they'd already released it. The sketch. It went on the news half an hour ago."

Nolan peered through a window. The house was dark and still, except for the frantic dog. Lucy tracked him as he walked to the other end of the porch and looked through the breakfast-room window.

"Dax tells me tips are pouring in," Talia said, "but it's going to take an army to sort through them all."

A light was on in the kitchen. The back door stood open, and Nolan could see through the screen door and into the backyard. The TV on the kitchen counter was on, and a saucepan on the stove was bubbling over. Rice? Grits? Looked like someone had been here recently but left in a hurry.

"I can't believe they released it," Talia was saying. "If he sees it, he'll be in the wind, Nolan."

His gaze returned to the television as a police sketch appeared on the screen. Nolan squinted through the glass. The face in the picture hit him like a sucker punch.

"No fucking *way*," he muttered.

"What is it?"

"I know him."

CHAPTER 26

The pit was taller than Grace. But not by much. If she could just get a foothold, she might be able to pull herself up and out. Grace took a series of shallow breaths. One. Two. Three. No deep breaths, or it felt like slivers of glass cutting into her lungs.

She grasped the rock, then planted her foot on a bump in the stone. Bracing for the pain, she pulled herself up, then planted another foot on a small ledge. Squeezing her eyes against the hurt, she pulled herself up and reached for another handhold.

Grace looked down, breathing hard. Her shoulder was on fire. Sweat streamed down her neck, and she was plastered to the cool stone. Her feet were bare—her whole body was bare—but the lack of shoes seemed to be helping as she curled her toes over the rock.

She looked up and squinted at the sunlight. Ignoring the burn in her side, she reached up and grasped a weed dangling down from the edge of the pit. It felt flimsy, so she groped around some more, and her fingers closed around something thick and ropy, like a tree root. Praying it would hold her weight, she pulled up.

Please, please, please, God. You owe me.

Her foot slipped, and she gasped, clinging to the root and the wall with every fiber of her being. She hung there, heart pounding, as she moved her foot around, looking for a bump in the rock. She found one and used it to lever herself up while at the same time reaching her arm over the ledge.

Thorns and grass pricked her skin. Tears burned her eyes again, but they were tears of joy this time—joy and disbelief, as she heaved her body up and threw her leg over the ledge. Clawing at roots and weeds, she dragged herself across the ground and rolled onto her back.

She blinked up at the sky. Tears and snot and spit slid down her face as she lay there, squinting at the brightness.

She turned her gaze to the cliffs. The tall limestone rock face was a creamy white in the morning sun. Trees lined the top. It looked like a slab of cake with green frosting, and just the thought made her stomach yearn.

Food. Soon. If she could just find the energy to stand up and move. But every limb felt like it weighed a thousand pounds.

A low rumble sent a jolt of fear through her. A car. She rolled over and scrambled to her feet. Glancing around frantically, she took in her surroundings for the first time. There was a cliff beside her. And scraggly trees all around. The engine noise grew louder. In a panic, Grace lunged behind one of the trees, yelping as she stubbed her toe on something hard.

She knelt behind the bushes, clutching her hurt shoulder and peering through the branches as a little green car came into view and pulled over. Grace cowered lower and glanced around, but this clump of trees was the best cover out here. The car door popped open, and Grace held her breath as someone got out.

A woman, thank God. Relief flooded her. The woman looked old, too, with curly gray hair in a loose bun on top of her head. She reminded Grace of her grandmother. As she walked around the car, Grace stood up and stepped toward her.

"Are you *crazy?*" the woman shrieked.

Grace froze.

"Have you *lost* your *mind?*" Her voice was shrill and piercing, and Grace stood paralyzed as she realized there was someone else nearby.

A low male voice answered, and Grace swayed on her feet. *Him.* She ducked back behind the tree and crouched as low as she could, trying to melt into the rock.

Her heart jackhammered. She couldn't hear what they were saying. Didn't even try. She was too petrified to move or think or do anything but try to be invisible.

The volume escalated. Grace pictured the blue eyes, the twisted mouth, the skin that looked ghoulish in the flashlight beam. Her chest convulsed, and she couldn't breathe as the voices got louder.

"You idiot! You ungrateful, worthless—"

Thunk.

Grace registered the sickening sound of rock against flesh, then a body hitting the ground.

Then nothing.

Grace didn't pause to think or plan or even breathe. She turned and ran.

Talia called Nolan from her car.

"Where are you?" he demanded.

"On my way. I just got off with Santos."

"What's he got?"

"Bryce Michael Gaines, age twenty-five."

"Younger than we thought."

"Yep. And you're right, the police sketch they're running is pretty good." Talia flipped through her scribbled notes as she drove. "Mother, Katherine *Hansen* Gaines. Looks like she had Bryce when she was eighteen. She was arrested for possession of narcotics, let's see . . . age twenty. Died of an overdose that same year."

Nolan cursed on the other end of the phone. "So he was raised by his grandparents. The widow knew something was up, and she was covering for him. That's why she lied to me."

"That's speculation, but yeah, that's what it looks like. You want the rest of this?"

"Yeah."

"If Bryce has any juvie charges, I don't have them yet, but from Google, I learned he graduated from high school here in town and got a scholarship to Belleview Bible College in western Tennessee. He didn't last a year."

"Expelled?"

"I called the college, thinking maybe I could get something about an on-campus assault, rape, cheating, whatever, but the college would only tell me he withdrew from school for undisclosed reasons. Few months later—this was five years ago—he was arrested in Rocky Shoals Park for illegal camping."

"Timing works."

"I know." Talia flipped a page. "Then he dropped off the radar for a while. Santos has an arrest for him three years later on a DUI in Maverick, near Big Bend National Park. And get this, a ranger out there knows him."

"You're kidding."

"Santos talked to this guy. He caught Gaines sleeping in his car in the park a few times. Felt sorry for him. Helped him get some work inside the park doing odd jobs. Apparently, he was pretty good at the work, because this ranger later recommended him for their summer internship program. He didn't make the cut, and then he disappeared. This was three years ago. Guy said he hasn't seen him or heard from him since."

"Yeah, that's about when we got him," Nolan said. "He joined Allen County Search and Rescue that same year."

"How did that happen, anyway? Doesn't ACSAR vet its people?"

"No idea. But even if they do, it's probably not thorough. Illegal camping isn't a felony. Neither is sleeping in your car."

"I bet he did some shit at that college, and that's why they kicked him out."

"Yeah, well, if it was sexual assault, it probably got swept under the rug and wouldn't be on record. Anyway, I talked to ACSAR," Nolan said. "They haven't seen him since last weekend, when he rescued a pair of dehydrated hikers up in Dove Canyon. Nobody's heard from him since."

Talia spotted the turnoff and shifted lanes. "Question is, where is he now?"

"We're working on it," Nolan said. "We're taking this place apart."

"You got a search warrant already?"

"Exigent circumstances."

He meant Grace Murray. If there was a chance they might find her alive, they could let themselves in and look around.

"What have you found?" Talia asked.

"So far, zilch. We've got a hysterical mutt closed up in the utility room, a car up on blocks in the garage, and an empty house. Elaine Hansen is missing, and so are her other vehicles. We've got an APB out for her Volkswagen and the Chevy."

"I'm almost there," Talia said. "And be on the lookout for Dax Harper. He's on his way, too."

"Tell him to step on it. We need all the help we can get."

Sara bumped along the gravel road, looking for any sign of a low-water bridge. This was the right place. Had to be. A mile back, she'd passed some pumpjacks and then a sleepy herd of black cows with white stripes down the middle. Oreo cows.

She checked the map on her cell phone. But she wasn't getting service, and it still wouldn't refresh. She curved around a bend, and her pulse sped up as a low-water bridge came into view. She followed the dip in the road, then passed through a narrow canyon. As the walls sloped down, she took a hopeful look at her phone. Bars. *Finally.*

A gate came into view, and Sara pulled over. This had to be the place. She got out of her car and glanced around. Everything looked right—the ground, the trees, the craggy cliffs rising up to her left. There had to be caves nearby, the very caves Will Merritt had written about and possibly where he'd held his victims.

Sara grabbed her phone and called Nolan.

It went straight to voice mail, so she searched through her contacts and found Talia.

"Hey, it's Sara Lockhart," she said. "I'm trying to reach Nolan. Any chance he's with you?"

"Yeah, he's a little busy right now. We ID'd our suspect, and we're conducting a search of his house."

"You mean . . . it's official? You've identified Will Merritt?"

"Merritt? No, Bryce Gaines. He's local."

Sara's blood ran cold. She pictured the lanky rescue worker with the friendly blue eyes who'd lent her his rappelling helmet. "Bryce Gaines, the S-and-R guy?"

"Yeah, he's been ID'd by several witnesses, including a bouncer in Austin. His sketch is all over the news. You didn't know?"

"No, I—" She glanced down at her phone and saw she'd missed a call from Nolan. Had he gotten her message? She'd told him to meet her here with backup, but it sounded like he was sidetracked. *Shit.*

"Talia, listen to me. I think I know where Grace is," Sara said. "I think he took her to a cave complex not far from the park."

"Where?"

"Just east of White Falls. I'm out on Red Hawk Road, and we need to get a search team here ASAP, including a tracking dog—"

Her gaze fell on a man who stood on the side of

the road, watching her. Sara's stomach dropped. It was Bryce Gaines. He must have sneaked up on her while she'd been focused on her phone call. He stood less than twenty feet away, and he held something black in his hand. A stun gun? A pistol?

Sara's throat went dry. It was a stun gun. But she was no less afraid. She'd seen what those could do to a body.

"Hello?" Talia's voice sounded small and distant. "Sara?"

"He's here."

"What? Who's there?"

He stepped toward her, and she took a step back.

"Bryce," she croaked, as it all fell into place. "Talia, he's *here!*"

He stepped closer. "Give me the phone, Sara."

"It was *you.* You were the local guide who took him around."

She clutched the phone in her hand like a weapon and took another step back. A distraction. She needed a distraction.

She stepped back again. "You showed him the caves, didn't you? Where's Grace?"

His mouth curved into an eerie smile. And then he lunged.

Sara brought her fist up, smashing his chin but dropping the phone. He grabbed her arm, but she wrenched free and lurched away. She stumbled and ran, screaming at the top of her lungs. Adrenaline flooded her as her limbic system kicked into gear, and she sprinted as fast as she could, as fast as her legs would move with her thin leather sandals slowing her down.

Sara's heart galloped inside her chest. His footsteps slapped behind her, getting closer and closer, even as she ran so hard she thought her lungs would burst.

Fire blazed through her. She dropped to her knees. Another searing burst, and then there was nothing.

CHAPTER 27

Nolan raced down the highway, gripping the steering wheel until his knuckles burned.

"How much farther?" He shot a look at Talia.

"Uhh . . ." She fiddled with the map on her phone. "As the crow flies, only about a mile. But we've got to go around this whole pasture and—"

"Lemme see."

She showed him the phone with their route highlighted in red.

Nolan stomped on the brakes and skidded to a halt. He threw the truck in reverse, shot backward, then threw it into drive and hit the gas. "Hold on."

"What the— *Nolan!*"

The engine roared as they burst through the barbed-wire fence, scaring up a flock of birds perched in a nearby mesquite tree.

"What are you *doing?*"

"Cutting through the pasture."

They bumped and lurched over the uneven terrain, hitting rocks and ruts. Nolan swerved around a giant prickly pear cactus. His heart felt like it was about to pound out of his chest as he thought of Sara. She'd been in the middle of a conversation about Bryce Gaines, and Talia had heard a struggle, then the call cut off.

He had her. Nolan felt it in his bones.

They hit a rut and pitched down, then up again. Nolan's head jerked forward with a tooth-rattling snap. He looked at Talia beside him, gripping the door.

"Don't look at me! *Drive!*" she yelled.

Nolan pressed the gas again, navigating the terrain as best he could, swerving around bushes and cacti. In the distance, a line of trees came into view, paralleling a barbed-wire fence.

"That has to be it," he said. "Red Hawk Road."

Sara's body throbbed. She opened her eyes, then immediately closed them as pain ricocheted through her.

Bryce Gaines.

The name echoed inside her head.

He has Grace.

Sara sat up, wincing. Every cell, every nerve in her body was on fire. She looked around. She was surrounded by bushes. She wasn't in the road anymore, but she could see it, maybe ten feet away at the top of an incline. How the hell had she gotten here? Glancing down, she realized her hands were tied.

Sara stared at the purple bindings with shock. She tried to move her hands, but the bindings were too tight. Her ankles were bound, too. She glanced around frantically, then looked at the bindings again with disbelief as she remembered the autopsy photos.

A hot wave of rage washed over her.

"Fuck. You," she whispered. She went after the twine with her teeth. Gnawing and biting, she tried desperately to get through the cordage.

A distant noise.

She stopped. Her heart thrummed as she listened. Had she imagined it?

The noise was back, louder now, and it was definitely an engine. It was coming closer. It was coming *here*. Sara craned her neck to look at the road, and another shock hit her as she saw her black Explorer speeding toward her.

Holy, holy, holy hell. He was going to, what, abduct her in her own vehicle? Use it to dump her body somewhere . . . and then take off? He needed a getaway car now that his face and his white SUV were plastered all over the news.

She couldn't run or hide, so instead, she played dead. She was motionless, completely still, until she could find a time to strike.

The Explorer skidded to a halt. She listened as the door opened and closed. Footsteps on the gravel. The cargo door squeaked open.

Fear gripped her. He was going to do it. He was going to load her in the back and take her . . . where? To his cave?

Sara's heart squeezed. She broke out in a cold sweat.

Footsteps again. Getting closer. Closer. She kept her eyes shut and tried to make her face blank. She was unconscious. Inert. Harmless.

He reached down, and Sara's heart skipped. He wedged his hands under her shoulders and knees. With a low grunt, he heaved her up. She remained still, dead weight, even as her mind was racing a mile a minute. She had to do something.

In the distance, another noise.

A car? A truck? *Please, God.*

He halted. Did he hear it, too?

His grip tightened, and he moved faster, hauling her up the incline, which meant he was nearing the road.

Sara fisted her hands together and thrust them into his face.

"Fuck!"

She bucked and threw an elbow as she crashed to the ground, knocking her head against something that felt like a thousand needles.

"Fucking *bitch.*"

She brought her legs up, kicking at his knees and his groin, as he cursed her and reached for her again.

She nailed him between the legs, and he bent over, gasping. Sara logrolled away. Then the ground fell out from under her, and she careened down a hill.

• • •

Nolan plowed through the fence and fishtailed as he turned onto the road. He hit the gas, glancing around for a black Explorer, a white Tahoe, a green Volkswagen.

"Nolan, *look!*"

He slammed on the brakes as he spotted a glint of something behind a tree. A windshield.

"That's the VW," he told Talia. "We're close."

"Why is it parked there?"

"It's not parked, it's hidden." Nolan sped up again, searching the road ahead for any more cars or people. Where the hell was Sara? His palms were slick on the steering wheel as he pictured her with Bryce.

He spotted a rusted pumpjack up ahead. Nolan scanned the pastures on either side of him and saw a trio of cows lazing under a tree.

"We're getting close," he said. "It's around here."

"How do you know?"

"The oil wells, the black-and-white cows. This is what Sara wanted to show us. There are caves near here."

Up ahead on the road was a cloud of dust. A vehicle was speeding toward them.

"There!" Nolan pointed. "Look, that's her."

"Are you sure?"

He tried to make out the shape of the driver behind the wheel.

"Shit. No, it's him."

Nolan's gut clenched. *Where was Sara?* The Explorer sped closer.

"Hang on."

He stomped on the brake and yanked the wheel right, blocking the road. There was a screech of tires and then a deafening crunch of metal as the Explorer slammed into the back of his truck.

Nolan unlatched his seat belt and looked at Talia. "You okay?"

She nodded dazedly.

He shoved open the door, drawing his weapon as he jumped out. The Explorer's airbag had deployed, and the driver's-side door was open.

A blur of movement at the back of his truck caught his eye.

"Freeze! Police!" he boomed.

"On the ground!" Talia yelled.

Nolan heard scuffling on the other side of the Explorer. He darted around it as Gaines tried to make a dash for some trees.

Nolan raised his weapon. Gaines tripped into a ditch. Nolan bolted after him, landing on top of him and jamming a knee into his back. He shoved his forearm against the back of the man's neck and aimed his gun at his spine.

"Hold him, I've got cuffs!" Talia yelled, leaping down into the ditch with a pair of handcuffs in hand.

Nolan yanked Gaines's arms behind his back, and Talia slapped the bracelets on.

"Where is she?" Nolan demanded.

He didn't respond. Nolan jumped to his feet, leaving the prisoner facedown in the ditch. He nodded at Talia, a few feet away now. She had her Glock in a two-handed grip, aimed straight at Gaines's back.

"Keep a bead on him," Nolan ordered.

He leaped out of the ditch and ran back to the Explorer. He raced around it, checking the windows, and jerked open the cargo door. His heart felt like it dropped out of his chest when he saw a woman curled up in a ball.

But it wasn't Sara.

Grace peered around the tree where she'd been hiding. She struggled to her feet and took a few wobbly steps. Pain shot up her ankle, and she knew she'd injured it. She felt light-headed. Disoriented. She'd heard the car crash, then doors opening and closing. What was happening? She wanted to yell for help, but what if he came back and found her? She had to get out of here. She had to find help.

Grace hobbled forward. Something sharp cut into her foot. Her shoulder throbbed, and her ankle was ablaze with pain. But she kept moving forward, one painful step at a time, trying to stay hidden behind the trees.

Through the bushes, she saw a pile of honey-blond hair. Grace's heart skittered. She stopped moving and stared through the branches. It was a person. A woman. She was covered with dirt and leaves, as though she'd rolled down a hill. Grace stepped back behind a bush, watching the lifeless body with a feeling of dread.

Then the woman moved.

Nolan jogged along the road, searching the land-scape for any sign of her. All he saw were scrub trees and bushes and those damn cows. *Where was she?* And where was the backup he and Talia had called?

"Sara!" His voice was hoarse from shouting her name.

Sweat streamed down his back, soaking through his shirt. He kept a steady pace along the road, searching the trees.

A flash of movement. Nolan's heart missed a beat as Sara emerged from the bushes.

He broke into a run. She staggered toward him. Her shoulders were cut and bleeding, her eyes wide with shock. Nolan caught her around the waist.

"Are you okay? Christ, you're bleeding."

She slumped against him. Scratches covered her arms, and he realized she wasn't wearing anything but a black sports bra and torn yoga pants.

"Sit down. I got you." He tried to lower her, but she pulled away.

"We have to go. She's here."

"What?"

"She's *here*. She has a twisted ankle, but she untied my hands, and I gave her my shirt and—"

"*Who's* here?"

"Grace. Nolan, she's alive."

CHAPTER 28

Dust swirled like a tornado as Sara watched the helicopter from the back of the police car. She had the door open, her feet out, and she shielded her eyes from the grit as a pair of paramedics loaded Grace's stretcher into the chopper. After Grace came a second stretcher with Elaine Hansen strapped to it. The woman had suffered a serious head injury at the hands of her grandson.

Despite the powerful downdrafts, Sara couldn't tear her eyes from the spectacle as the helicopter lifted into the air and then swooped east toward San Marcos.

A shadow fell over her. "Ten more minutes, I promise."

She looked at Nolan. "There's no rush."

But she knew it was futile to protest. He'd been insisting for the past half hour that she needed medical attention. He'd wanted her to go in the chopper. But Sara had balked, and they'd ended up in an argument in front of half the Springville Police Department.

His phone buzzed, and he gave her a long look before stepping away to take the call.

The moment his back was turned, Sara slumped against the vinyl seat. She ached everywhere. Even her teeth ached. And for the past five minutes, she'd been battling the urge to puke.

"It sucks, I know," Talia said, stepping over. "We went through it in training." When Sara didn't respond, she frowned. "He stun-gunned you, right? That's what Nolan said."

Sara nodded.

"Takes about a day to wear off." Talia crouched beside her. "I haven't had a chance to thank you."

"Why?"

"We wouldn't be here without your help." She glanced up at the sky. "I doubt Grace would be alive."

Sara's chest tightened at the thought of her. She'd been in terrible shape. Sara's cursory examination had revealed a fractured clavicle and a sprained ankle. She had contusions on her arms and legs, suggesting sexual assault, and she showed signs of severe dehydration. All that was in addition to her emotional wounds, which were unfathomable.

And yet she'd rescued Sara. She'd hobbled over to her and untied her bindings and helped her to her feet, before nearly collapsing herself from dehydration. Sara had thought she was dreaming when she saw Grace's dirt-smudged face looming over her.

"You sure you're okay?" Talia asked.

"I'm fine."

Talia stood up. "No need to be a hero, you know, Sara. Every last one of us is ready to kiss your feet. Nolan included, even though he's being an ass."

Sara forced a smile. "Really, I'm okay."

"Hey!"

Talia turned to look at Bryce Gaines, still seated cross-legged on the side of the road near Sara's wrecked Explorer. His arms were cuffed awkwardly behind him, and he had to crane his neck to look at them.

Talia glanced at Sara. "Excuse me." She walked over and glared down at the captive.

"You guys sat me in a fucking *ant* bed."

Talia put a sympathetic look on her face. She knelt down and said something, and Sara wished she could have heard it, because his face went slack. Talia stood up and sauntered off, leaving him sweltering in the dirt.

An unmarked police car pulled up to the scene, and a man the size of a refrigerator got out. This would have to be Dax Harper from APD, the only task force member Sara hadn't met yet. Talia strode over, and they were joined by Nolan. The three huddled together, and Sara leaned her head back against the seat as a new surge of nausea gripped her.

CSIs buzzed around the scene, collecting evidence. Besides the newly discovered cave complex, the sprawling crime scene included Sara's SUV and Nolan's truck. The front of the Explorer looked like an accordion, and Sara doubted she'd ever drive it again. Not that she wanted to. She watched with detachment as a photographer leaned into the cargo space and snapped a picture of the bloody carpet.

Suddenly, Sara's stomach churned, and her mouth filled with saliva. She clutched her middle and tried to breathe through it.

Nolan glanced at her and did a double take. He walked over.

"We're about to head in." He leaned his hand on the top of the police car and bent down. "You okay?"

"Yes."

"Let me get the prisoner loaded, then I'll be right back."

"Aren't you taking him in?"

"Talia's taking him, and Dax will ride with them."

"It's your arrest. Aren't you going to question him?"

"After I take you to the ER."

"But—"

"He can wait. I'm taking you."

By nightfall, the police station was a madhouse. People from everywhere congregated by the flagpole, including a rabid pack of reporters who shoved microphones in Talia's face as she made her way inside. Joanne was at the reception desk, frantically fielding calls, and she didn't even make eye contact as she buzzed Talia into the bull pen.

Every badge in Allen County—and several from surrounding counties—seemed to have found an excuse to show up tonight. Talia spotted Dax's head above the rest and threaded her way through the crowd. He nodded for her to follow him into the hall beside the restrooms, where they at least had room to talk.

"How'd it go at the house?" he asked.

"They're just wrapping up." Talia combed her hand through her stringy hair. The Hansen home was overrun with FBI agents, who had taken over for the local CSIs. "Should be finished within the hour."

"Anything new?"

"No murder weapon yet," she said. "But definitely some weird shit."

Dax arched his eyebrows.

"There's a closet off the main hallway. Has a dead bolt. The walls inside are all scratched up. Looks like someone used to lock a child in there."

"Gaines?"

"And maybe his mom, too, when she was a kid? Who knows."

Talia shuddered, refusing to let herself picture

Gaines as a child. She didn't want to feel sorry for him. She didn't want to feel anything for him.

She nodded at the pair of closed doors—an interrogation room and an observation room beside it. "How's it going here? Is that him in the box?"

"No, they took him into County."

"You're kidding."

"They've got the grandmother in there, seeing what they can get out of her."

Frustration swelled inside her. Talia maneuvered her way through the cops milling in the hallway and let herself into the observation room. Nolan shot her a glare. He stood beside Rey Santos. The FBI agent wore his typical suit and tie, even though the stuffy room was about a hundred degrees.

"Shut that door," Nolan ordered.

Dax eased the door shut behind him as he squeezed in beside Talia, and all four of them focused their attention on a monitor. Black-and-white footage from the camera next door showed Elaine Hansen seated across the table from the police chief. The woman had a thick white bandage wrapped around her head and a box of tissues in front of her. Just the sight of her made Talia's blood boil.

"What is this?" Talia asked. "I thought we wanted Gaines."

"He's not talking," Nolan said tightly.

"Want me to take a crack at him? Maybe he'll let his guard down with a woman?"

Nolan shook his head. "He clammed up. Asked for a lawyer."

Talia looked at the screen again and tuned in to the conversation.

"Something's not right with that boy," Elaine said tearfully. "I knew it the day he was born. I saw it in him. His mother dumped him on us when she was eighteen, went on about her wicked life." She plucked a tissue from the box. "He's been an albatross around my neck every day since."

Hank patted her hand. "You did the best you could, Elaine. God knows."

Talia looked at Nolan. "What the hell is this? We're coddling her now?"

"It's called building rapport."

"It's called bullshit," Talia retorted. "That bitch abused him and made him into a monster. This guy killed *seven* women that we know of— probably more. Four of them while he was *living* with her. You think she didn't know about it or at least have a clue? She's covering her ass!"

"She's our best shot at getting Gaines to talk," Nolan said.

"So what if he talks?" Talia thought of Grace Murray with her cuts and bruises and her glassy eyes. Fury bubbled up. "We've got mountains of evidence against him. Why do we care if either of them talks? We should throw the book at them, let them rot in jail."

Nolan gave her a sharp look. "There could be more, Talia. And he's the only one who can tell us where to find Kaylin."

The reality of his words smacked her. She looked at the screen again. Hank sat there calmly, nodding and listening, when he probably wanted to shake the woman until her teeth fell out. Kaylin Baird was his grandniece.

". . . twenty-five years," she said tearfully. "All that time, he's been my cross to bear. And now *this*."

Hank patted her hand again. "The Lord never gives us more than we can handle, Elaine."

The woman bowed her head and cried until her shoulders shook.

"Here it comes," Nolan muttered. "He's going to flip her. Watch."

Hank leaned forward and looked her in the eye. "Bryce knows where Kaylin is. We both know it. Tell him to talk to us. He'll listen to you."

"He won't. He never has."

"*Talk* to him, Elaine. It's time for Kaylin's family to bring her home."

Sara's windows were dark.

Nolan pulled up to the curb and studied the red-brick building with a clench in his chest. He thought he saw a slight glow on the kitchen side of the apartment, but maybe that was wishful thinking.

He cut the engine. It was after one. Sara needed rest. After spending half the day in the ER, she'd spent four hours at the police station, giving a statement and filling out paperwork. She had to be beat.

He got out and walked to the door, where he scrolled through the digital keypad until her name appeared. He called, and she picked up.

"Hey, it's me."

She buzzed him in.

Nolan took the steps two at a time and found her standing in her doorway in that silky white robe he remembered from this morning. It felt like a lifetime ago. Her hair was disheveled, and he felt a stab of longing. He wanted to kiss her and wrap her in a bear hug, but he was afraid to touch her.

"Sorry to wake you up," he said.

"You didn't." She let him inside. "I couldn't sleep."

She led him into the living area, where a mug sat on the coffee table. The TV was tuned to the news, but the volume was muted.

"Want something to drink?" she asked. "I can do better than tea."

"I'm good."

She sat down and looked at him. He sat, too. She leaned against him and slid her arms around his waist, and for the first time since Talia had told him about the phone call, Nolan felt like he could breathe again.

He kissed the top of her head.

"I tried to get away sooner," he said. "I wanted so badly to be here earlier."

"Why?"

"I didn't want you to be alone tonight."

She looked up at him. "I'm alone every night. Alone is my default state."

Not anymore.

But he didn't want to push her. Not tonight, when her emotions were ragged. He just wanted to hold her. He breathed deeply, taking in the clean scent of her hair. Her arms tightened around him, and he felt his chest loosen.

"The last few days have been . . ." She trailed off.

"Scary."

"Soul-sucking." She tipped her head back, and he saw the shadows in her eyes. "The cruelty people are capable of—" She shook her head. "I feel so hopeless."

"Don't."

He shifted her closer and stroked her shoulder. She felt warm against him. He wanted to stretch out with her, but it seemed like she wanted to talk.

"I don't know, Nolan." She sighed. "I thought I was up for this work, but . . ."

"Give yourself a break. You've had a shit day. Tomorrow will be better."

Another sigh.

"Hey." He gently tipped her chin up. "It's not all bad. Not everything. People help each other. People go the extra mile for each other."

People love each other.

She nestled her head against him. When her body finally relaxed, he felt a measure of relief. He stared at the muted news channel, not even watching it, really, as she lay against him, breathing softly. There was nowhere else in the universe he wanted to be right now.

"Everything hurts," she murmured.

He wasn't sure if she meant physically or emotionally or both.

"Did the ER doc give you some painkillers?"

"I took one earlier. And I keep thinking how Grace spent twelve days with that man without painkillers or clothes or even solid food."

Nolan pictured the dungeon-like cavern. He pictured the dried blood puddles and the empty packets of sports gel. Gaines had installed bolts in the stone and linked carabiners together to keep her chained to the rock. The place would have been Sara's worst nightmare, and he was glad she hadn't seen it. But she could imagine, especially after seeing Grace's condition.

"I'm so tired," she said. "Don't even want to crawl into bed."

He kissed her head. "Just sleep."

She lay there quietly with her head against his chest.

"Nolan?"

"Yeah?"

"Did you guys get it?"

The confession, she meant.

"Yeah," he said. It was probably the last thing Hank would do as a cop. "We got it."

CHAPTER 29

Kaylin Baird was buried in a shallow grave not far from the cave complex where her killer had kept his victims. Less than twelve hours after Elaine Hansen helped elicit Gaines's confession, Nolan, Sara, and her team had arrived at the grove of trees near a weathered deer blind. Within five minutes of arriving, Peaches had located the spot. Sara and her team spent the day toiling in the sun, and by nightfall they'd completed the excavation and loaded everything into the van to take back to the lab.

The Hansens had once owned the twenty-acre property and leased the mineral rights to an oil company. But the wells and the money had stopped flowing, and the property was sold for next to nothing, creating one of the many hardships that set the stage for Bryce Gaines's tumultuous childhood.

Not that Nolan gave a shit.

He saw it over and over—the endless cycle where cruelty begets cruelty, abuse begets abuse. Nolan no longer focused on excuses. People had to be held accountable, and holding Bryce Gaines accountable for the rape, torture, and murder of seven women was Nolan's chief objective now.

Now he peered through the window into the autopsy suite where Sara was finishing up. She made a few notes on a clipboard and then set it aside on the counter where Aaron stood at a laptop. The two exchanged words, and then Sara stripped off her latex gloves and tossed them into a trash bin before scrubbing her hands and stepping out of the laboratory.

"Have you been here long?" She checked her watch. "I thought we said nine."

"We did." He nodded toward the lab. "How's it going?"

Sara heaved a sigh. "It's done."

Nolan was surprised.

"I still have to write up my report, but my findings are complete. You have a minute?"

"Yeah, of course."

She perched on the edge of her desk and took a deep breath. "Cause of death, blunt-force trauma to the skull. The instrument was something long and heavy."

"We recovered a tire iron from the Tahoe with some blood on it." As Nolan had expected, Gaines's vehicle was a treasure trove of evidence.

"An instrument like that would fit," Sara said. "We can have our tool-marks examiner take a look to confirm."

"Okay, what else?" Nolan braced himself.

"No further fractures. The only other sign of bone trauma is an old injury to her arm, which matches the X-rays provided by the family."

"From when Kaylin was thrown from a horse." Sara nodded.

"So you're saying . . ."

"She was not tortured and held captive like the others. No signs of further bone trauma, no garrote marks. It appears to have been a blitz-style attack from behind. She was buried soon after, clothes intact, in an eighteen-inch grave, which is pretty standard."

Jesus. She had a standard for what constituted a shallow grave.

Nolan studied Sara's face. She looked tired. She *was* tired. She'd had less than four hours of sleep last night before waking up and embarking on an excavation, followed by an autopsy. It had been a marathon day.

"So." She checked her watch. "What's the plan?"

"After this, I'm headed to the Bairds'." He needed to do it tonight, even though he was dreading it.

She nodded. "I'll come with you."

"You don't need to do that."

She stood. "Just give me a minute to clean up."

Nolan put his hand on her shoulder. "You've had a grueling day."

"So have you. And the worst part isn't over yet.

I *know,* Nolan. I've done this before. Talking to families is the hardest part."

Her eyes glinted with determination. She wanted to come, and if he was honest, he wanted her at his side.

And in that moment, it struck him. She was the strongest person he knew. He'd always thought he was tough, but Sara was tougher.

"Nolan, these people are grieving and heart-broken. They're going to have questions, and I can help you answer them." She took his hand and squeezed it. "Let me come with you."

"All right." He nodded. "Let's get this done."

Talia went straight to the hospital after work and nearly bumped into Dax as he walked out the door.

"Hey." He stopped in front of her. Talia hadn't seen him in the two days since Gaines's arrest.

"I'm here for Grace. Is she—"

"You just missed her," he said. "They discharged her twenty minutes ago. She went home with her parents."

A nurse appeared behind him, pushing a man in a wheelchair. "Excuse me, sir?"

"Sorry." Dax stepped out of the doorway, joining Talia on the sidewalk.

She hadn't expected to see him here, and she wished she'd brushed her teeth after the Italian sub she wolfed down for lunch.

"Are you here for an interview or . . . ?"

"No, nothing like that," she said. "I just wanted to check in, see how she's doing." She paused, searching his face. "Better, I guess, since she's been discharged?"

His brow furrowed. "Better. Not good, but better."

Another plainclothes cop stepped through the door, this one with a fat brown case file tucked under his arm.

"Hey, I'll catch up," Dax told him. The guy headed for the other parking lot, and Dax turned back to Talia.

"How'd the interview go?" she asked.

He blew out a sigh. "Fine. That was our last one, I hope. She needs to be left alone for a while."

"Was it as bad as we thought?"

"Worse."

Talia's heart squeezed. "I'm sorry."

"Yeah, me too."

She looked at him more closely. "You okay?"

"Yeah." He rubbed the back of his neck. "Sometimes this job . . ." He shook his head.

"I know."

Their gazes locked. It wasn't often she heard people talk about the stress. Men almost never did.

"I just sent you an email," she said. "We ID'd one of our Jane Does from the park."

His expression perked up. "Who is she?"

"Teresa Marin. Turns out she's from Abilene."

"How'd you find her?"

"Basically, wading through missing-persons cases from the last two years. Her physical description was consistent, so I ran it down. She disappeared two summers ago. She was estranged from her family, so it took a while for her to be reported. When she missed paying her rent, her landlord tracked down a relative, and her family ended up filing a report."

Dax nodded. "ID?"

"Her sister recognized a gold pendant found with the body. We confirmed through dental records."

"Good work."

"Thanks."

He held her gaze, and the moment stretched out. "You parked out here?" He looked over her shoulder. "I'll walk you."

They started toward the parking lot, and Talia tried to think of something to say. She came up empty, and soon they reached her car. She fished her keys from her purse. She had no more excuses to linger with him. Or even see him again.

"Thanks for your work," Dax said.

"No problem."

"I mean it. Without your help, Grace might never have made it home."

Talia nodded. He was right, and it was the one

thing to feel good about in this whole disturbing case.

She popped her car locks and opened the door. "Well. Take care."

"You too." He stepped back. "And if you get up to Austin, call me."

"Why?" she asked before she could stop herself.

"We could go get a drink together. Or listen to some blues somewhere." He smiled, and she felt it down to her toes. She'd told him she liked blues music, and he'd been listening. And he wanted her to know he'd been listening.

Talia smiled up at him. "I'd like that."

CHAPTER 30

Sara woke with a start as her front door swung open. She felt a spurt of panic, but the familiar sound of Nolan's boots against the floor made her relax.

She glanced at the clock. It was one fifteen. She listened to Nolan's footsteps as he made his way to the kitchen, where she'd left a light on. She heard the *swoosh* of his jacket landing on the armchair and then his gear hitting the bar: keys, holster, handcuffs.

More footsteps, and then the bed sank with a *creak*. One by one, his boots hit the floor, and then he stretched out behind her and hooked his arm over her waist as he kissed her neck.

"Umm. Hi." She rolled over to look at him. The light from the kitchen cast shadows across his face.

"Sorry I'm late." He kissed her. "Liquor-store hold-up."

"Are you hungry?"

"Yeah, but not for food." He dipped his head down and nibbled her neck.

"Seriously, I can heat something up for you."

He smiled.

"*Food,* Nolan."

Another kiss. "I'm good."

She searched his eyes and noticed the tension. "What's wrong? Were there fatalities?"

He propped himself up on his elbow. "Nothing like that."

Dread tightened her stomach as she looked at him.

He brushed a lock of hair from her face. "Hank is retiring."

"Oh." She tried to clear the haze of sleep so she could think about the implications.

"The mayor wants to appoint me acting chief. And he's recommending me to the city council as the permanent replacement."

Sara sat up. The sheet slipped down around her waist, and Nolan's gaze went to her skimpy black nightgown as she scooted back against the headboard.

"Damn, now I'm *really* sorry I'm late." He leaned in for a kiss, but she held him off.

"Nolan, that's great. What did you tell him?"

He eased back. "Nothing."

"What do you mean? You had to tell him *something.*"

He looked at her evenly. "I told him I needed to think about it."

Sara watched him, trying to read his thoughts. Her heart was racing now, and she wondered if he was worried about the same thing she was.

It was the fifth night this week he'd shown up at her apartment after midnight. In the three weeks since Gaines's arrest, they'd spent every single day shuttling back and forth between houses—mostly sleeping at her place, meaning that Nolan dealt with four hours of driving, which cut into his sleep and his time off. Sara traced her fingers over his hand, wishing things were different. He'd just gotten here, and he'd have to be up and gone again in a few hours.

They couldn't keep this up if he became chief of police. But just the thought of limiting their relationship to weekends or—God forbid—ending it felt like a knife in her chest.

"I've been thinking." Nolan cleared his throat, and she braced herself for more news she wasn't going to like. "We'd have more time together if we lived in the same place. Yeah, we'd still work long hours, but at least we'd see each other coming and going."

"You mean move in together."

He nodded.

"Where would we live? Your place, I assume?"

He tipped his head to the side. "It's possible. I mean, when you get callouts, the person's already dead, right? They've been dead a while. It's not as time-sensitive as, say, a robbery in progress."

Sara's nerves started up again, and she had a flashback to how she'd felt with Patrick, when he used to make everything revolve around him. His career, his schedule, his life plan.

"So I should move," she stated, trying to keep the tightness out of her voice.

"I was thinking I should."

"But . . . if you're going to be chief, you need to be there. In Springville."

"Hear me out." He squeezed her hand. "I *do* need to be near my jurisdiction. But right now, I'm living on the far west side of town. If I moved to the far east side, I'd be the same distance from the police station but half an hour closer to San Marcos. We'd still have a drive to deal with, but it wouldn't be as bad."

"You mean you'd get a new place?"

"*We* could get a place." He kissed her knuckles. "Something we choose together."

She stared at him. "But that's your grandparents' house, Nolan."

"So?"

"So . . ." She shook her head. "How would this work? I want to hear your hypothesis."

He smiled. "Always the scientist."

"*Yes.* Explain to me the logic of you selling your family home to shack up with a woman you haven't even known very long."

"Well, for starters, I don't think of it as 'shacking up.' Fact, I'm pretty old-fashioned, so I'd prefer to have a commitment first." He paused, searching her reaction, and Sara was

427

pretty sure her shock was written all over her face. "But if you want a trial run, I'm open to that, too."

Her mind was reeling. A commitment, as in an engagement?

"Uh-oh." Nolan frowned. "You look worried."

"I'm just— I've never lived with anyone."

"Same."

This was news to Sara. And the fact that she didn't know this little tidbit about his life just showed how crazy it was to be talking about moving in together so soon.

"But you love that place. You know your neighbors. And that house has been in your family for generations."

He shrugged. "A house is just a building. It's the people in it that matter. I can move closer to where you work."

"You'd do that for me?"

His look turned serious. "I'd do anything for you."

It took a moment for the words to sink in. As they did, warmth spread through her entire body. That giddy, euphoric feeling that had been sneaking up on her for weeks now was back, but stronger.

"Nolan, I think—" Her throat felt tight, and it was hard to speak.

"What?"

"I love you."

He laughed and rested his head on her shoulder. "What's so funny?"

He smiled up at her. "You're just now figuring this out? I figured it out weeks ago."

She frowned. "That *I've* fallen in love with *you* or vice versa?"

"Both." He scooted closer on the bed and cupped the side of her face as he kissed her. "I love you, Sara. I want to be with you. I don't give a damn where we live, and if you want to stay here in this loft, I'll turn down the chief's job and stick to being a detective if that means this can work between us."

Tears filled her eyes as she watched him. She didn't want him to turn down anything, but his willingness to make sacrifices for her overwhelmed her.

"I want to go to sleep with you. And wake up with you." He brushed a lock of hair off her shoulder. "Even if it's at oh-dark-hundred when one of us gets called to a crime scene and has to leave."

She kissed him, and that was all the encouragement he needed to wrap his arm around her and drag her down on the bed to ease himself on top of her. He kissed her long and deeply, putting all the emotions swirling inside of her into a perfect kiss. He pulled back and propped his weight on his elbows.

Sara gazed up at his deep brown eyes that could

so quickly go from sharp to passionate to loving. She traced her finger over his jaw.

"So, you really want to move in together?" she asked.

"That's just the start of what I want, but yeah." He stroked her cheek. "What do *you* want?"

"I want that, too." More of that giddy warmth rippled through her. It seemed impossible. They hadn't known each other that long. So much had happened so fast, and her mind was spinning.

Her heart was spinning, too.

"This is crazy," she said. "What are we doing?"

His smile faded, and his eyes grew somber. "I don't know, but it feels right. I know my mind, my heart. And this feels right."

She smiled up at him. "Feels right to me, too."

| Books are produced in the United States using U.S.-based materials | Books are printed using a revolutionary new process called THINKtech™ that lowers energy usage by 70% and increases overall quality | Books are durable and flexible because of Smyth-sewing | Paper is sourced using environmentally responsible foresting methods and the paper is acid-free |

Center Point Large Print
600 Brooks Road / PO Box 1
Thorndike, ME 04986-0001 USA

(207) 568-3717

US & Canada:
1 800 929-9108
www.centerpointlargeprint.com